Mr. Darcy's Challenge

Volume II of

THE DARCY NOVELS

Monica Fairview

Other Books by Monica Fairview

Mr. Darcy's Pledge

Steampunk Darcy

The Darcy Cousins

The Other Mr. Darcy

An Improper Suitor (Regency)

Mr. Darcy's Challenge

ISBN 978-1503363526

Copyright © 2014 by Monica Fairview

An Imprint of White Soup Press

Cover design Jane Dixon-Smith

Prologue

A man in possession of a fortune may be in need of a wife, but there were many ways to choose one. Writing a list of required qualities was perhaps not the best approach. That, at least, was Darcy's conclusion as he rode away from Longbourn, his thoughts on how best to convince Elizabeth Bennet that marriage to him was not as disagreeable a prospect as she seemed to think.

He tore up the list he had made into many pieces and threw it behind him. The list of requirements for a wife was gone. Darcy was no longer bound by it, nor was he bound by society's restrictions. He was free once again to follow the dictate of his emotions. A huge burden shifted from his shoulders. Now all he had to do was find Wickham and rescue Miss Lydia from the scoundrel's clutches. Darcy could then return to fulfill his pledge to woo Elizabeth until she gave him her hand in marriage.

The torn bits of paper were taken up by a light breeze. They floated back towards him like blossoms tossed over a bride and groom, as they would be tossed one day over him and Elizabeth. He imagined the two of them emerging from the small chapel at Lambton, surrounded by well-wishers, with Elizabeth by his side, smiling and radiant.

Darcy was not normally given to flights of fantasy but, fired up by the conviction that he would find a way to make things right for Elizabeth and her family, he indulged himself in an altogether pleasant daydream. He was a knight on horseback, like the Darcys of old, and an evil knight threatened his fair lady. He was riding off to challenge the evil knight to a duel, and, to prove himself the hero once and for all. He would return, having vanquished his adversary, and would find his fair lady awaiting him, her fine dark eyes full of admiration – and love. She would run out of her home and cast her arms around him. The daydream culminated with him leaning over to receive the kiss he had craved for so long.

A branch brushed against Darcy's face and awakened him from this happy trance. He was half-asleep on his horse and likely to fall if he did not pay attention. His childish fantasy embarrassed him. How Wickham would have mocked him for his ridiculous notions! Darcy had always loved tales of valor and bravery when they were children, while Wickham had always scoffed at them. Once, Darcy had tried to creep inside the old suit of armor in the Picture Gallery at Pemberley and had been stuck inside, unable to get out. Wickham had laughed at his discomfort and refused to assist him, saying he should shout for a knight on a white horse to come and rescue him. In the end, Darcy had to bribe Wickham by promising him two of his toy soldiers in return for going for one of the servants. Wickham had agreed to the bargain, but instead of bringing someone to help Darcy, he had fetched Darcy's father. Darcy had been whipped for desecrating one of his family's oldest possessions and lectured for days afterwards about not taking enough pride in his ancestors.

In any case, this was not the time for dreaming. It was the time for action. He needed to sort out this business with Wickham and return, as he had pledged, to woo Elizabeth until she agreed to become his wife, even if it meant taking up residence in Meryton for the next five years.

He spurred his horse onwards. His aspirations, however, came to a sudden and complete standstill when his horse slowed down to a trot then halted, refusing to go any farther. She had found a particularly juicy clump of grass and she intended to enjoy it.

Darcy sighed, recognizing in the horse his own bone-deep weariness. Driven by Lady Catherine's letter informing him of Miss Lydia's elopement and the Bennet family's disgrace, Darcy had ridden as fast as he could to Longbourn, intent on showing Elizabeth and her family his support. He was thirsty, hungry and sore. The mare he had hired from the last posting-inn felt much the same, he imagined. Unlike him, she did not have the impetus of being heroic. She needed a good rub-down and some rest.

Now that they had stopped, Darcy realized where he was. The uprooted oak tree lying on its side by the road signaled that he was drawing closer to Netherfield. There was the path that forked left and led across the fields toward Bingley's estate. This was undoubtedly the way Elizabeth had taken when she walked from Longbourn to attend to her bed-ridden sister. He had not even known he had been looking for it until he found it.

"At least six inches deep in mud," Caroline Bingley had said and had pointed out the mud, but he had not noticed it. His gaze had been drawn to the brief glimpse of a fine-turned ankle that had been revealed as she had shifted her skirts self-consciously under the onslaught of probing eyes.

Hardly conscious of what he was doing, Darcy descended, tethered the horse to the oak tree and took the path left. He followed the path until he reached an old cross-step turnstile. He climbed it awkwardly and jumped down the other side. Unsurprisingly, his boots sank with a squelch into the mud. He grinned with delight at the thought that he was experiencing what Elizabeth had experienced, stepping into the very same mud that she did. Then he felt embarrassed and hastily rearranged his features into a more serious expression. Fortunately, no one but a group of brown cows clustered together had witnessed his exhibition.

Passing through hazel copse, he continued, drawn as if spellbound towards his friend's house. Then suddenly the view opened up and a lavender field spread before him, row upon neat row of purple sprigs waving gently in the breeze. The aroma drifted up towards him, an irresistible blend of sweetness mingling with the scent of the earth. In the distance, the grey stone edifice of Netherfield sat on the slope of a knoll, looking out to the apple orchards beyond it. He stared at it, his heart filled with myriad emotions. His gaze sought out a particular window. She had slept there, in the bedchamber closest to her sister Jane. She had been under that same roof. If he had only known it then, he would have made every effort to make a good impression on her. He had departed from Longbourn just two days later, believing he was putting an end to the whole story.

It was just the beginning.

He stood gazing at the house for a moment longer, contemplating his blind, naïve confidence that day, then turned away. He was wasting time. He had a mission to accomplish, and he would not do so stopping in the middle of a field and reminiscing about the past. He strode back to where the horse had been contentedly feasting and mounted, turning towards the direction of London.

A light breeze came up and a piece of paper drifted lazily across the green expanse to settle near the horse's hoof. He thought of the pieces of paper he had tossed behind him and a sudden panic gripped him.

He had stupidly left his list behind on the grounds of Longbourn for everyone to see. What if Elizabeth were to chance upon them? Would she connect the pieces of paper to him? He had torn them up but the segments were still large enough to be legible. He tried to dismiss his sudden fear, to rationalize that she could not guess that it was his list, but he knew the evidence would incriminate him. Paper was not commonly found strewn around the countryside, with most of the population illiterate and without access to the expensive material. Besides, Elizabeth had seen him write on that memorable day in Netherfield. Caroline had drawn Elizabeth's attention to his handwriting. She would very likely recognize it.

He could not afford to have her find the list. If she did, she would have nothing but contempt for his cold-blooded manner of acquiring a wife. He had to go back and retrieve the pieces at once.

He turned back towards Longbourn. The mare shook her head as if to question his sanity in deciding to retrace the same path they had taken so recently, and then responded to his urgency by breaking into a reluctant trot.

As he approached the spot where he had thrown the paper, he distinguished a feminine figure approaching from a distance, walking with confident strides and swinging her bonnet in her hand.

He was too late.

Chapter One

"I wonder where Mr. Darcy could have gone?" said Mrs. Annesley as Georgiana sat down to breakfast.

Georgiana was taken aback by the question. Mrs. Annesley discouraged speculation generally, calling it *detrimental curiosity* and she certainly never showed interest in William's comings and goings. Yet here she was, asking a question which Georgiana could not answer.

"What do you mean, Mrs. Annesley?" she said. "Surely it has nothing to do with us."

Mrs. Annesley took a nervous sip of her coffee. "Naturally, I did not mean to question Mr. Darcy's whereabouts. I simply wondered if you knew where his travels were taking him this time."

Georgiana was so startled at this unexpected revelation that she dropped her fork.

"Oh," said Mrs. Annesley, hurrying to pick it up from the floor. "I did not mean to startle you, Miss Darcy. I am very sorry to have done so."

"My brother is travelling? *Again*? What could have possessed him to do so?"

She ought not to be critical of her brother in front of Mrs. Annesley, but really, it was very puzzling. Why had he not informed her he was leaving? She would be forced to admit that she had no idea where her brother had gone, nor for how long. She would not even have known that William had left Pemberley if it were not for Mrs. Annesley's question.

"Are you certain he is traveling?" said Georgiana.

"Yes. I know I should not be eavesdropping, but the window was open and I overheard him say to young Ebenezer when he brought the horse that he would be away for a few days. Mr. Darcy gave specific instructions about exercising the new mare he acquired."

"I do not understand," said Georgiana. "He said nothing to me at all last night."

Georgiana could scarcely credit it. So Darcy had departed yet again. Of course, William was a free agent and being her older brother, he was not obliged to inform her of his movements. There was nothing remarkable about that. He was a man. He was free to go and come as he pleased, and it was not up to her to question his reasons. Perhaps he had received a last minute invitation to a house party.

However, that did not mean she did not feel provoked that, after she had believed they had come to trust each other a little better, he had departed without even saying goodbye. It pained her that he disregarded her presence so completely, quite as if she was no more than a child and not the current mistress of Pemberley at all. The least he could have done was leaving her a note.

Perhaps he *had* left one and she was growing upset over nothing. Georgiana tugged at the bell-pull.

"I would like to speak to Timmons," she said, when the footman answered the summons.

She wished she did not need to question Timmons. When she was a little girl, she had quailed under his disapproving eye and solemn expression. Now that she was older, she knew he was an excellent butler, but she still preferred to have as little interaction with him as possible.

Timmons appeared promptly.

"Did Mr. Darcy leave a message for me?" she asked.

"He did not," said Timmons, his tone implying what was obvious: namely, that if Mr. Darcy had left a message, it would have been delivered.

Georgiana hesitated. She had to find out where her brother had gone, but she did not wish the staff to know that William had not informed her. She did not feel secure in her position as mistress of the household and she could not help feeling that her ignorance of her brother's departure would lower her status in their eyes.

"Did he inform you when he would return from his trip?"

Timmons' expression did not change, but Georgiana noted rather gleefully that his body had stiffened. So, the butler did not know either. She felt less mortified now.

"He did not," said Timmons.

"Thank you, Timmons. That is all. Could you send Mrs. Reynolds to me? I will be in the parlor."

The old butler bowed and withdrew. As she Georgiana walked with Mrs. Annesley to the parlor, she debated inwardly whether to reveal her ignorance to the housekeeper or not.

Fortunately, Mrs. Reynolds solved the problem for her.

"I am glad you sent for me, Miss Darcy. I was just wondering if you knew when Mr. Darcy would be returning. Cook is desirous to plan her menu for the next three days, but I was wondering if I should advise her not to put together any formal dinners."

Georgiana smiled, happy to be saved the embarrassment of asking.

"I know nothing about my brother's plans," she said. "I did not know that he was leaving."

One would have thought that he might at least have said something to Mrs. Reynolds, but the housekeeper was quite as mystified as Georgiana was. Not that she said anything, of course. She was far too loyal.

"Well, I am sure Mr. Darcy has his reasons," said Mrs. Reynolds, folding her hands in front of her, which was something she tended to do when she was baffled. "I just wish he had taken an overcoat with him in case of rain."

"Your concern does you credit, I am sure," said Mrs. Annesley, which was irksome because it was precisely what Georgiana herself had been about to say.

"Thank you, Mrs. Annesley," said Mrs. Reynolds. "Miss Darcy, about dinner?"

"Dinner in your room might be best, Miss Darcy," said Mrs. Annesley.

"Yes, of course. I would prefer that, Mrs. Reynolds. There is nothing more dreary than dining alone at a big empty table," she replied. She already felt the weight of the loneliness. It had been so busy the last few days, and now everyone was gone, including William, and she was left behind.

"I thought so," said the housekeeper, giving Georgiana a warm smile. "You must be missing all the company we have had lately. The house seems very quiet."

Thank heavens for Mrs. Reynolds, who knew her so well she seemed to read her mind sometimes. She ought not to think that way, of course, but she felt that Mrs. Reynolds was the closest to a mother that she had. She had been a constant support since her mother had died so many years ago. It was probably silly of her to think this way, but she could not help it. Mrs. Annesley was all very well as a companion, but she did not know her half as well, and besides, she took her duties as much too seriously to attempt to discover Georgiana's feelings about anything. If she had as much as mentioned loneliness to Mrs. Annesley, she would have found Georgiana more sewing to do, or sent her out into the garden to sketch lavender or whatever happened to be blooming at the moment.

"It is certainly much more peaceful," said Georgiana, catching the housekeeper's eye, "especially with Lord and Lady Matlock gone." It was probably foolish of her to make so much of it, but Georgiana had been flattered when Mrs. Reynolds had come to her to complain that two of the chambermaids had been in tears after Lady Matlock had dismissed them without a reference for bringing bath water that was too cold. Georgiana had spoken to her aunt rather firmly, reminding her that as a guest in the house she did not have the right to dismiss any of the staff. She had been trembling in her shoes while she did it, but astonishingly her aunt had not argued the point.

"Your servants are very slack," had been Lady Matlock's response. "Clearly a mistress is needed at Pemberley to take over the reins. Not you, my dear Georgiana, naturally – no one would expect it of a schoolgirl. That brother of yours has a great deal to answer for. What is he waiting for? When is he going to find himself a wife?"

The servants had been reinstated and sent to another side of the house, all without Mrs. Annesley even knowing a thing. It made Georgiana feel like a guilty kind of pleasure at accomplishing something without Mrs. Annesley looking over her shoulder.

Mrs. Reynolds returned her look but was too discreet to say anything further.

"I will convey your decision to Cook, then."

"Thank you, Mrs. Reynolds."

The moment the door closed behind the housekeeper, Mrs. Annesley put down her needlework.

"I hope you will not take it amiss, Miss Darcy, but it is best not to make remarks about persons of higher rank like your uncle and aunt to the servants. I cannot think it quite right that you were discussing Mr. Darcy's departure, either."

Mrs. Annesley was really very kind, but sometimes she grated on the nerves, particularly since she seemed to constantly find fault. Lately Georgiana was beginning to feel a need to take charge more. Being on a short leash strained her patience. How was she to learn her responsibilities if she did not have the opportunity to practice? She had been hoping to talk to William about it once all the guests had departed, but now he was not here.

She sighed, wondering yet again why William had dashed off without a word. She could not help feeling worried about it. There was no getting around it. Her brother was no longer the same brother she had known for seventeen years of her life. This new Darcy was unpredictable and erratic. The fact that she knew the reason for this great transformation went by the name of Elizabeth Bennet did provide some explanation, but it did not make it any less troubling. She had witnessed how restless he had been before Elizabeth Bennet had arrived in Pemberley. He had even been on the verge of becoming engaged to someone else – to Miss Marshall, of all people. Georgiana could not think of a worse choice of a wife.

At least William's sudden trip had nothing to do with Miss Marshall, who, as far as Georgiana knew, was still resident in Lambton. Georgiana could not rest easy, however. This new William was not to be relied upon not to make imprudent decisions on the spur of the moment. The more she thought about it, the more concerned she became. It was not like William to go away without informing anyone at all. Perhaps he had received an urgent summons or heard bad news.

With a sense of sudden urgency, she rang for Timmons to enquire if any letters had arrived this morning.

"Yes, there was a letter for Mr. Darcy," said the Butler.

"Do you know who sent it?" she asked.

There was a slight flicker in the butler's eyes, as if he was considering whether answering would betray his master's confidence or not.

"I believe it was from Lady Catherine, to judge by the handwriting," he said.

Georgiana could not help but feel that answering her question was a big concession on his part. With a surge of gratitude, she smiled at him. "Thank you for the information. You have been very helpful."

The butler did not react. He bowed gracefully and retreated.

Old Stoneface, she thought, but at least he had given her the information. So now, she knew there was a letter involved. What could Lady Catherine possibly have said that could have sent her brother running? If there had been an emergency of some sort – an accident or illness – Georgiana was certain William would have told her. After all, there would have been no need to keep it a secret.

If it was a secret, then it very likely had something to do with Miss Elizabeth Bennet. What connection could there be, however, between Lady Catherine and Elizabeth? Perhaps Timmons had mistaken the writing. Elizabeth had also left Pemberley very suddenly. Was William's departure related to hers?

The clang of the front doorbell interrupted her thoughts and Timmons appeared again.

"Mrs. Renwick. Mrs. Marshall. Miss Marshall."

Georgiana groaned inwardly. Miss Marshall was the last person she wished to see at the moment.

12

"Good afternoon, Miss Darcy," said Miss Marshall. "We thought we would keep you company now that Mr. Darcy has abandoned you. We ladies must stick together."

Georgiana frowned. How did Miss Marshall know that Darcy had left?

"You may well look surprised," said Mrs. Marshall. "We have come straight from visiting Mrs. Parris, you see, and she told us that Mr. Logan came across Mr. Darcy this morning. Darcy informed him that he expected to be away a few days."

"I see," said Georgiana.

"What an exciting life Mr. Darcy appears to lead!" said Miss Marshall. "Always travelling hither and thither! I cannot imagine why he has returned to London so soon after leaving it."

"I am not privy to my brother's private business," said Georgiana tightly, not wishing to encourage any discussion in that direction, even though she was desperately curious whether William had told Mr. Logan that he was going to London. "He is free to come and go as he pleases."

"In any case, that is not why we are here. We came to take our leave as well," said Mrs. Marshall. "The countryside is all very well, but when there is no hunting and everyone is away, it is quite abysmally dull. We have been invited to a house party in Kent – Lady Anthorpe, you know, everyone longs for an invitation from her – then we shall return to London. Perhaps we will see you there soon?"

"Possibly," said Georgiana, hoping fervently that Miss Marshall would find an eligible partner at Lady Anthorpe's house party.

"I shall be counting the days, Miss Darcy. I have become very attached to you, you know," said Miss Marshall, "even though we have known each other but a short time."

Having informed her of their plans, they did not stay long, claiming to have a great many things to do before they traveled. Georgiana could not imagine what could possibly occupy them in a tiny village like Lambton.

"Will you not open the window, Georgiana? The scent Miss Marshall is wearing always seems to bring on a headache," said Mrs. Annesley.

"That is because you do not like her," said Georgiana, with a little smile.

"No, indeed," said Mrs. Annesley, "I would not be so forthright as to venture an opinion on the matter, for as far as I know, Mr. Darcy is considering asking for her hand in marriage."

Her eyes were round and unhappy.

With a sigh, Georgiana looked out of the window. The carriage had not yet left and the two ladies were inspecting the stable area as though Pemberley belonged to them. As they approached, she could hear them speaking.

"He seems to keep good stables, at any rate," said the mother.

"A pity the house is so musty. I am sure no one has bothered to redecorate since Lady Anne died," said Miss Marshall, with a giggle.

The two women entered the carriage and drove away.

Georgiana watched until they disappeared into the avenue of trees then turned to Mrs. Annesley. She was not going to let Miss Marshall get her claws into her brother or into Pemberley for that matter. She loved both too much.

"My brother is not going to marry Miss Marshall," said Georgiana, firmly.

"Just because you do not wish it," said Mrs. Annesley "does not mean it will not happen."

Georgiana thought of Elizabeth Bennet and the expression on her brother's face whenever he looked at her.

"It will not happen," she said, crossing her fingers behind her back.

One thing was certain. If Miss Marshall was to be in London and there was a chance that her brother would be there too, then Georgiana's purpose was clear.

She would go to London as well.

Chapter Two

The situation was exactly as Darcy had feared. The white incriminating pieces of paper lay on the path, clearly visible, and Elizabeth was bending down to pick them up and fitting the pieces together. Darcy prayed for a sudden downpour that would wash away the ink, but the heavens did not oblige. It was vexing to think that he had just come from a muddy field, while the bridleway was perfectly dry. Meanwhile, Elizabeth bent down to pick up several pieces of the paper and held them together.

He raced towards her in a desperate effort to prevent her from reading them.

"Why, Mr. Darcy," said Elizabeth, looking up, her cheeks dimpling as he approached. "You appear to be riding in the opposite direction from London. Have you perchance lost your way?"

She put her bonnet on her head and shielded her eyes from the sun to look at him.

He had been so intent on reaching her that he had not thought of a possible response to that question. The sight of Elizabeth after all his recollections was in itself enough to make him tongue-tied. Having to come up with an explanation for riding towards Longbourn rather than away from it proved entirely beyond his ability. He tried to sort out his jumbled thoughts but his mind refused to assist him.

"Erm," he said. It was as much as he could say.

"I did not mean to challenge you, sir. I was merely curious," said Elizabeth, laughing. "Your secrets are your own to keep. I will not attempt to ferret them out."

Secrets? Why was she speaking of secrets when he was doing what he can to prevent her from discovering the list? Did she already suspect something? If so, he had to distract her.

This sense of purpose enabled him to find his tongue – as well as a creditable explanation.

"I have no secrets," he said. "I was on the verge of taking the London road when I recalled that I had not asked for your uncle's address. I intend to call on the Gardiners when in town."

He felt guilty for lying, but he could think of nothing better. Of course, he knew exactly where the Gardiners resided. He had paced outside their house on Gracechurch Street and even knocked on their door.

A shadow came over her face and the laughter disappeared.

"That is very kind of you, sir," she said, looking pained, but as you know, my aunt and uncle are very preoccupied with— the whole business, and will very likely not be receiving anyone until the matter is resolved."

Now he had unintentionally upset her. He felt an irresistible impulse to alight from the horse and draw Elizabeth to him to comfort her. He struggled to bring the impulse under control.

"I am much obliged to you, sir," said Elizabeth, bending down once again to pick up the bits of paper. "However, I cannot write the address for you. We have plenty of paper; it seems, but no quill." She took up one of the larger pieces and peered at the handwriting. "I wonder what such fine paper is doing here."

Flustered, Darcy sought desperately for a way to distract her from reading what he had written.

"I need to be on my way," he said, abruptly. "I cannot delay any further. If you will ride with me, we could go back to the house where we could obtain one."

The moment he said it, he wished it unsaid. Had he really suggested taking her up in front of him? The prospect of having her so close put him in agony of anticipation. He waited tensely, hoping she would say yes.

She looked at the horse uncertainly.

"Do you ride, Miss Bennet?"

"I am a poor rider," she said, "I prefer to walk."

The sense of disappointment was intense, but he acknowledged to himself that it would have been madness to have her so close. It would have stretched his self-discipline too far.

"Then I shall walk with you," he said, sliding down from the saddle.

"I see you have already been walking," she remarked with smile, indicating his mud-splattered boots.

Darcy hoped she would not wonder why he had been walking about instead of riding off to London.

"I found the lavender fields irresistible."

"Did you, indeed?" she asked, looking pleased. "They are my favorite place to visit. I have a particular tree that I like to go to. I often sit with my back against the tree trunk and read, while the bees drone on around me and the delicious scent fills my head. It is my secret hideaway when I need to escape from home. I am glad that you liked the fields as well."

For now, they were in perfect accord. He cherished this moment in which Elizabeth spoke to him freely, her expression unguarded.

"Perhaps one day I shall come back and we could visit the field together," he said, envisioning a holding of hands or even a kiss.

"Then you shall have to bring a book to read, for I shall insist on silence."

The vision dissipated.

"As you may recall, we both share a love of books."

Now that he was on the ground, he took the opportunity to pick up several of the papers closest to him.

She observed him in astonishment. "There is no call for you to do this, Mr. Darcy."

"I noticed them from a distance. They are an ugly blot on a pristine landscape."

"I did not realize you were so particular. Allow me to assist you, in that case."

17

She moved to help, but he shooed her away. "Miss Bennet, I beg you, leave this to me."

She did not insist, but took out the pieces in her hand and smoothed them out.

"Your mother seems to be taking the situation ill," he said, seeking to draw her attention away.

"Very ill indeed. And she is likely to make us all ill." She kicked an acorn with her foot and watched it as it skidded down the path. "Though in truth I can hardly blame her. The situation is very grave indeed, and I do not think anything can be made of it."

"You must not be too hasty to reach that conclusion," he said, "I am sure a solution will be found that will enable her to be married."

"What, and have Wickham be forever a part of this family?" She paused to consider it. "Yet that could be the best possible outcome to an impossible situation. My foolish sister can have no idea of the pain she has caused."

He thought of Georgiana and her near-brush with Wickham.

"She is but fifteen. She does not think of the consequences," said Darcy, consolingly.

"She is more like a child of two – heedless of others and free with her tantrums." She gave him a quick look. "But I must not burden you with what is, after all, a family affair. Let us talk of better things. These pieces of paper, for example."

As she peered closely at them, his palms grew slick.

"You happened upon me when I was reading someone else's writing. I am afraid I am guilty of being wickedly inquisitive. However, I cannot repent because I am too excessively diverted," she said. "This person has itemized his requirements for a wife. Can you conceive of such a thing? Quite as if he meant to prepare a plum pudding or a blancmange!" She laughed. "I cannot conceive what kind of person would do such a thing!"

Any moment now, she would put two and two together and produce Fitzwilliam Darcy. If she did, all would be lost. After everything that had happened, she would never believe him if he said he meant none of it. What a pickle he had landed himself in. Whatever had possessed him to throw the list away on her property? How embarrassed she would be to discover that the raillery she had engaged in was focused on him.

She was frowning. He could tell that any moment now it would dawn on her that it was he who had written it. A diversion was needed, desperately, but he could not imagine how he could create one without alerting her to the reason.

Then a diversion came to him. It was perfect in every way since it was what he had wished to do for a long time.

He would ask her to marry him. He had planned to do so when Elizabeth was in Pemberley, only her unexpected departure had prevented him. If she accepted him, she would forget about the pieces of paper. Even if she discovered that the list was his afterwards, they could laugh at it together. She would tease him endlessly about it, no doubt, but it would not matter, because he would have her.

Fortunately, he knew what to say this time. He was not unprepared as he had been the first time. He had rehearsed his speech with Bingley's help and had honed it until Bingley's romantic notion had been satisfied.

"Miss Bennet," he said. His tone was so intense that she threw him a searching look.

"I am aware that in the past I have behaved like an utter fool. You were right to chastise me when I approached you at Rosings and proposed to you. My behavior was quite unforgiveable. I desire you to know that I attach no blame to you for either your rejection or the manner of your rejection. The fault was entirely mine. I was too arrogant to consider that you might reject me. In fact, I thought it quite impossible. Knowing how determined your mother was to arrange a suitable marriage for you, I assumed that your presence in Rosings was intentional, and that you were endeavoring to attach my interest."

He paused, trying to gauge her reaction.

"Mr. Darcy, there is no reason to apologize," she said, biting her lower lip. "Neither of us behaved well on that unfortunate occasion. I said some things I have come to regret. Let us put the incident behind us entirely. Can we not set our differences aside and be friends?" She put out her hand to him with a smile.

19

He took it and clasped it to his heart.

"I cannot forget. Every moment of our interaction is branded into my heart. You do not know how often I have re-lived that occasion and regretted my words. Your response is stamped into my very being—"

She pulled her hand away. "Mr. Darcy, you must not!"

He could no more help himself than he could stop the flowing of a river. Part of him knew he was making a mistake, that she was not yet ready. He wanted to stop himself, but now that he had begun, the words seemed to take on a life of their own. The speech he had prepared so carefully eluded him. It was as if all the frustration of months had chosen this moment to be released. He wanted to make her know him. He wanted to make her love him.

"You must understand, Miss Bennet, I have been a selfish being all my life, in practice, though not in principle. Unfortunately an only son – for many years an only *child* – I was spoilt by my parents and encouraged to think well of myself. I have believed in my inherent superiority for many years. There was nothing to keep my high opinion of myself in check. You have met the Earl and his wife. You have met Lady Catherine. I was reared to be like them. I believed that my status in society entitled me to arrogance and my view of the world was defined by that status. I have come to realize that not everyone shares the same perspective, and you have taught me that, dearest, most precious Elizabeth. This change I owe to you and you alone."

From her heightened color, the quickness of her breathing and her determined refusal to look him in the face, he knew he had struck a chord in her. It was as he had thought. His civility to her at Pemberley, his solicitude for her aunt and uncle's welfare as well as his marked attention to her had reaped their rewards. What more could any young lady wish for from a gentleman of influence and position such as himself? No doubt, too, seeing the magnificence of Pemberley itself and imagining herself the mistress of such an estate had had a strong impact on her. A surge of triumph rose up in him and encouraged him to press on. His efforts had not been wasted. Finally, the prize was within his reach.

"Do not think that my feelings have changed since that day I spoke to you at Hunsford. Rather than diminishing, they have multiplied threefold. The ardent love and admiration I felt for you then was nothing to what I feel for you now. Our time apart only served to increase my love for you. Then, that day when I saw you in the carriage, with blood on your head —I was terrified that I had lost you. I wanted nothing more than to protect you. Destiny played a role in bringing us together that day. "

She was silent.

He was driven to fervor by his own words, by the belief that the hand of fate had intervened on his own behalf. "Surely you cannot deny any longer that what lies between us is a special bond? That we belong together?" he insisted.

She wrapped her arms around herself and turned away, considering his words. Her familiar profile was etched against the falling darkness, a black silhouette against the orange of the setting sun. He waited with bated breath for her acquiescence. In a moment now, she would be in his arms. In a moment, he would finally press his lips to hers and know the happiness he had been denied so long.

"Mr. Darcy," she said. "I am very flattered that your feelings for me are so strong in spite of my less than civil rejection at Hunsford. I am heartily ashamed of my response to your offer. I can only excuse myself by saying that I allowed anger to cloud my judgment. I realize I have misjudged you in the past and I ask your forgiveness for it. I am very much in your debt for the assistance you provided during my uncle's injury. Your consideration towards me and my relations despite what had occurred between us does you credit." She took a deep breath. "Now that Mr. Wickham—" She bowed her head and gazed at the ground, "— suffice it to say I no longer believe his account of you. His falsehood and duplicity have become apparent. It was an unfortunate serendipity that brought both of you to Meryton at the same time, however, I have thought about it obsessively these last days, and I still cannot understand why Mr. Wickham would have any interest in running away with my sister."

Darcy frowned. Why was she invoking Wickham now? What relevance could he possibly have at this juncture? Surely, she was not still under Wickham's spell?

"Why must the conversation always turn around Wickham?" he said, gritting his teeth against the rush of jealousy that reared up inside him. "I must ask you as I did before, on our previous occasion – what is your interest in that gentleman? Surely now that your sister—?"

"Enough," said Elizabeth, raising her hand. "I merely wished to clarify that, while your feelings have remained steadfast, so have mine, even if I now no longer give any credit to any of the poison Mr. Wickham poured into my ear. Having enjoyed your kind hospitality at Pemberley, moreover, I am more aware than ever of the falseness of his accusations. However, I am no more likely than I was before to think marriage between two such different people with such different social positions could have any hope for success. If anything, the insulting behavior of your aunt, who insisted on offering me a position as her companion, confirmed to me the absurdity of thinking that I could live in such exalted circles as you are accustomed to. And I still can neither forgive nor forget the fact that you deliberately and unrepentantly set out to cause the unhappiness of my sister even while you pursued me yourself."

Darcy had been smoldering ever since Elizabeth had first mentioned Wickham. Now he could scarcely see straight. Was she turning him down? Even after he had told her he had changed, that he no longer saw things the same way? Even when he had made such a particular effort to prove amiable to her, and had condescended to be nice to the Gardiners despite their background in trade?

"Besides," said Elizabeth, "It seems to me there is a lack of sensibility in renewing your attentions to me when you know our family is in a high state of anxiety about my sister."

Darcy felt the sting of the accusation, felt the injustice of it. Did she not see that what she termed lack of sensibility was in fact concern for her welfare? How was he to blame for loving her to distraction? For months now, he had stood accused of wrong-doing only because he had expressed the depth of his feelings.

A leaden anger settled inside him, heavy and aching, squeezing out his fervor.

"I see you are still determined to think ill of me," said Darcy, coldly. "However, perhaps you should consider things another way. Your family has been disgraced, your chances of desirable suitors all but destroyed. It is unlikely that Wickham will marry your sister. Your situation in the world since I last offered you my affection has declined significantly. You future is bleak indeed – with no brother and no wealthy relatives to support you, your only possibility when your father dies is to find a genteel occupation. While you take great exception to my aunt's offer of employment, it would in fact be extremely desirable for you to accept such a position – provided my aunt would still be willing to extend it when she hears of your family situation."

"No more!" said Elizabeth, bringing her hands to her face to cover it. "Do you think I do not know that?"

The cold anger that had seized him did not abate. "Yet you are contemptuous of my aunt. You say I lack sensibility. You accuse me of pride? It is you who are full of pride, you who refuse to acknowledge the reality of your situation, you who think that somehow you possess the moral high ground. On what do you base this? I have come to you in supplication and offered to save you from such a situation. It is within my means to save your whole family from penury and to rescue your sisters from living out their lives in neglect and dishonor, yet you are too proud to accept. Why, I ask you? I have a great deal to offer you, including my love. What do you have to offer me?"

Elizabeth brought down her hands to stare at him.

"Nothing," he said, his pain pouring from him. "Nothing but a sharp tongue, a propensity to laughter and a pretty face. Oh, and perhaps I should mention that the papers you now hold in your hand are mine. That was my list for a bride. I had hoped I would have no need for it, but it appears I have no choice."

Elizabeth blushed bright red. He felt a strong sense of satisfaction at causing her embarrassment. Let her think about it for a while. "I am done with you, madam. You need not fear any renewal of my attentions again. Ever. Good day to you, Miss Bennet."

He bowed to her stiffly, swung up onto his horse, and turned towards London, with Elizabeth's eyes boring into his back.

Chapter Three

Darcy did not ride to town, that day or the next. He rode as far as he could from Longbourn and humiliation, not caring what direction he was taking. All he knew was that his life was wrecked, his heart in tatters and his hopes cast on the wind. It was obvious that Elizabeth's feelings towards him had not changed since he had first asked her to marry him. If anything, her impression of him would have deteriorated after knowing he was the owner of the list.

He had deluded himself. She would never give him a chance.

To make matters worse, the heavens decided to empty their chamber pots on his unprotected head. He had set out from Pemberley without his greatcoat. Wretched and wet, hungry, tired and ready to fall from the saddle, he plodded onward he knew not where. All he needed was for his horse to turn lame or lose a shoe to complete his misery.

He stopped at the first inn he found. Luckily, it looked like a decent, clean place, though it was not one of the usual posting inns. The innkeeper was hardly welcoming, looking Darcy up and down as if he were a vagabond. For a moment, Darcy stood bewildered at the entrance in a puddle of his own making, the rain following him in through the open doorway.

"Shut the door, then, sir," said a sprightly barmaid, giving him a cheery smile. "Looks like you could do with some warm food and a chance to dry your clothes. Are you staying the night?"

Her good-natured kindness almost unmanned him as tears sprung to his eyes. He blinked the tears back.

"Yes, I would like a room," he said. "And if you could have my horse taken care of—."

The innkeeper's scowl disappeared as he heard Darcy's educated accent. Satisfied that he was not dealing with a brigand out to rob them, he quickly gave orders for a room to be prepared and the horse to be stabled. Darcy ascended the stairs to his room gratefully, asking for private parlor to eat in. He had carried a change of clothing in his saddlebag, just in case – as he had foolishly dreamed – the Bennets would ask him to dinner, but when he opened it, it was just as sodden inside as out. At least these clothes were not mud-splattered and were more appropriate for dinner.

Spreading his muddied clothing on any surface available in the room, he hoped the warm weather would help dry them out by the next day.

A scratch at the door and a chambermaid announced that dinner was ready and did he wish for a hot bath afterwards? Darcy could do little more than nod. He was so weary he considered the possibility that he might fall asleep in the bath and drown, but it would go some way towards soothing the aches and pains that now tormented him from his long hours on horseback.

He was shown into a private parlor where a dinner of jugged hare and a ragout of roasted beef awaited him, but he was in no mood to eat just yet. He needed oblivion first. He swallowed down a sifter of brandy then poured himself another one and, tipping it back, gulped it down. The brandy was not first class, but no matter. It burned his throat and pulsed through his blood, soothing away the pain and warming his stomach so he began to feel less empty and hollow inside.

Darcy saw everything from a great distance, as if it were happening to someone else.

He did not feel like eating, but as he had not eaten all day, and drinking on an empty stomach was unwise, he forced himself to take a few bites. The food was better than he had expected. He began to eat with some eagerness. Then the face of Elizabeth rose up before him, her expression hard and bitter as he berated her and the food suddenly weighed in his stomach like a stone. Pushing the food away, he ordered more brandy to be brought up.

It was all over. He could do nothing any more to convince her to love him. It was clear that nothing he did would change how she felt about him. He supposed that he should be glad that she was principled enough to refuse to marry him without affection, but that was little consolation for being rejected so completely.

Why would she not have him, even in a dire situation such as hers must be? He was not an ogre. Certainly, he had his faults, but they were minor. He did not have some of the faults other men had – drunkenness, wenching or gambling. He was not a spendthrift and he did not lead a debauched life. He was not a thief or a criminal. He was not a penny-pinching miser who valued money above his loved ones. Nor was he disagreeable – reserved, yes, but hardly brutal or ill-tempered. He was a man of his word, honorable and upright without being too rigid in his principles. He was guilty of no excesses of any type.

Her refusal might have been more understandable if his appearance was repellent. However, he had been told on many an occasion by the ladies that he was a handsome devil, and he had no reason to suppose otherwise. Ladies generally did favor him – not just ladies pushed by their chaperons and mothers to try and capture him. He had had more than a few women widows and married ladies fancy themselves in love with him. He was from an old family, wealthy and well connected.

Though he considered the matter for some time, no answer came to him beyond the fact that he was not as persuasive as other gentlemen were.

It could be said that his manner of proposing was not the most romantic, but he suspected that even if he had come to her on bended knee it would not have mattered. She was a sensible woman. She did not set much store by such gestures. Perhaps he should have courted her more, sent her flowers, for example. Women liked receiving flowers, though why that was the case when they could pick them from the garden or a field, he had never quite understood. He could have easily given her flowers while she was at Pemberley. It was not his style, however. He would have felt foolish. Besides, how could a flower reflect the raw immeasurable longing he felt for her?

He shut his eyes against the pain. He would not think of it. It was over, done with, gone forever. There was no going back. He had burned all bridges, irrevocably, destroyed all hope.

Pouring more brandy into his sifter, he stared into the golden liquid as it sloshed about, thinking of everything he should have said but did not.

He had lost Elizabeth. His ridiculous pledge had not even survived the day.

His musings were interrupted as the innkeeper scratched at the door and stepped in, looking apologetic.

"I am extremely sorry, sir, but I was wondering if I might move you to the tap-room? The parlor was promised to a young lady, but since she had not yet arrived and it was late I assumed – wrongly, it turns out – that she was not arriving until tomorrow. She is here, however, and is too genteel to be expected to eat in the tap-room."

Well, too bad, he was in no humor to be giving up his privacy and dining in a room full of strangers just because a spoilt young lady wished it. She had arrived too late. She could jolly well dine in her bedchamber. Darcy had no intention of giving up his privacy and dining with a roomful of strangers.

"I will not be removed," said Darcy, ready to defend his right to this space with his fists, if necessary. He was aware that he sounded childish and petulant but really, he did not care what the innkeeper thought of him. His life had come apart at the seams. He had the right to be as petulant as he wished.

"But, Mr. Darcy," protested the innkeeper, "the young lady—"

"You need not remove Mr. Darcy from the private parlor on my behalf," said a soft voice as an elegant young lady appeared on the doorway. She was dressed in a grey travelling gown, with grey gloves and a striped black and white turban with a black heron feather, clearly in half-mourning. "I have a perfect solution to the problem. I have no objection to sharing the parlor." Her somber appearance contrasted with the lively smile on her face.

28

However, Darcy did have an objection. He had been in too many situations where young ladies found ways to waylay him in the hopes of being compromised.

"I thank you," he said, arrogantly, "but I am not one to enjoy the company of strangers, particularly in the form of young ladies travelling alone."

"Neither am I," said the young lady. "However, I am not alone. My companion and my maid accompany me and will be partaking of supper with me, so you see there will be no problem. I am simply desirous of having my meal away from the public eye and then retiring to bed. I am Mrs. Deborah Fortin, by the way," she said.

The fact that she was married sat more easily with him, and her somber attire suited Darcy's mood. He did not wish to be impossibly churlish, so he stood up, leaning on the table as he was not as steady as he had hoped, and executed a small bow.

"Mr. Darcy at your service, madam" he said. "I daresay the table is large enough for both our parties. I hope you do not mind if I am not particularly sociable."

"I expect nothing of you, sir."

Her calm tone reassured him. He turned his back to her and continued his contemplation of his brandy. However, the quiet conversation of the lady and her companions intruded, and, even though they ignored his presence, he found it difficult to indulge in his fit of self-pity with them in the room. Good manners dictated that he make some effort to converse. Despite Elizabeth's criticism of his behavior at the Meryton Assembly, he was *not* so uncivil as to turn his back on a lady.

Waiting for a lull in the conversation, he intervened. "I see you are in mourning, madam," he said, since that was the most obvious topic he could fix on.

Mrs. Fortin looked a little surprised, but she answered readily enough.

"I lost my husband a little over a year ago. He was wounded at Salamanca. He was to be brought home to recover, but unfortunately, he did not endure the journey."

Darcy felt an unexpected surge of sympathy for her situation. The unhappiness in her eyes mirrored his own. He, too, had lost something precious.

"We have something in common, in that case," said Mr. Darcy, swallowing down a large gulp of brandy.

"You have lost someone you cared for," she said, sympathy in her eyes.

In many ways, Elizabeth was as lost to him as if she were dead. "Yes."

He did not elaborate any further because a wave of misery brought a glimmer of tears to his eyes. He turned away to hide them, but she had already seen them.

"The heartbreak will improve," said Mrs. Fortin, "and the pain will diminish. I did not think I would ever recover from my loss, but we find the fortitude somehow to continue, and I am now thankfully over the worst. You will discover a well of strength inside you, I am certain, even if you do not see it now."

Darcy shook his head. Her words echoed in the darkness that filled him. He felt so destitute he could not imagine himself having the strength to endure. How did she understand him so well? He felt a sudden rush of affection for her. She knew how he felt as nobody else had done.

"How did you become so wise?" he said, peering at her more closely. She looked hardly older than Georgiana, certainly no more than eighteen or nineteen. "You do not look old enough to have married and become a widow."

"I was married when I was sixteen. I had known my husband since childhood and we –" she gave a small smile. "—we did not wish to wait. We were very much in love. We had a little more than two years of marriage, though he was on the Peninsula fighting most of that time. My father approved of the match, so it seemed at the time that everything was in our favor." She sighed. "Only it wasn't, was it?"

Tears trembled in her eyes. She looked so tragic and heartbroken Darcy felt his own tears well up in response, though whether at her situation or his own he could not quite tell.

Damn the brandy. It had made a sop of him. The pain of his loss made him feel physically ill.

"I want nothing more than to crawl under a table and roll myself into a ball," he said, feeling so horribly maudlin he wanted to howl.

"I see you know exactly how I felt," murmured Mrs. Fortin. "She must have been a special person."

Special? Elizabeth Bennet? She had made him laugh. She had made the world a different place to live in. She had made him question himself and become someone better. Yes, Elizabeth had been special.

Darcy nodded, not trusting himself to talk. He was quite appalled at his lack of self-control but his limbs felt languid and he was experiencing a desperate need to unburden himself to someone who understood. The bedchamber that he had so recently wished to escape to now seemed desolate as a desert.

Scarcely knowing what he was saying, he began to speak.

~~X~~

Someone was pounding on the door. Darcy raised his head and discovered that the pounding was in his own head. The sun was pouring blindingly through the window. Groaning, he covered his head with a pillow and tried to return to sleep but it was impossible.

Then he remembered he had an urgent mission. He had to go to London to save Lydia Bennet. He sat up quickly in his bed and winced as his head proved to be too heavy for his body to hold. Memories came washing over him like a tidal wave and he shrank back at the impact. He recalled now that Elizabeth had destroyed his dreams.

There was no urgency to go to London after all. He was no longer the knight who aspired to her favor.

He returned to sleep.

He awoke some time later when someone scratched at the door and the door opened. The head of the amiable barmaid who had welcomed him the night before appeared.

"Mr. Darcy, seeing as it's so late, I was wondering if you would like breakfast brought up."

The thought of breakfast filled him with nausea.

"No, nothing. A strong coffee, perhaps?" He rubbed at the sides of his temple.

"I have just the right thing for your headache," she said. "A family recipe. You'll be up and about in no time, sir." She gave him a significant look. "You were rather wild, sir, yesterday."

Grinning, she shut the door.

Wild? What did she mean by wild? What had happened?

He realized now that he was in a state of undress. He was wearing nothing more than his shirt. A sudden panic set in as he recalled nothing of last night. He did not remember underdressing. A look around the room revealed clothes scattered all around the room.

Wild.

He jumped to his feet. Who had undressed him? How did the room come to be in such chaos? He always placed his clothes carefully on a chair when he undressed.

Wild.

He had a fuzzy recollection of Mrs. Fortin helping him up the stairs. He remembered her soft, gentle voice coaxing him into the room and shutting the door.

He sat back on the edge of the bed, horrified. The evidence was all around him.

The door opened again and the maid appeared with a glass.

"This should put you right as rain, Mr. Darcy, never you worry," said the barmaid.

"Did I—" How could he ask her? How could he even mention Mrs. Fortin? To mention her would be to acknowledge something had happened, and he did not wish to besmirch a lady's name. However, he could not bear the idea that he could have done something like that and not even remember.

The chambermaid bustled around the room picking up his clothes. "Looks like they're all dry now. Lucky for you the weather's so warm. This is a very fine shirt. That's what I told Mr. Holmes – he's the innkeeper – I told him, you can tell he's a gentleman, even under all that mud. We don't get many gentlemen coming this way. No call for it, this not being a coaching inn."

He wished she would stop talking. Her lively chatter clamored through his head. He took a tentative sip of her concoction. It tasted as horrible as it looked.

"What did you put in this?" he asked.

"Sorry, sir, but it's a closely-kept secret. Now you swallow it down and you'll be glad you did."

She seemed to be waiting for something. Then his thick brain registered that she was expecting something from him. He reached for his purse and took out a coin.

She looked at it but did not take it.

"I could see you were very taken with that young lady last night, sir," she said, casually. "The one who helped you up to your chamber."

Darcy's heart plummeted as his worst fears were confirmed.

"Are you engaged, sir?"

"Engaged?" said Darcy, thunderstruck.

"Well, she seems like a respectable young lady, sir," she said, winking at him. "Never you worry, Mr. Darcy, your secret is safe with me. I'm not one for idle gossip, not me."

Again, she was waiting for something. Clearly, she expected him to grease her palm.

"It is nothing of the sort," said Darcy, his aching head protesting as he moved it sharply. "It was a chance encounter, nothing more. I have never met the lady before."

The chambermaid seemed disappointed.

Darcy decided that it would kill two birds with one stone to grease her palm but for an entirely reason. He took out some coins and jingled them.

"I would appreciate it, however, if you will discover what you can about the lady. What do you know about her?"

"I know little enough, though I am sure I can find out more. She is a woman of means, to judge by the carriage she came in and by her clothes. Her maid thought herself quite important, I can tell you – didn't so much as say a word to any of us, and put on airs, but the lady herself seems kind. She was quite generous, at any rate. Though I must admit I was surprised she departed so early this morning. I suppose she had to be somewhere soon."

That was little enough to go on.

"I need to know where she came from and where she lives, if possible, and anything else you can discover."

The chambermaid curtseyed. "Very well, sir."

After she left, Darcy sank into the armchair and passed his hand across his face. What a spot he was in! How could he have done such a thing? It should teach him never to indulge himself in drink.

His only consolation was that she was a widow and therefore experienced in the ways of the world. It was not entirely unusual to have an encounter at an inn. In fact, at this moment, across the breadth and width of England, there were many gentlemen doing precisely that. However, this was a respectable inn, he was a respectable gentleman and Mrs. Fortin was a young, respectable widow. Had she been older, he thought, he might well have been tempted to forget about the whole affair. He winced at the term. Affair was the wrong word. However, she was young and quite innocent. From what Darcy remembered, she had not been married more than two or three years before her husband had been killed fighting Napoleon.

He cursed his deuced memory that seemed completely unable to recall what had happened. That empty blank worried him. If he had been able to speak to Mrs. Fortin before she left he would have at least been able at least to discover what had happened. However, Mrs. Fortin had eluded him and he could only imagine that he had embarrassed her, otherwise why depart so early without a chance to say goodbye? It was not a good sign.

The chambermaid returned.

"I asked around, but no one seemed to know much about Mrs. Fortin apart from the fact that she was on her way to London."

"She did not leave a forwarding address?" said Mr. Darcy.

"I'm afraid not, sir. The rooms were bespoke and paid for ahead of time, by a Mr. Thompson."

That would not help him. London – or anywhere else for that matter – was full of Mr. Thompsons. There was a veritable surplus of Mr. Thompsons.

Fortunately, the name Fortin was more unusual. That would be easier to track down, surely.

It was very clear what he had to do. Mrs. Fortin may have been a widow, but she was young and inexperienced and he had taken advantage of her.

He was a gentleman, and gentlemen did not do such things with well-bred young ladies.

He almost felt a sense of relief. His duty was clear, his future determined. He would find Mrs. Fortin and ask her to marry him.

Chapter Four

Was he any better than Wickham?

That was the question that faced Darcy as he rode away from the inn, his head reeling. How could he have done such a thing? The weather had cleared but he could not say the same about his head, which pounded like the blow of an anvil with every step his horse took.

He had always been scrupulous about drinking. He was no puritan, but unlike many of his acquaintances, he prided himself on not dipping too deep. Perhaps not all gentlemen considered sobriety an ideal, but he disliked excess and preferred to err in the direction of sobriety than dissipation. He had never been the type of youth to use drunkenness as an excuse for licentiousness. He had witnessed what Wickham was capable of when deep in his cups and had made sure never to allow himself to be in such a situation.

He recalled Mrs. Fortin from the night before – at least as far as he was capable of doing so. There was a hole in his memory. She was a lovely young lady who had lost her husband a year ago and was in half-mourning. They had spoken for some time –she about the husband she had lost, he about Elizabeth. He knew he had given her the false impression that Elizabeth was dead. What other falsehoods had he committed? It was hopeless trying to remember what he had said beyond a certain point, but he had a vague recollection of leaning his head on her shoulder. Even that much seemed incredible enough. Matters must have progressed beyond this at some point, but there was no recalling when or how.

There was nothing inherently wrong in dallying with a widow, of course, particularly if she was willing and provided the two parties were discreet. Doing so without even being aware of it was beyond enough, however. Besides, he was in love with someone else, and even if Elizabeth had rejected him, that was no reason to turn to another woman the very same day.

Though perhaps he had good reason, after all. He was flesh and blood, and the reality was that Elizabeth had rejected him a long time ago. He had been deceiving himself all this time, believing that somehow he would be able to win her over. He was no closer to doing so than he had been months ago.

As for his courtly ideals – well, they had disappeared into the mists of history. The days of knights' challenges and jousts were over, and young ladies these days were not likely to be won by a show of chivalry. He had been chivalrous when he had rescued Elizabeth's uncle from the carriage. He had brought him the best physician and extended his hospitality to the Gardiners. It had not affected Elizabeth Bennet's view of him, not in the least.

It was charm that won the ladies over, charm that he did not have, and charm that men like Wickham had in abundance. No longer did a man have to be a hero to win his fair lady. He had only to smile and weave his magic and all the ladies around fell under his spell. Then, when they discovered the deceit, they cried foul and it was men like him who had to come to the rescue and to pick up the pieces. Darcy seethed with the injustice of it all, because, in fact, if he had been more like Wickham, Elizabeth would very likely have been attracted to him. Instead, here he was, riding to London with a pounding head, intent on rescuing Elizabeth's sister from Wickham.

He had made a pledge to Elizabeth Bennet that involved rescuing her sister Lydia. That was when he believed he could win Elizabeth over, however. Now with no hope at all, how could he be expected to hold to the conditions of the pledge? Of course, Elizabeth knew nothing of the pledge. He had not made it to her but to himself.

Apart from the near-disaster with Georgiana, he had had to do his share of placating in the past. One particularly notable occasion had been after Wickham had been sent down from Oxford. It had involved the niece of one of the Dons, a young girl around sixteen who had fallen madly in love with Wickham, only to discover him in bed with someone else. Wickham had laughed it off. He had justified it by saying he had done the chit a favor— she had been hounding him for weeks, thinking herself in the midst of a passionate romance. If she had been disenchanted, it was only because she had allowed herself to be enchanted in the first place.

The girl had been heartbroken and Wickham had been expelled. Darcy had been unwise enough to try and intervene on Wickham's behalf, believing him for once to be the innocent part. He had almost been expelled himself for his efforts.

Now again he was expected to repair the damage Wickham had done, with no reward other than his own satisfaction in putting things right.

Well, he had had enough. He could see Wickham's perspective, which was simple. If a young lady was foolish enough to fall for his empty talk, then so be it. The responsibility was hers, no one else's. Take Georgiana, for example, she had escaped narrowly because she had been wise enough to inform Darcy of their plans. True, he had had to work hard to minimize the damage afterwards, but at least Georgiana had known to extricate herself before it was too late.

Elizabeth, on the other hand, had been very taken by Wickham. Subsequent events had shown her Wickham's villainy, but it had not made her any more predisposed towards Darcy. Not even a position of influence and a promise of a large and noble fortune made up for his lack of charm.

He had tried to be charming with Elizabeth at Pemberley, or at least to prove to her that he could be civil, but he had been too tongue-tied to succeed. Why was it villains like Wickham were never tongue-tied in a lady's presence?

Darcy seethed with the injustice of it all, because, in fact, if he had been more like Wickham, Elizabeth would very likely have been attracted to him. Instead, here he was, riding to London with a pounding head, intent on rescuing Elizabeth's sister from Wickham. True, he had pledged to rescue her sister Lydia, but that was when he believed he could win Elizabeth over. Now with no hope at all, surely he was not bound by that pledge any more. It was not as if anyone knew about it. He had not even told Elizabeth of his resolution.

He could not forever be trying to undo the damage that the scoundrel left behind him wherever he went. Darcy was not responsible for his childhood companion's mistakes. It was time Wickham – and others – realized that they had to take responsibility for their actions.

Tightening the reins, Darcy slowed down. Elizabeth's rejection had freed him of the necessity of going to London. If he wished, he could return to the calm and peace of Pemberley. Georgiana would be there. She would play her music and he would be soothed. He would look across at the land he owned and know that he was destined for something entirely different, that his duty lay with his ancestors, with the continuity of the land and, last but not least, with his family.

Time passed as he sat there on his horse at the crossroads of the London Road and the Great North Road, considering that prospect. The harvest was still in progress. There was fishing, and soon it would be the hunting season. There were plenty of things to do on the estate. He neglected things of late.

The draw of Pemberley was so strong that he turned and began to head in that direction. A sense of relief rose up in him. It was the wisest course. Then the image of Elizabeth standing by the edge of the river, putting out her hand to pull him out of the water returned to him in full force and he stopped. There would be no peace for him there, now. Pemberley was imprinted with her presence. He thought of Georgiana, too. She was not as restful as she once was. She had demands of her own, and she would have questions for him that he would not be able to answer. As if those two considerations were not enough, there was Miss Marshall, who no doubt would be making demands of her own.

In any case, there was no possibility of shirking his responsibility. Even if he decided not to pursue Wickham, he had another crucial reason for going to Town. He needed to find Mrs. Fortin and offer for her. He was too much of a gentleman not to do so.

Perhaps it was not a mistake, after all, to have dallied with Mrs. Fortin. Maybe it was just what he needed to sort out his life. He had made a hash of things, but he could make amends. He already knew Mrs. Fortin was a caring kind of person. From what he had gathered, she seemed kind, well-mannered, gentle and not unattractive.

Turning his back on Pemberley, he took the London Road. No one was in the Townhouse, so he would be left in peace. He would go there, recuperate for a while then search for Mrs. Fortin. They would marry in time for Georgiana to have a chaperone for her London season. It was certainly not what he had planned, but the outcome might not be so very bad after all.

Georgiana did not know what she would have done if it were not for young Ebenezer, the coachman's son. He was a shy young man with a differential manner, and the moment Georgiana explained to him that she needed his help to travel he was more than willing to help. He even arranged travel for Georgiana's maid and Darcy's valet, who would be following close behind.

"I know exactly where to stop," said Ebenezer, "I've travelled this way with Mr. Darcy so many times I've lost count. Never you fear, Miss Darcy. I'll have you safely in London in no time."

It was a tremendous relief to Georgiana that at least one person did not oppose her. She was tired of trying to justify herself. Mrs. Annesley clearly had everyone on her side; even Mrs. Reynolds had tried to convince Georgiana not to go. It vexed no end to think they all talked about her behind her back and made decisions for her as if she were still a child. Yes, she was inexperienced, but that did not mean she was entirely devoid of sense.

She clung obstinately to the idea that William needed her. That was what carried her through as Mrs. Annesley finally bowed to the inevitable and accepted that, for once, Georgiana was not going to obey her strictures blindly.

It was strange, but she had never before noticed how much her life was confined by those around her. She had always thought of them as working for her, but the last two days had brought home to her clearly the fact that they did not. They worked for her brother, not for her. Perhaps she should not mind it; after all, it was William who paid them their wages. Nevertheless, she felt a sense of dissatisfaction with it all. It was churlish, perhaps, to complain about being imprisoned when she lived in such luxury, yet she did not feel pampered at all. She felt as if her life were not her own, and that she was ruled by an army of servants.

It was therefore with a sense of escaping prison that she mounted into the carriage. For the first time in her life, she felt in control. It was a strange, heady feeling. It was frightening, too. It was she who knocked on the wall to ask for the carriage to begin its journey. It was she who knew ahead of time – thanks to Ebenezer – which inns they would be stopping at.

Mrs. Annesley stared out of the window silently as the familiar landscape began to fall behind them.

"I do believe we should turn back before it is too late, Miss Darcy. I shudder to think what your brother will say to your gallivanting around the countryside in this manner."

Really, Mrs. Annesley was such a dear, even if sometimes Georgiana had little patience with her.

"Gallivanting around the countryside?" Georgiana smiled and shook her head. "Hardly gallivanting, Mrs. Annesley, and certainly not around the countryside. My destination is London and I hope we will be proceeding in a straight line. Besides, I have told you already, Mrs. Annesley, my brother will not blame you. He knows I can be very obstinate once I have set my mind on something."

At least, she hoped he knew her well enough to be aware of that. In either case, she would ensure that Mrs. Annesley did not bear the brunt of the blame. It was entirely her doing, and Georgiana would make it clear.

The sense of freedom singing inside her increased as she crossed the bridge leading away from Pemberley. It was not as if she did not love her home. Quite the opposite. Pemberley was very precious to her. She could not, however, continue to live in it like an unwanted poor relative. Sooner or later she would have to take matters into her own hands and prove herself the mistress of Pemberley, at least until William married and brought a wife with him to shoulder that responsibility.

Georgiana very much hoped that wife would be Miss Elizabeth Bennet, which was partly why she felt it essential for her to be in London. Eventually, both William and Miss Marshall would be in London at the same time, and Georgiana did not wish to leave William at the mercy of Miss Marshall's wiles.

"So be it," said Mrs. Annesley. "I have done what I could to prevent you. I wash my hands off the whole enterprise."

A sudden attack of conscience came over Georgiana. Was she acting unreasonably? Was she being selfish? Was she presuming too much? Did she have a right to interfere in her brother's life? The answer was simple. She did not have that right and she would never have dreamt of interference under normal circumstances.

However, she reasoned, her brother was not himself and had not been since he had lost his heart to Elizabeth. She could never have imagined the old William would need her council in any way, but this new Darcy seemed at the mercy of his emotions and too easily swayed in one direction or the other. A rash decision made in a moment of despair could have a detrimental impact on all of them.

Naturally, she could not say any of this to Mrs. Annesley, who was convinced that Georgiana's behavior was irrational. She knew she had upset her companion. However, returning to Pemberley was out of the question. Not only for her own sake, but also for her brother's as well.

"You have done your duty, Mrs. Annesley," said Georgiana. "It is I who has been hopelessly obstinate. I hope you will forgive me."

Mrs. Annesley shook her head. "Nothing good will come of it, mark my words," she said and with that, she leaned against the squabs and settled herself down to sleep.

Chapter Five

The Holland covers had scarcely been removed and the bed prepared when the front doorbell sounded and Georgiana heard her brother's voice in the entrance. By and by, his footsteps could be heard coming slowly towards them.

"Georgiana?" said Darcy. "What in the world are you doing here?"

"William! You are in town after all! The servants did not know. Were you staying at your club?" said Georgiana, hurrying over and giving him a delighted peck on the cheek. She had done the right thing, apparently, to come here. It was such a relief to know that Darcy was not off somewhere else after all.

"I have only just arrived," said Darcy, with a little frown, "Though I will admit, I am rather puzzled to find you here. Where is Mrs. Annesley?"

"She is upstairs, seeing to the bedchambers."

He was displeased. Georgiana could see that at once. He was smiling that twisted smile of his that meant he was agitated. Perhaps he was dealing with something private and she was intruding. She twisted her hands together behind her back and wondered how he would react if she tried to explain the sudden sense of urgency she had experienced.

"I felt rather abandoned now that all the house guests have left and there was no one to talk to," she said, feeling an explanation was necessary.

She had meant it to be a white lie, but now that she said it, she knew it was also true. She did feel abandoned and restless at Pemberley. She was no longer content as she had been before to wander around the great house with no one else but Mrs. Annesley. Georgiana felt guilty at the direction of her thoughts, but her companion was hardly a substitute for her brother, let alone a wider social circle.

Darcy's expression softened. "I am sorry I had to leave so suddenly, little sister, but I was required on an urgent matter."

"Well, we have brought you your valet," said Georgiana, with a smile. "He was rather unhappy at having his services dispensed with, particularly since you took almost no clothing with you. He has prepared a trunk for you."

"That was thoughtful of you, Georgiana. I am indeed in need of a few shirts." He hesitated. "I hope you will not mind if I do not dine with you tonight. I am planning an early night. I fear you will not find me as good company as you hope. I am rather tired."

"Your time is your own, William. Please do not feel constrained by my presence here," said Georgiana. "There is always enough in town to amuse me, even if many of the fashionable circles have left. When we passed by Hyde Park today it was the fashionable hour, and to me it seemed no less crowded than usual."

"Did it indeed?" said Darcy, looking weary. "I am glad to hear it. And now if you will excuse me— I need to change out of these clothes and retire."

As she watched him walk to the door, she felt a fierce gladness that she had come. Her instinct told her that once again, her brother was in trouble and would very likely be in need of support.

~~x~~

The next day, Georgiana did not see William all day until dinner, where conversation was very muted and mostly consisted of polite observances between Mrs. Annesley and herself.
William appeared entirely distracted and barely answered any of their questions. It was not until breakfast the morning after that she had an opportunity to talk to him.

45

"William," said Georgiana, after she had asked him a question, which he had not answered. "Did you even hear a word I said?"

Darcy looked up from a plate of uneaten food.

"Hmm?"

"Clearly not," said Georgiana, with a smile. "You seem rather listless. I hope you are not coming down with some illness."

"No need to fuss, Georgiana. I am perfectly well," said Darcy, with a note of finality.

Georgiana considered her brother. There were dark circles under his eyes, his hair was disheveled and he had not eaten so much as a bite of his food. He had a helpless, lost look in his eyes. She restrained a sudden impulse to reach over and hug him.

He would not appreciate it.

"I can see that," said Georgiana. She could not help smiling. It was perfectly obvious that something was gnawing at him, or rather someone possibly with the name of Elizabeth Bennet.

If only she could write to Elizabeth and tell her how her brother felt! It was such a pity he had not had the chance to propose to her when she was at Pemberley. Georgiana felt that Elizabeth might have been predisposed to like her brother then. However, Caroline Bingley's insinuations that she was to marry Darcy did not help matters. There had been no opportunity to set the record straight. Perhaps if she wrote a letter to Elizabeth explaining the situation—?

No, it would not do. She would be no better than her aunt and uncle if she intervened in a private matter that concerned only her brother. It would likely cause more harm than good, leading to the embarrassment of all parties. Unless William provided her with more information, any conclusion Georgiana could reach would be more than guesswork.

She cast a quick glance at William, whose attention was focused on his plate. He had taken up his knife and was idly engaged in cutting each of the capers in quarters with concentrated precision. Georgiana plucked up her courage and decided that there could be no harm in asking. If he did not wish to answer her, he would not.

"William, do you know why Miss Bennet left us so suddenly at Pemberley?"

Darcy put down his fork and knife with a clang, pushed back his chair, and stalked off to the side table to help himself to more food he would not eat.

"Why do you ask?" he said.

"Because it was strange of her to leave so abruptly," said Georgiana. "I know there was that business with Caroline, and then our aunt and uncle. I was thinking, perhaps I could write to her, explaining. I know you cannot, since it would not be quite proper, but I can write her an apology."

Darcy stared at her for a moment with such intensity that she shifted uncomfortably. Was he actually considering her offer?

"I—" he broke off, looking completely defeated. "No. Writing will not help. She did not leave for any of the reasons you suggested."

"Then why?" she said, feeling her heart clench. Had someone made improper advances to her? Why the mystery? If so, who could it be?

"I am not at liberty to say," said Darcy, with an air of finality. "I appreciate your offer, but I suggest you forget the whole thing. I have promised to provide some business advice to the Gardiners and, once I have done so, I intend to consign the Gardiners and the Bennets to the past. I suggest you do so as well."

With that, he strode to the door, and, without waiting for the footman to open it, he stepped out and slammed the door loudly behind him.

Alone in the library, Darcy struggled to reach a decision. On his way to town, things had been clearer. He would not look for Wickham. The situation with Wickham was not of his making and he did not have a role to play in it. However, seeing Georgiana had triggered memories for him. What if Georgiana had been in that situation?

One part of him, the part that dealt self-preservation, told him in no uncertain terms that he should have nothing to do with the Bennets. Why should he save the Bennet girls' reputation when Elizabeth wanted nothing to do with him and would very likely marry someone else? Why prolong his own unhappiness instead of walking away and leaving the Bennets to deal with the problem themselves?

The other part of him, the one that still believed in being a gentleman, was appalled at such blatant self-interest. The gentleman in him insisted that he could not abandon Elizabeth Bennet in her hour of need. He could not be so self-interested as to refuse to help her because she would not marry him.

He sat behind his desk, trying to convince himself that he had the right to protect himself, that he desperately needed that distance, but it was in vain. In the end, it was the gentleman in him who won. He knew his conscience would never allow him to walk away and leave Elizabeth stranded. Besides, he had made a pledge, even if Elizabeth did not know it, and he was honor-bound to fulfill that pledge.

Having reached his decision, he tugged at the bell pull. He would have to locate Mrs. Younge at once. He had wasted enough time. She would undoubtedly know where Wickham was hiding.

Then he realized that he had a problem. He did not have Mrs. Younge's address. He had corresponded with her before employing her to take care of Georgiana – and what an ill-considered decision that had turned out to be – but of course the letter would have been filed by Darcy's secretary, Mr. Abbott. Unfortunately, Mr. Abbott was away on leave and would not be coming back until next week. He had gone to visit an aunt somewhere in Devon – Darcy could not remember where. Even if he had left an address, there would be so much time wasted sending an express that it would hardly be worthwhile trying to recall him.

However, Mr. Abbott was a methodical man and meticulous to a fault when it came to retaining records of Darcy's correspondence. It should be reasonably easy to find Mrs. Younge's letter of application for the post of companion to Georgiana. Even without his secretary's presence.

When Darcy ordered the boxes of papers related to the previous year brought to the library, he had had a vague idea of two or three boxes. He had been unprepared for the parade of servants who appeared, each carrying a large box. His desk was surrounded. Where the devil did all these boxes come from?

"How many boxes are there left?" said Darcy to a footman who had just deposited yet another box near his desk.

"Not too many, sir," said the man cheerfully.

Darcy looked through the files, at first careful not to disturb Mr. Abbott's careful organization. However, he soon realized he could discern no method to the madness. If Mr. Abbott did have a system, it was not apparent to anyone other than him.

An hour later, Darcy was no closer to finding the letter than he had been at the beginning.

There was a scratch at the door and having obtained his permission, the butler appeared, holding a tray with steaming hot tea and a large piece of venison pie.

His empty stomach gurgled at the sight. He was hungry and thirsty and for a moment, he was tempted to indulge himself in some food and drink and to forget about his frustrating search. Then the image of Elizabeth as he had last seen her, lines of worry marring the smooth skin between her brows, rose up before him. The urgency of his mission returned, stronger than ever. He had no time to waste, eating or drinking, much as he was tempted.

Darcy dismissed the tray with a wave of his hand.

"Later," he said, turning back to the files.

He surveyed the boxes that still remained to be examined in dismay. It was a herculean task. How in heaven's name was he going to find Mrs. Younge's application letter? He needed help, but he did not wish to engage any of the servants in this work. He could not risk any information leaking out.

There was nothing else to be done. He was going to have to ask Georgiana for her assistance.

Darcy had barely set his foot outside the library when he was approached by an apprehensive Mrs. Annesley.

"Now that Miss Darcy is upstairs, may I have a word with you, Mr. Darcy?"

"Of course," said Darcy, wondering what was amiss.

"I wish to make it clear that I would have none of it, Mr. Darcy," said Mrs. Annesley, looking so stern that Darcy wondered if it was possible he had gone to the other extreme by hiring such a forbidding companion for his sister after Ramsgate. He made a mental note to ask Georgiana if she found her companion too harsh. "The fact is, I tried to stop her, but she showed an unexpectedly stubborn streak and refused to back down."

Darcy was beginning to feel alarmed. Georgiana? A stubborn streak? What was Mrs. Annesley suggesting?

"I did not realize Georgiana was proving difficult to manage," said Darcy. "I hope she has not been in any trouble?"

Surely, Georgiana had learned her lesson and was not engaged in any improper relationship?

"Well, sir, I will admit that I did not handle the situation as well as I could have. I should have guessed I would set her back up if I forbade her from doing it. Young people are like that, are they not? But I never thought she would go through with it."

What the devil was this "it" she was talking about?

"I would appreciate it if you told me what incident you are referring to, Mrs. Annesley. I am afraid Georgiana has not informed me of what happened."

It was Mrs. Annesley's turn to look bewildered.

"Did anything happen?" she said, with alarm. "I am sorry, Mr. Darcy. I knew nothing about it."

That infernal "it" again.

"Neither do I," said Darcy, struggling to be patient, "which makes two of us. I am merely trying to ascertain what it was you disapproved of in Georgiana's behavior."

"Why, the trip to London, of course. I wished to let you know I objected strongly to it. In fact I did everything I could to dissuade her."

Was that all? Darcy felt such a palpable sense of relief that he almost grinned at Mrs. Annesley. He refrained only because he suspected she would not appreciate it.

"Ah, I see. You did not wish her to come to London?"

"Precisely. I knew you would not approve."

"Well," said Darcy. "Under normal circumstances, you would perhaps be right. However, I am rather pleased she has come as I require her assistance in something."

Relief spread over Mrs. Annesley's features. "Do you indeed, sir. I am very happy to hear it. Then you are not angry?"

"Not at all," said Darcy.

"Well then." She seemed at a loss what to say.

Darcy felt sorry for her. She clearly had worried about Georgiana's decision to travel. "I have in fact been meaning to tell you that you have done very well with Georgiana. I am very pleased with the improvement in her character."

He was rewarded with a big smile.

"Why, thank you, Mr. Darcy," said Mrs. Annesley. "I am happy to be of assistance."

She curtseyed and walked away, leaving Darcy to reflect on the situation of ladies like her who, through misfortune or being impoverished, were so completely dependent on the goodwill of their others.

He only had to hope that Elizabeth Bennet was never reduced to such a situation.

He slammed his right fist into the palm of his other hand. If only the wretched woman would see sense. Why, oh why did she have to be so deucedly proud?

Georgiana expected her brother to be too angry with her to even appear for dinner, but to her surprise, he joined her in the music room while she was singing and seemed to have recovered enough of his humor to make an effort to show concern for her.

"I have sent a note around to the Bingleys to inform them that we are here. The situation is awkward between Caroline and myself, but that does not mean you cannot enjoy her company. I know you do not know too many people in town and I do not wish you to be isolated."

"You need not worry, brother," said Georgiana. "I have some old school friends I could call on -- that is, if they are in Town -- and there are plenty of places to visit. As long as I have Mrs. Annesley's company, we can explore the museums and galleries and generally find things to do."

"Very well," said Darcy, absently. He gave the appearance of a person struggling with himself.

Georgiana had already found herself in trouble earlier in the day for speaking up. She decided to let him be; hoping that at some point he would choose to explain what it was that troubled him.

Darcy cleared his throat suddenly and looked as though in preparation for an important announcement to make.

Georgiana immediately set down her fork and prepared to give him her full attention. Was he finally going to confide in her?

"I have been meaning to ask something of you. However, you must promise me to tell no one I asked you for this, not even Mrs. Annesley."

Now her brother was behaving mysteriously. What could he possibly have to hide?

"Of course I promise, William."

"Good. I would like you to cast your mind back. Do you remember Mrs. Younge?"

As if she could ever forget the woman who had been the cause of her disgrace.

"How could I not remember her, brother?"

"I am asking for a specific reason. It is imperative that I get hold of her immediately. Do you perchance remember her address?"

Georgiana's heart sank.

So Darcy's sudden absence had nothing to do with Elizabeth Bennet at all. She had had it all wrong. Her sudden trip to London had been ill-conceived and unnecessary.

A darker thought occurred to her. Did any of this have to do with what had happened at Ramsgate? Surely her recklessness would not be coming back to haunt her one year later?

"I do believe I recall where she lived," said Georgiana, uncertainly. "I cannot tell you the address, but I believe I can take you there."

Darcy looked at her sharply. "Do you mean that she actually had the temerity to take you to her home?" said Darcy. "For what purpose?"

Georgiana hung her head. "I did not know at the time it was wrong to visit her, but that is where I first met Wickham before we travelled to Ramsgate."

"She took you to a questionable area of town? Why did I not hear of this?"

"It appeared to be a respectable area. Her house was not grand, of course, but it did not seem improper to me, though perhaps I was not the best judge of such things. I was completely taken in by her."

"Well, you must not blame yourself, Georgiana. If I, much older and more experienced in such matters, was deceived by Mrs. Younge, then I do not have a leg to stand on." He gave her a kind smile. "Are you certain you can find the place again?"

She nodded, relieved. William was not angry with her. He actually needed her help.

"Absolutely. We can drive past it and I will point it out to you." She shuddered at the thought of meeting the woman who had betrayed her so badly. "I hope you do not require me to speak to her."

"No, not at all," said her brother. "I will have the coachman drive you straight home."

"Then in that case, brother, I will be more than happy to help."

Chapter Six

Georgiana had scarcely had time to take off her bonnet when Caroline Bingley appeared on their doorstep. The butler, who had known her for years, made no more than a half-hearted effort to announce her. She was a frequent visitor at the Darcy townhouse with her brother, having interfered in Darcy and Bingley's games many years. It was only now that she was grown up that William had taken to calling her Miss Bingley.

"My dear Georgiana," said Caroline, advancing towards her quickly and kissing her on the cheek. "How I have missed you! It seems like months since we last met."

Georgiana was at a loss to understand Caroline's sudden enthusiasm. The last time she had seen her was when William had informed Caroline in no uncertain terms that he intended to offer for Elizabeth Bennet. Caroline had appeared heartbroken then. It seemed Caroline had recovered from the shock far more quickly than Georgiana would have given her credit for.

With a sense of relief, she returned Caroline's embrace. After all, she had known Caroline for several years now, and did not wish to lose their association.

"I am glad we can still be friends," said Georgiana warmly. "I was worried when—"

"Oh, that," interrupted Caroline. "It was of no significance at all, I assure you. I have already put it completely behind me." There was an airy blitheness to her statement that made Georgiana look at her more closely.

Caroline Bingley was dressed even more carefully than usual, in a burnt orange walking dress that complemented her grey eyes. A matching turban with a single ostrich feather completed her fashionable appearance. Overall, the effect was quite stunning and Georgiana found herself feeling dowdy by contrast in her morning dress.

As they walked to the parlor together, Caroline drew Georgiana's arm into her own and patted her hand.

"You do not know how delighted I am to see you again," said Caroline. "Is there somewhere we can talk privately?"

Georgiana was more bewildered than ever at Caroline's high spirits. Much as she tried, she could not account for them.

"Not in the parlor," said Georgiana. "Mrs. Annesley is there."

"Are you not tired of having a companion watching your every step?"

Georgiana sighed. "Yes, although Mrs. Annesley is very kind. However, I would like to be trusted to make my own decisions sometimes."

"Well," said Miss Bingley, taking her hand and squeezing it. "Perhaps your brother will soon take a wife and you will no longer need a companion. If I were to marry Mr. Darcy, for example, I would immediately relieve you of her presence."

Georgiana frowned at this statement. Something must have happened for Miss Bingley to make such a statement, so soon after William had dashed her hopes so clearly.

Curiosity consuming her, she led the way to the bedroom. She felt a little odd doing so. She did not make a habit of entertaining anyone in her bedchamber, but perhaps she would now find out what had happened to change Caroline's mood.

She rang for tea and was forced to wait until the servants had retreated to question Caroline.

"So," she said, as soon as the footman closed the door behind him. "I see you have some important news to convey to me."

Miss Bingley gave a wide grin. "You understand me so well. Yes, I have news that you will very probably be relieved to hear. It concerns Miss Elizabeth Bennet."

Of course it was about Elizabeth Bennet. Everything seemed to revolve around Elizabeth Bennet these days. Perhaps she was finally to find out what had gone so wrong at Pemberley.

Miss Bingley fished inside her reticule and produced a letter. It´was closely written and heavily crisscrossed in a rather childish, rounded hand.

"I have my contacts in Meryton, as you can imagine, since we have taken an estate there. One of my correspondents is inclined to gossip, which I normally would not encourage as I have no interest in knowing the trivialities of life in the country. However, in this case I have to admit I was very pleased to hear from my friend."

She paused dramatically. Georgiana had been trained not to squirm no matter how impatient, but she could barely contain herself from asking Miss Bingley to hurry up.

A delighted smile settled onto Miss Bingley's face. "My dear Georgiana, this has occurred just in time. Miss Elizabeth Bennet's youngest sister – a girl barely fifteen years old – has run away, and you will never guess with whom!! This is so deliciously ironic! With our own *Mr. Wickham* – your father's steward's son. You cannot imagine the scandal. And as if that were not bad enough, it is not known whether the two are actually married..."

Georgiana was aware that Miss Bingley was still talking, but she could not hear another word. She was certain she was going to faint. She took in some deep gulping breaths and strove to control herself.

It was too utterly horrible. This would have been what people would have said had she ran away with Wickham. People would have gloated as Miss Bingley was doing, said the things Miss Bingley was saying, had she not averted that terrible mistake and confided in her brother at the last moment. She trembled as she thought of what her fate would have been. She would have lost everything, including her fortune, which would have belonged to Wickham. He would have married her, of course, but only because he would then have possessed everything she owned.

She had no illusions now what he would have done with it.

Her heart went out to that foolish, foolish girl who had fallen for Wickham's charms. What must she be suffering now, knowing she was abandoned, friendless and without resources to fall back on! She could only hope she had enough of a fortune to guarantee that he would marry her.

"Georgiana, what on earth is the matter? You look as pale as a sheet."

"I need my smelling salts," she said, rising to look for them in her drawer.

"I knew you would be shocked. Imagine if that had happened after your brother had announced his engagement! I am not surprised you are overwhelmed. Fortunately, it happened at the right time."

"Oh, pray stop, Caroline. I do not wish to hear anything more!" said Georgiana. She was desperate to be alone. However, she dared not say anything because she did not want to betray herself. She did not want Miss Bingley to guess at her guilty secret.

She took in deep whiffs of the smelling salts and tried not to hear anything Miss Bingley was saying.

"There, there," said Miss Bingley. "You need not be so very alarmed. It was a narrow escape, indeed, but the timing could not have been better."

Georgiana pulled herself together with an effort. She must control herself. She must not allow her feelings to give anything away.

"Perhaps your brother will now reconsider his marital prospects," said Miss Bingley, giving a malicious smile.

Georgiana did not like that smile. She wanted Miss Bingley to go away and leave her alone, but she could not reveal anything.

"I think it may be too soon for him to reconsider his prospects," said Georgiana, measuring her words carefully.

"Georgiana, while I appreciate your concern, I am far more experienced in the ways of the world than you are. Gentlemen often make impulsive decisions if the lady they love repulses them."

"But we do not know yet that my brother has heard the news, and we do not know what his reaction to it may be." Even as she said it, however, she remembered her brother's despair in the morning. She realized that, not only had William heard, but also he had made up his mind what to do. After all, what had he said to her?

I intend to consign the Gardiners and the Bennets to the past. I suggest you do so as well.

For the first time that she could remember, Georgiana felt angry with her brother. Surely, he had not abandoned the woman he loved because of a mistake her sister had made. Surely, he remembered that Georgiana had almost done the same.

She could not credit her brother with being so cold, so hypocritical.

Then suddenly she understood why he had needed Mrs. Younge's address. He was looking for Wickham. Of course! Her brother had not abandoned the Bennets; he was trying to save them.

All her anger dissipated. She had misjudged him. He must have rushed to Longbourn to find out as much information as possible, and then come straight to town to locate Wickham. She was touched. Her heart swelled inside her. She was lucky to have such a wonderful, caring brother.

"Miss Darcy? Do you find what I said amusing?"

She looked up to find Caroline watching her. She had no idea what Caroline had been saying, but she knew it was crucial to discourage her from setting her sights on her brother again.

"Even if my brother did hear the news," said Georgiana, "I do not believe it will make any difference."

"Indeed?" said Caroline, raising her brow. "I find that difficult to believe. It is one thing to ignore the Bennets' inferior social standing, and quite another to marry a young woman whose family are social outcasts."

"I believe my brother too much of a gentleman to abandon the lady he is practically engaged to, because of something that is no fault of hers."

Caroline rose to her feet, looking agitated. "Well, Miss Darcy," she said, suddenly turning very prim and formal, "I do believe you are quite mistaken in this matter. We shall continue this discussion at another time, however. I have just recalled a prior engagement. I hope you do not think me rude if I take my leave?"

"Not at all, Miss Bingley," said Georgiana.

As Caroline hurried away, Georgiana felt a qualm of conscience. She should not have said that her brother was practically engaged. Very likely William would be upset at her if he knew. He would certainly not appreciate her interference. If she did not hold herself in check, she mused, she would soon be in danger of becoming very much like her aunt Catherine.

It was a sobering thought.

~~X~~

Georgiana was right, thought Darcy, casting a glance around him. Mrs. Younge did in fact live in a respectable neighborhood. The terrace house was located in an unfashionable area of London, but it showed no sign of being disreputable. The yellow terraced houses here were not very high and with their small double-hung sash windows, they gave the impression of being shabby genteel.

From inside there was a sound of girlish voices and laughter. Did Mrs. Younge keep a boarding school? There was no sign indicating it. Perhaps Mrs. Younge was more upright than he had given her credit for. But she could not be, not after what she had been willing to do to Georgiana. If this was a boarding school, Darcy could only pity the parents who entrusted the care of their daughters to a woman like her.

Darcy rapped on the door with the knocker. Within seconds, a young servant woman came to the door.

"I would like to speak to Mrs. Younge," said Darcy.

"She is not receiving visitors at the moment, sir," said the servant woman in a sing-song tone that told him it was a speech she gave frequently. "If you would like to leave your card–"

"I would not like to leave my card," said Darcy. "She will see me. Tell her Mr. Darcy is here."

"Very well."

He blocked the door with his foot, giving her no chance to close it. The servant walked away hesitantly, looking behind her to see if he meant to force his way in.

As he expected, he did not have to wait for long. Mrs. Younge came sauntering down the corridor and stopped just inside, blocking his way in.

"Mr. Darcy," she said, a hollow smile on her lips. "To what do I owe this great honor?" He noted that she did not acknowledge his bow with a curtsey.

"I am looking for Wickham," said Darcy.

"Why do you assume I know where he is?"

"Because you are clearly well acquainted with that gentleman. I never was able to determine the nature of your relationship with him. I assume you were lovers."

"Ha, you must not know Wickham very well if you think that would count for anything with him," she said, sneering. "Not that it's any of your business. As it so happens, I have no idea where he is. I have not seen him for some time."

Did she really think he would be convinced that easily? She must take him for a real fool.

"It behooves you to tell me where Wickham lives, or I will be forced to hire a bow street runner, and he may discover unsavory things about you."

She gave a mocking laugh. "He would have to hang around a long time to find out anything worthwhile. The trouble with your sort, Mr. Darcy, is that you assume the worst of others, simply because they are not from the same class as you,"

Her statement stung. It was true. He had done the same with Elizabeth and her family. Still, it was clear that whatever she was, she was not a suitable companion for a young girl.

"You turn up here and try to intimidate me, even though you know absolutely nothing about me."

"I know enough to be certain that honesty is not a strong point of yours."

"I would ask you, sir, not to slander me in front of my girls." She looked pointedly behind him.

Darcy turned.

An uncommonly pretty young girl stood there. A student? She gave him a pretty smile. "Excuse me, sir."

He stepped back to let her pass. Her voice was genteel, but there was rouge on her cheeks, and the scent of cheap perfume clung to her.

This was no scholar.

Darcy's blood ran cold. Surely even Mrs. Younge would not stoop so low—. No, it could not be possible.

She regarded him with a lopsided smile.

"The direction of your thoughts is only too clear. However, it is not what you think," she said. "I run a respectable house. These are lodgings for young actresses. I teach elocution lessons -- they all want to talk like ladies, and I am very much in demand."

It might very well be true. This was a respectable neighborhood. Anything else would not go unnoticed. Darcy gave a brief nod. "What you do to make a living is none of my concern, Mrs. Younge."

She leaned placidly against the doorway.

"I go by a different name now, Mr. Darcy. My name is Mrs. Carter."

"And where is Mr. Carter, pray?" said Darcy, coldly.

She gave him an amused look. "Now why would you want to meet Mr. Carter, I wonder? I assure you he does exist, otherwise how would I come to have all this?"

Darcy looked over her shoulder at the long corridor. It was clean and in good repair.

"As I said, it is no longer my concern, as long as you have no contact with my sister. I am here for one reason and one reason alone. Where is Wickham?"

"What is it you want with him? He has not tried to run off with your sister again, has he?"

"It is a private matter."

She sighed.

"As long as you are not here to start a fight," she said. She gestured with her head. "He is upstairs, if you must know."

So he was here! It was much more than Darcy could have hoped for. Still, he had wasted precious time talking to Mrs. Younge. Had she engaged Darcy in conversation to give Wickham time to get away?

"Is there a rear entrance, by any chance?"

Mrs. Younge regarded him with insolent amusement. "Of course there is. You surely cannot think I'd set up a house without a rear exit, did you? You never know what unpleasant people may come calling."

"Bow Street Runners, for example."

She was blocking the way.

"Tradesmen, Mr. Darcy. Tradesmen. They show up, every time of day and night. No consideration for honest folk."

"Debt collectors, more likely," said Darcy, curtly.

"Call them what you like," said Mrs. Younge, with a shrug.

"Well, *Mrs. Carter*, step aside, then." She did not move. "This is what I'd like to make clear. If Wickham takes it into his mind to run away, then I will hold you personally responsible for his escape. If you manage to delay him, however, much as I dislike it, you will have a handsome reward."

Mrs. Younge's eyes glittered. "I may just take you up on that."

She stepped aside to let him pass. "Upstairs, second door."

Wickham was probably gone by now.

Darcy took the stairs two at a time. At the top of the narrow stairway, there was a long hallway. He cursed under his breath. Did she mean second door on the right or the left?

He rapped on the door loudly with his cane and listened for sound of movement. There was a slow shuffle and a young woman – also extraordinarily pretty – opened the door.

"I beg your pardon," said Darcy, peering into the room. The bed was made up and there was no sign of other occupants. The window overlooked a blank wall. Wickham would choose a room that overlooked the street.

"Sorry to disturb you. It is the wrong room."

She gave him a shy smile and shut the door.

He knocked on the left hand door. Not that he expected Wickham to answer. He was quite prepared to break down the door if necessary.

To his surprise, however, the door opened instantly.

"Darcy!" Wickham smiled agreeably, as if this was nothing but a social call. "I saw you from the window talking to Mrs. Carter. To what do I owe this great honor?"

Darcy hated that Wickham was echoing Mrs. Carter's words in such a manner, making it clear he had been listening to their conversation. Darcy wanted nothing more than to slam his fist into that arrogant face, but he had another purpose in mind and he did not want to destroy his chances.

"Hardly an honor," he said. "I am looking for a young lady."

"A young lady? Lord, Darcy, I did not know you wished to take up with an actress. Well, you have come to right place. This is a boarding house for young actresses. But I warn you, you will not find it easy to have your way. You cannot use your money or position here. They are not looking for protectors. You will have to charm them first if you wish to take advantage of them. Not a strong point of yours, I must say."

Darcy gritted his teeth.

"Do not play the fool, Wickham. It does not suit you. We both know that I am speaking of a *particular* young lady."

He peered over Wickham's shoulder into the chamber but could not see anything. It did not escape his notice that Wickham had his foot placed behind the door, making it difficult for him to enter.

"Wickham, I warn you that I will haul you before a magistrate on charges of kidnapping a gentleman's daughter if you do not hand over the young lady immediately."

To his surprise, Wickham stepped aside and swung open the door.

"I was not aware that you had an interest in this particular young lady, Darcy," said Wickham. "However, I do think we should give the young lady in question a choice in the matter, do you not think so?"

Darcy stepped inside the room. It was a small room that once might have looked quite pretty. The rose wallpaper was curling off at the edges and the floor was unswept. The appearance of the room was not improved by the strings of ladies' underthings hanging across the room on a rope and dirty plates with dried food on them covering the table.

Darcy's gaze swept past these to the bed and the form of the young lady lying in it, covered in a sheet that was clean but worn thin and patched in a number of places. A naked calf was in plain sight, tangled in the sheet.

Darcy grimaced at the intimacy of the scene. There could be no doubt at all that Lydia Bennet had succumbed to Wickham's charms entirely. It was too late for him to do anything but try to negotiate a marriage. It would not come cheap, of course. Wickham would milk the situation for what it was worth, but if it meant salvaging Elizabeth's reputation, the price would be well worth it.

"You need to wake up, my dear," said Wickham, sitting on the edge of the bed and uncovering Miss Lydia's head. "I'm afraid we have company."

Miss Lydia giggled. "You take care of the company and I will stay here. Make it go away."

"I cannot do that. This gentleman here wishes to take you with him."

"Miss Lydia," said Darcy, looking away quickly as the cover shifted and a naked arm and shoulder emerged from behind the sheet.

"I am here on behalf of your family—"

"Miss Lydia? *Lydia Bennet?*" said Wickham. "Is that who you are looking for?"

Darcy ignored him. "I am coming to take you home," he said, gently.

The girl giggled again. "If you please," she said very prettily. "I am quite happy where I am. I have never met you in my life, so I do not comprehend why you would wish me to go away with you."

She sat up in the bed, holding up the sheet to cover herself.

Darcy stared at the young woman in astonishment. What trick was this?

Unless he was very much mistaken, this young lady was not Lydia Bennet.

Chapter Seven

Darcy narrowed his gaze in suspicion. This was very clearly a trick. Wickham had had enough time to remove Miss Lydia from sight and substitute the actress. He felt ridiculous doing it, but he bent down and looked under the bed, then stalked over to the cupboard and flung it open. No other young woman materialized. Of course, that meant nothing. She could have hidden in any of the other rooms.

"Where did you hide her, Wickham?"

"I have no idea what you are talking about."

Darcy stepped forward menacingly. "You will tell me at once where she is, Wickham, or I will search every chamber in the house from top to bottom."

Wickham watched him with amusement.

"I sense that you are very perturbed, Darcy, though I admit I do not know the reason. Why would I be hiding Miss Lydia Bennet in my bedchamber, or anywhere else for that matter, when I am very pleasantly engaged with a much more agreeable young lady? Besides, the last I heard, Lydia Bennet was under the protection of Colonel Foster."

"I am not in the least deceived by your casual manner, Wickham," said Darcy. "Miss Lydia herself penned a letter advising us she was eloping with you. You were traced travelling with her from Brighton as far as Clapham."

Wickham looked surprised. "There must be some mistake. I did travel from Brighton to Clapham but with only one young lady, and that is Miss Penelope Woodruff here. You can ask her yourself. Penelope, my dear, meet Mr. Fitzwilliam Darcy. The circumstances are rather awkward, certainly, but it seems you are forced to make his acquaintance."

The young lady extended her arm prettily. Uncertain what to do under the circumstances, Darcy took her hand and bowed over it before dropping it hastily.

"You may think me ill-mannered, Miss Woodruff, but I need to ask you to account for your movements in the last few days."

He was determined to get to the bottom of this. It would be easy enough to expose her lies.

"Of course, sir," said the young lady, smiling confidently. "We left Brighton last Wednesday at ten o'clock at night. I remember because I had just finished performing at the Regent's summer gardens – I was singing, you understand -- and dear Wickham was waiting to return me to Mrs. Carter. I would not have left Brighton so late, only I was needed to return to town to rehearse my new role. I am engaged to appear in Vauxhall. Not as a main singer, of course, but I am in the chorus. My name will appear on the program, if you care to see it. We had supper at The Black Swan in Pease Pottage and changed to the post at the George in Crawley in order to get here quicker."

It sounded plausible. Wickham would not have eaten at the George. It was beyond his means. Could it be true? As far as Darcy knew, Miss Lydia had disappeared around that time, but he was not in possession of any of the details of the elopement. He felt remarkably foolish for not making more of an effort to discover the details of the young couple's journey before turning up to question Wickham. He should have called on the Gardiners first. How could he verify anything when he knew next to nothing?

However, it was quite possible that Wickham had coached the young woman and told her what to say. Miss Woodruff was on the stage, after all, and would be able to repeat anything with conviction. The question was, to what end?

As if sensing his confusion, Wickham now spoke. "Come, Darcy. You could not possibly believe me so stupid as to elope with Lydia, who is under the protection of my superior officer."

"I believe you capable of anything."

"Anything but stupidity," said Wickham. "Please acquit me of that at least."

Darcy gave that some thought and nodded reluctantly. "Yes, I will acquit you of stupidity."

"I could have no possible motive for running off with Lydia Bennet. She is penniless."

"There could be other motives," said Darcy, darkly, aware that the woman on the bed was listening.

As if reading his thoughts, Wickham reached for the woman in his bed.

"I had no motivation at all. She is not even particularly good looking."

It was true that Lydia Bennet paled when compared with Wickham's current partner, but was it enough? Darcy stood uncertainly in the middle of the chamber. The carpet had been pulled from under his feet. He could not tell if Wickham was telling the truth. Past experience did not help at all in determining what he was up to.

"Speaking of stupidity," said Wickham. "It occurs to me that it is rather odd for you to come after me to rescue Lydia Bennet. What is your interest in her? She is scarcely out of the schoolroom and not particular in her favors at all."

Darcy controlled his temper with an effort.

"Kindly do not speak of a well-bred young lady in that manner, Wickham," he said, in his coldest voice.

Wickham lay back on the bed with studied casualness. "I *will* speak the truth and you cannot prevent me. What I am trying to work out, is exactly why you are willing to come to her defense so readily. I would have thought Lydia Bennet is one of those young ladies that you would be very quick to condemn."

The fact that Darcy *had* condemned Lydia Bennet outright to her sister did nothing to assuage his anger at Wickham.

A sly look came into Wickham's face.

Oh, no. Darcy suddenly wished he had never come here personally. It would have been far better to employ someone to capture Wickham and bring the villain to him. The last thing he needed was for Wickham to guess that he had an interest in Elizabeth.

"You are not here for Lydia at all, are you? You are here on behalf of someone else entirely."

The woman in the bed was beginning to look bored.

"Who is this Lydia, Wickham?" she said, looking sullen.

"Do not trouble your pretty head with her, she means nothing at all to me," said Wickham. "Although she does seem to mean something to this gentleman here."

Darcy was growing more incensed at Wickham's insinuations by the minute.

"I would suggest you tread carefully, Wickham. You do not have a leg to stand on. A word from me will have you released from the militia."

"You are not as powerful as all that, Darcy, for all the airs you put on."

They stood facing each other, all their old animosities rising to the surface. If Darcy had had a sword with him, he would have challenged Wickham to a fight, right then and there.

"I hope you are not going to exchange blows," said Miss Woodruff, in alarm. "I am going to call Mrs. Carter." She rose from the bed, dragging the sheet behind her.

Darcy was grateful that she had stopped him from something he would have regretted. He turned away.

"You need not worry, Miss Woodruff," he said. "I am not here to fight. Only to find someone. I hope you would tell me if you knew something about her."

Miss Woodruff shook her head petulantly. "I know nothing about this Lydia you are talking about, and I do not wish to know anything, either."

It was quite futile to keep asking questions, Darcy decided. He felt completely inadequate to the task of discovering the truth. He did not have a detective's ability to search out clues and discover them in unexpected places. There was no point in staying here any longer.

"Very well, then, I will take my leave. But you have not heard the last of this by any means, Wickham."

Wickham gave him a mocking smile. "Do your worst, Darcy. You will find that I have nothing to hide." He turned his back on Darcy and strode over to the bed.

"Now where were we, Penelope," he said to Miss Woodruff, "before the nasty man came in and interrupted us?"

Darcy closed the door on a giggle.

That had not gone well at all. He would obviously need to come up with a much better strategy to discover the truth than to issue empty threats.

Darcy left the building no wiser than he had been when he entered it. Standing outside the building, he considered his options. He was loathe to leave the house unobserved. His best recourse was probably to find a detective to watch the house, but it would take time to find someone and set things in motion. Meanwhile, there was nothing to prevent Wickham from whisking Miss Lydia away and depositing her somewhere else. The new location could potentially prove worse than Mrs. Carter's boarding house, which at least was clean and safe.

Wickham opened the window and waved to him.

"Have you lost your carriage? I do believe I can see a glimpse of it farther down the road."

"Thank you," said Darcy.

He began to walk reluctantly in the direction of the carriage, turning over the problem in his mind.

A young urchin with a thick mop of raggedly cut hair was sweeping the street with a large broom. He looked to be about ten years old, though it was hard to tell with the dirt and grime that coated him from top to toe. The smell of horse dung hung around him like a thick cloud.

"You, boy," said Darcy. "Are you reliable?"

"Can't say, sir. Don't know what it means."

"Can I trust you to do a job for me?"

The urchin took off his cap and scratched his head with blackened nails.

"Now that depends, don't it, what type of job it is and how much it's worth to me. I ain't willing to do anything criminal, mind, not 'less you pays me really well."

Darcy named a sum that would keep the boy clothed and fed for a month at least – more if he did not spend any of it on gin.

The boy's eyes widened, but he gave no other indication of being impressed.

"Well, now," said the boy, with cunning. "Don't know as it's worth it. The master expects me to keep the streets clean an' if I'm off doing somefing else – well then I'll lose my job, won't I? This here's my corner, you see."

There was intelligence in the boy's eyes, thought Darcy, intelligence that was wasted on such a menial job. Perhaps he would find him something else if he proved reliable.

"You don't have to go somewhere else, at least, not unless you have something to report, and you can keep up your sweeping as much as you need to. I want you to watch that house over there. I want you to report to me if a gentleman comes out with a young lady." Darcy described Miss Lydia to the best of his ability. "He might come out of the back door, so keep an eye out for anything unusual."

"There's lots of girls that lives there. How do I know I got it right?"

Darcy gave that a thought. It was a good question.

"I expect there will be baggage involved," said Darcy. "If anyone gets into a hack or a carriage, I want you to listen carefully to the address and remember it. Can you do that?"

The boy nodded earnestly.

"What's your name, by the way?"

"David McKee."

"Very well, David. When you have something to report, I want you to come to my address and tell me. Can you stay here at night? Do you have another boy you can trust to watch through the night? Wickham may likely make his escape under the cover of darkness."

The boy nodded his head. "Don't you worry about nofing, gov'ner."

He made the boy repeat the address of his townhouse three times. The boy learned it instantly, which gave Darcy the satisfaction of knowing that his initial instinct about the boy was right.

Darcy sighed. If only his instinct served him as well in the case of Wickham. He was reluctant to leave, but other than by skulking in the shadows himself there was no way of catching out Wickham. Hopefully the boy would prove trustworthy.

Meanwhile, he would have to go home to wait for the boy to report to him.

~~X~~

As he entered the Darcy townhouse, Georgiana appeared at the top of the stairway. She must have been waiting at the window for the carriage to return.

"May I talk to you, William?" she said.

"Of course," he replied. "Shall we go to the parlor? Come."

He wished now he had not involved her in finding Wickham. Of course, it was all very well to say that in retrospect, but he knew Georgiana; she was insatiably curious and would want to know what was going on. He considered telling her the truth but it was not his secret to reveal.

"I just wanted to ask if you had succeeded in finding Miss Lydia Bennet?" she asked, as soon as they were private.

He stared at her, stunned. How did she know? Had he revealed something accidentally? He had made such an effort to make sure she did not suspect anything. Was he really that obvious?

He gave her a lopsided smile. "I am bound to ask you how you know before I answer your question, little sister. I thought I had done a reasonable job holding onto my secret. However, it seems you somehow ferreted it out."

Georgiana looked uneasy. "I do not think you are going to like this, brother, but I did not suspect anything. It was not you who gave away the secret, it was Caroline."

Darcy let out a loud exclamation. "Confound it! How did she come to know?"

As Georgiana obligingly began to explain, he raised his hand to stop her. He felt tired deep in his bones. "It does not matter. It was a rhetorical question. Of course, she would know. There is no such thing as a secret in the *ton*. Even a country gentleman's family like the Bennets who rarely come to town become the object of gossip when there is a fall from grace. Let it be a lesson to you, Georgiana."

Georgiana smiled. "I hope very much I will not need that lesson," she said. "Now you must answer my question, since I have answered yours."

It was very awkward. He had not expected to be held to account by his own sister, but there she was, looking expectant, and he really had no choice but to tell her.

"I found Wickham as I expected at Mrs. Carter's – that is, Mrs. Younge — but he denies having anything to do with Miss Lydia."

She looked shocked.

"Does that mean he does not intend to marry her?"

"I wish I had better news but, yes, I do not believe he has any intention of marrying her."

Georgiana paled. "I cannot believe that he could be so heartless."

Darcy said nothing. He knew Georgiana must be wrestling with her own demons. All this must have brought home to her how lucky she was to have escaped Wickham.

"Would he have actually married me if I had run away with him?" she whispered.

He gave her a reassuring smile. "Of course he would. He would have been a fool not to. You are an heiress to a fortune."

"And Miss Lydia is not," she continued, in that half whisper.

He could only nod.

Georgiana bowed her head. When she looked up again, her eyes were blazing.

"You must find her, William. You must find her and *make* him marry her."

"I will do whatever is in my power," said Darcy.

She laid her hand on his arm. "Do it for my sake, as well as for hers," she said, and left the room, leaving him to ponder whom exactly she had meant by "hers".

Darcy climbed the stairs to his chamber hurriedly. He needed to go to his club to talk to a friend of his with contacts who might help him search for Miss Lydia.

He rang for his valet.

"I'm going to my club, Briggs. Please put out my black superfine."

The little valet bowed, looking pleased with himself.

"Do you have something you wish to say, Briggs? Out with it."

"As a matter of fact, I do, sir. I have good news for you. You asked me yesterday to find a way to locate Mrs. Fortin. Well, I am very pleased to inform you, Mr. Darcy. I know where Mrs. Fortin lives."

Darcy's heart sank. Devil take it! Did Briggs have to be so very efficient? It would have been far better news if Briggs had told him that Mrs. Fortin had disappeared off the face of the earth, or that she had set out on a journey to the West Indies.

"Are you sure this is the right Mrs. Fortin?"

"Yes, sir, the widow of Colonel Fortin who fell at Salamanca. That's how I found her, sir. Through her husband, so to speak."

Darcy had expected it to happen sometime, but not so soon. He had not been really prepared for it. Until she had been found, it had all seemed unreal – a nightmare of sorts, along with the nightmare of his botched proposal. Now he was faced with the reality.

"If you were not desirous of finding Mrs. Fortin, Mr. Darcy," said Briggs, observing him shrewdly, "you might have dropped a hint and I would have taken my time."

"No, Briggs, you did the right thing. I did wish to find Mrs. Fortin. It is a matter of honor. However, I have been occupied with other matters and I am unable to deal with the issue at present."

Briggs was clearly suppressing his curiosity with difficulty. He stomped around the bedchamber, shifting hairbrushes, examining clothing in the wardrobe and fiddling with the bedclothes, obviously trying to find a way to ask Darcy about Mrs. Fortin without causing offence. Finally, Darcy could stand the aimless fidgeting no longer.

"And in case you were planning to ask," said Darcy, irritably, "I will not be revealing any information about Mrs. Fortin to you or to anyone else."

"Oh, no, Mr. Darcy," said Briggs, "I would not dream of intruding upon your privacy, sir. You know I am the very soul of discretion."

If Darcy were not in a very ill humor, he would have laughed at that statement. As it was, he found it amusing enough to deem it worthy of a response.

"I know no such thing, Briggs. It is news to me. In fact, I sometimes wonder at the wisdom of keeping you on." He sighed.

Briggs grinned. "Now that's more like it, sir. I'm happy to see you showing a little spirit. I've been quite worried about you."

"Have you, indeed?" said Darcy, "well you have better stop worrying about me and start worry about saving your own skin. I find impertinence very unappealing in a valet."

"Very well, sir," said the valet, with a wide grin. "I shall endeavor to be more pertinent."

With that, he made good his escape, leaving Darcy with no option but to laugh.

If only there was really something to laugh about.

Chapter Eight

Darcy did not go to the club to seek his friend in the Home Office. As Briggs disappeared from his room, Darcy realized suddenly that Providence had stepped in to remind him where his real duty lay. Briggs had found Mrs. Fortin, which should have been a clear reminder to him of where his real path lay. However, Darcy had been so intent on pursuing Wickham that he had not asked Briggs a single question. His thoughts had been somewhere else entirely. It simply would not do. He could not pursue his search for Miss Lydia single-mindedly. He had other matters to take care of.

It also occurred to him that he had not thought to consult with Mr. Bennet and the Gardiners. He was going about this as if it was his own individual quest, but it was not. Mr. Bennet was waiting desperately for news. He should have gone straight from Mrs. Carter's house to the Gardiners to inform them that Wickham had been found, even if Miss Lydia had not. Perhaps they would be able to approach Wickham and find a way to discover the truth from him. Darcy doubted it, but he believed firmly in the maxim that two heads are better than one and, as he was at an impasse, he would very likely benefit from discussing the situation with others.

As he made his way to Gracechurch Street, however, he found himself hesitating. He would have to brace himself to meet Mr. Bennet and the Gardiners. After the words he had spoken to Elizabeth, he would not find it easy to look them in the eye. The encounter was going to be difficult and he was dreading it. However, since it was inevitable, he simply had to brace himself and plough through the awkwardness, hoping that he would feel more at ease once the initial encounter had happened. It was not unusual for him to experience some level of discomfort. This one was just more extreme.

Darcy paused on the steps of the house on Gracechurch Street as a flood of memories returned to him from the last time he had been here. Here he was again in front of the elegant white stucco townhouse. He remembered how torn he had been about whether to knock on the dark blue door or to turn away. Now he had no such hesitation. He would do his duty as a gentleman. There was some satisfaction in that, even if he knew he was destined not to receive anything in return. He had been honor bound to seek out Miss Lydia and he had done so. True, he had not found her, but he had found Wickham and that was close enough. Once he had told them where Wickham was, he could choose to walk out and never return. He would shut out the past once and for all and look only to the future.

The same steel-eyed butler who had spoken to him last time appeared in the door. He gave no indication whether he remembered Darcy's previous visit or not. Darcy gave him his calling card silently.

"If you would care to wait here, sir," said the butler, "I will ascertain whether Mr. Gardiner is available."

"I am also here to see Mr. Bennet," said Darcy.

The butler bowed and withdrew. In a matter of minutes, the butler returned, accompanied by Mr. Gardiner.

A strong rush of emotions overcame him at once. *Elizabeth emerging from the carriage, blood running down her face. He had wanted so much to protect her, to help her, to shelter her from harm.* He blocked the emotions and took refuge in arrogance. Arrogance had always served him well. It had protected him from being overwhelmed with the weight of grief and responsibility after his father's funeral. It would protect him now.

"Mr. Darcy!" said Mr. Gardiner. "What a pleasant surprise! We were speaking of you just this morning, and now here you are."

Darcy bowed stiffly. "I have some information that may interest you," he said, keeping his voice even and measured. "I would like to speak to Mr. Bennet as well, if he is available."

"Of course," said Mr. Gardiner, casting him a searching look. "Pray come in. Since you know Mr. Bennet is here, I assume you know the news. I will send for Mrs. Gardiner as well. I am sure she will be happy to see you."

He was ushered into a small parlor and offered a seat.

"I will find Mr. Bennet for you."

Darcy sat stiffly in his chair, not wishing to relax for an instant; thinking only of how best to give the news that Wickham may already have abandoned Miss Lydia.

Mr. Gardiner returned by and by, followed closely by Mrs. Gardiner.

"How kind of you to call on us, Mr. Darcy," said Mrs. Gardiner, with a flustered smile. "You must accept our apologies for leaving Pemberley so abruptly and for not answering your letter. I take it you have been informed of the circumstances and do not think too badly of us."

"I understand the reason for your urgent departure, yes." Then, because his words did not sound very sympathetic, he added. "This has been an anxious time for you, I am sure."

The door opened and Mr. Bennet shuffled in, looking greyer and more haggard than he had been when Darcy had last seen him.

"Mr. Darcy," said Mr. Bennet, "under normal circumstances I would say I was delighted to see you. However, we are under the grip of some trying personal business and I am not as merry as I should be."

"Mr. Darcy knows," said Mr. Gardiner.

"Ah."

Darcy could see Mr. Bennet struggling to imagine what Darcy was doing there if he knew about the Bennets' situation.

"I called on your daughters when I was in Meryton for some unfinished business," said Darcy, having decided it would best to mention his visit. "I had already heard the news. Since I know more about Wickham than any of you, I thought I might exert myself to find him."

Hope flashed into all their faces.

"And have you done so?" said Mr. Bennet, hopefully.

"Bless you for this," said Mrs. Gardiner, at the same time.

"I am afraid I bring no good news," said Darcy. "I have located Wickham, but as far as I can determine, Miss Lydia is not with him. I have questioned him and he denies any involvement. I cannot be certain that he is not lying, yet I cannot conceive of any reason he would keep the truth from me."

"But how—?" said Mr. Gardiner. "The Forsters forwarded her note. Lydia made it clear that she was running away with him."

"I cannot give you any explanation," said Darcy. "I only know that she is not now with Wickham. If he had forsaken her, I am sure you would have heard from her by now – if she ever came to town, that is. She would be able to find her way to Gracechurch Street, I am sure."

There was a long silence in which everyone contemplated the possibilities.

"I must ask this," said Mr. Bennet, in a broken kind of voice. "Does Wickham have any inclination towards violence?"

Darcy gave the question careful thought. Wickham was deceitful, yes, vindictive, yes, a spendthrift, yes, but he could not think of any incident in which Wickham displayed an inclination towards physically harming anyone, even as a child.

"I can only say that I have never known him to be violent and I would be surprised to find him so."

Mr. Bennet gave a sigh of relief. "Then Lydia must be somewhere," he said, his tone more hopeful.

Darcy rose to his feet. He took out a sheet of paper from his pocket and handed it to Mr. Bennet.

"Here is Wickham's address, if you wish to seek him out, though I am not sure that will accomplish anything. Meanwhile, I have left a boy to watch him."

He wanted to discuss possibilities with them, but they seemed too overwhelmed with the news to be able to come up with anything useful. Perhaps in a day or two he could approach them again.

"I will inform you the moment I hear anything new." He bowed, and turned to leave, feeling wooden and graceless as Mr. and Mrs. Gardiner followed him, thanking him profusely for everything he had done for them.

He had not done anything for them. He had done it all for Miss Elizabeth Bennet. It did not matter what the Gardiners thought of him. After the business with Wickham was over, the odds were he would never see them again.

As the door shut behind him, he set his walking stick firmly on the ground, looked down the stairs with resolution and smoothed out the inside of his beaver.

"Mr. Darcy!" said a much too familiar voice. "What are you doing here? Is there news?"

Darcy was so stunned he dropped the hat. It tumbled down the stairs and lay in the street on the dirty cobblestones. He stared at it for too long, unable to gather his thoughts together. By the time he registered the danger, a cart had come by and reduced it to pulp.

"Oh," said Elizabeth. "I am sorry to have startled you and ruined your hat."

He felt naked without it, totally naked and exposed. He could hardly say so, however. Years of practice in uttering polite phrases prompted him to answer. "It was entirely my fault. Say no more of it, I beg you."

His voice was so strained it sounded unfamiliar to him. He tried to steady his breath, which was coming as fast as if he had arrived from running uphill rather than from inside the Gardiner's house, but the more he tried to appear in control, the more breathless he became.

He watched her from the corner of his eye. She was wearing an alluring walking dress in a very attractive shade of green that showed off her ripe figure to perfection. It brought out the sparkle in her eyes and the wine-red color of her lips.

They stood there, staring at the ruined hat as if at some precious object that had been irredeemably destroyed. The specter of their last encounter stood between them.

Dodging the traffic, a street urchin dashed across from the other side and took it up, and, without so much as a glance towards Darcy, ran back to the other side where he proceeded to dust it and pat it back into a parody of a top hat, crooked and torn.

"Are you not going to stop him?" asked Elizabeth, curiously.

Darcy shrugged. "The hat – if it could still be called that – is no use to me. If he can sell it or use it himself, then I will not begrudge him that."

The urchin's theft – if that was what it could be called -- had served a useful function, in fact. It had given Darcy time to recover from the unexpected encounter. His pulse was still unsteady, but at least it was not galloping like a horse running from a fire.

"I did not expect to see you here," he remarked. It was a colossal understatement.

"We arrived last night. My mother was convinced my father would call Wickham out and be killed. Nothing would ease her fears but being here where she could prevent him."

"I see," he said, trying to think of something better to say but failing.

"You have not yet told me the purpose of your visit to my uncle and aunt," she said. "Has Wickham been found?"

Darcy took a deep breath. "Yes, he has."

"And--?"

He was behaving like an idiot. She needed reassurance and he was not providing it.

"I have found Wickham, but Miss Lydia was not with him, and he claims he has had nothing to do with her. I have not decided yet whether to believe him or not."

Elizabeth blinked. "Not with him? But what of Lydia's letter?"

Darcy shook his head. "I am more inclined to believe your sister's word than Wickham's. However, I do not know why Wickham would lie about it, unless he fears the repercussions. Perhaps he is afraid I would report him for abduction?"

"Would he believe you capable of it?" she asked.

It was good to be able to share the thoughts that had been turning around and around in his mind with someone, especially if that someone was Elizabeth.

"I doubt it. However, I have been thinking that he has no interest in revealing her whereabouts, and it is quite possible he is worried I would find a way to force him to marry her."

Elizabeth looked pained.

"I am sorry," he said, "but that is unfortunately the situation as I see it."

"I cannot believe that it has come to this."

"That is why a part of me wishes to believe Wickham. It would be far better for all parties that some mistake was made, or there is some other explanation. Yet, try as I will, I cannot think of any other possibility."

"Nor can I," said Elizabeth, "in which case I fear the worst. Unless his interest can be brought to be borne upon the situation, the only recourse would be to threaten him somehow, but how? I do not think either my uncle or my father would be taken seriously by a young man who is, after all, trained by the militia."

"No, they could not."

There was one thing that would tempt Wickham and only one and that was money, and the Bennets had none.

"Well," said Elizabeth, awkwardly, "I must express my gratitude to you for finding Wickham at least, even if Lydia was not found."

"I will do what I can to find your sister," said Darcy, with intensity.

She turned red. "I do not deserve—" she said, embarrassment written on her face, "—you are really too kind."

She curtseyed to him in some agitation.

"I must take my leave. My family will be wondering—"

"Yes," said Darcy. "You must. Goodbye, Miss Elizabeth."

He bowed and went blindly down the steps.

"Will you—?" she said, as she turned away.

He knew what she meant at once.

"Yes. I will inform you the moment I hear anything new. Meanwhile, you must come and call on Georgiana. She is here in London."

"Thank you, Mr. Darcy."

He noticed she did not promise to visit. The fact that she did not bothered him no end.

Well, if she did not visit Georgiana, then he would just have to bring Georgiana to visit her, it seemed.

For some reason, that thought was comforting, even knowing as he did that she cared nothing for him at all.

Chapter Nine

Darcy's encounter with Elizabeth left him too disturbed to return home. Instead, overcoming his reservations about meeting Caroline Bingley after their last unfortunate encounter at Pemberley, he fell back on old habits and called at the Bingley townhouse in Berkeley Square. To his relief, Caroline was not there. However, if he had expected to escape embarrassment, he was very much mistaken, because not sooner had Bingley set eyes on him than he dragged him unceremoniously to the library, shut the door and leaned against it.

"Darcy, you have a great deal to account for," said Bingley, looking grave and disapproving.

Needless to say, Darcy was very much taken aback, not least because he had rarely seen his friend disapprove of anything.

He sighed heavily. "I am sorry to hear it, Bingley, but I wish you would enlighten me further. I was unaware of causing offence."

"Well, you have," said Bingley, sullenly.

Darcy waited, but Bingley did not seem able to explain any further.

"Come, Bingley," said Darcy. "If you do not explain yourself I cannot be expected to comprehend your meaning."

Bingley wandered over to an armchair, threw himself into it and proceeded to ruffle his hair until it stood up like rooster's comb.

"For heaven's sake, Darcy, you could have told me what was going on. I thought we were friends." He shifted in his chair. "Instead, I had to hear about it from my sister – and from yours."

"Are you being deliberately obscure, Bingley, or am I slow-witted today?" said Darcy, frowning. "Why would Georgiana tell you anything?"

"I called at Darcy House after Caroline told me about Miss Lydia's situation, to see what you were planning to do about it, and Georgiana told me you had located Wickham. You can imagine how I felt when I heard that."

Darcy gave an impatient gesture. "Come, Bingley. You know very well that I am far better acquainted with Wickham than you are. What would have been the point of taking you into my confidence? You could not have found Wickham any faster than I did."

Bingley shook his head. "That is hardly the point. Darcy, I thought we were in this together."

He waited for some response from Darcy, but when nothing was forthcoming, he gave a sigh of frustration. "I suppose it is useless to continue, since you do not understand my perspective. Let us move on to another matter, then. I know you have found Wickham. Is the young couple married, or is it as everyone seems to fear?"

"I have found Wickham but not Miss Lydia."

Bingley stared at Darcy in shock. "Where is she, then?"

Darcy explained the situation in as much detail as he could. After he had finished, he sat still for a while, reflecting.

"You know what I think, Darcy?" said Bingley. "I think the problem is, Wickham has no motivation to reveal the truth. You need to give him a good reason to reveal Miss Lydia's whereabouts."

"Unfortunately," said Darcy, "there is only one incentive Wickham could possibly understand and that is to offer Wickham money to find and marry Miss Lydia."

Bingley nodded. "It is not ideal, I grant you, but it would solve the Bennets' problem and remove some of the sting of scandal from the family at least." He jumped to his feet. "What are you waiting for?"

"Certainly not for you. I will talk to Wickham alone."

"I must protest," said Bingley.

"You can protest as much as you wish, but the fact is, it would be deucedly awkward to meet with Wickham and offer him money to marry someone, with you as a witness. The situation requires a little more discretion than that."

Bingley raised his hands in surrender. "I concede your point."

Just then, Darcy heard the front door open and Caroline's voice as she addressed the butler. Since he had no intention of speaking to her, he waited until the coast was clear then sneaked out of the house as quietly as he could. He had just about had his fill of troublesome encounters and he had more to come. If he could avoid this one at least, he would consider himself ahead of the game.

Wickham, not surprisingly, did not arrive on time. They had agreed to meet in Bond Street in the early afternoon the next day, but as Darcy waited in his carriage, he became more and more infuriated, convinced now that the rascal had never intended to keep their appointment. However, showing impeccable timing, Wickham appeared just as Darcy was about to give up and ask young Ebenezer to drive on.

"I did not know you were into cloak and dagger intrigue, Darcy," said Wickham, stepping into the carriage. He looked around him, studying every detail. "Have you had new upholstery or is this a new carriage?" He ran his hand suggestively along the velvet squabs. "Soft as a woman's thigh. Certainly an ideal place for a seduction. How many wenches have you had on these plush seats, Darcy?"

Darcy sat quite still, refusing to be goaded into saying something unpleasant. Wickham, settled back into the corner and stretched his legs out onto the seat.

"A charming carriage, but hardly a substitute for good tea and refreshments. Why the secret meeting, Darcy? I always put you down as being a remarkably straightforward type of man. I see you have hidden depths. Why not invite me to your house?"

"I would not allow you within an inch of Georgiana," said Darcy, coldly.

Darcy realized his mistake as soon as he saw the expression of interest in Wickham's face.

"Oh, so Georgiana is in town? I look forward to renewing our acquaintance."

"Not if I can help it," said Darcy, grimly.

Wickham gave him a smug look. "Care to wager on it?" he said. "I am rather short of funds and would appreciate an opportunity to make good my losses."

At least this gave Darcy an opportunity to direct Wickham to his scheme.

"I will give you ample opportunity to make good your losses," said Darcy. "However, you will have to do something for it. I need you to find Lydia Bennet and marry her. If you do, I will give you a generous sum – enough to cover many of your debts."

"How much of a sum?" said Wickham. Upon hearing the amount Darcy proposed, he let out a whistle. A calculating look came into his eyes.

"So you wish me to marry the chit? Am I hearing you correctly? What does this involve, exactly? A *ménage à trois*, perhaps, an arrangement where we can share her between us while retaining the mantle of respectability yourself, Darcy? I have no object in principle, mind you. I only wish to know the terms of the agreement."

Darcy's fists curled. How dare he insinuate such a thing? How dare he suggest that he was after something as despicable as that? And with a young girl scarcely out of the schoolroom, no less. His stomach revolted at the very suggestion. For Wickham to even think he would be interested revealed the degenerate level to which he had sunk.

He leaned forward in the carriage and grabbed Wickham's cravat, hauling his face closer.

"I shall beat you within an inch of your life if you ever suggest such a thing again," he growled.

Wickham grinned.

"You are so easy to rile, Darcy. I always delight in poking holes in that cold, haughty exterior of yours. Sometimes you look so much like Lord Matlock that I can imagine exactly how you will be, twenty years from now. You have always been so deucedly predictable. If you will let go of your righteous indignation and of my cravat I would be more than willing to discuss business with you. Though I am not particularly impressed with your offer, I must admit. I would make more money abducting our dear Georgiana."

"You had better stay away from her, or—"

"Or what? What threat do you think is going to keep me away?"

"Or I will run you through with a sword. I have always been better at fencing than you are."

"If you challenge me to a duel, I will choose pistols. I am a better shot than you are. Think about it, Darcy, you cannot win this round. If you are willing to pay me this much to marry that little lightskirt Lydia, then you will certainly pay me more to stay away from that all-too-proper sister of yours. I know I am perfectly capable of reminding her of her affection for me."

"I do not think you will sway my sister so easily any more. She is no longer the naïve innocent child you tried to seduce at Ramsgate. Thanks to you, she has learned caution in her dealings with men."

"Darcy, Darcy! Do you not realize you are setting me a challenge? I am tempted to try, if only to prove you wrong. I smell another wager? Let us set the stakes. How about ten thousand pounds if I win?"

Darcy exerted a tremendous effort to prevent himself from landing his fist in Wickham's sneering face.

"You have my offer," said Darcy, his voice like ice. "Take it or leave it. You will receive no other."

"I have had my eye for some time on that diamond set of Georgiana's; you know the one that your mother left her? Perhaps if you threw that into the bargain, I would consider marrying the Bennet chit."

"Are you mad?" said Darcy, "those diamonds are worth a fortune."

"I am aware of that, naturally," said Wickham. "But what are diamonds to the reputation of a young girl…?"

"I have given you my final offer," said Darcy. "You are in no position to bargain. Now please leave the carriage before I give in to temptation and plant you a facer."

Wickham shook his head. "Now, now, Darcy, you must not allow your temper to force you into vulgarity. Remember what your father taught you about the importance of self-governance?"

Darcy pushed open the door of the carriage.

"Go, or I will not answer for the consequences," said Darcy.

"As you wish, Darcy, though I promise nothing. I will consider your offer – and whether it is worthwhile to shackle myself to that little hussy for a lifetime. *Au revoir*. We shall meet again soon. And give my love to Georgiana."

Darcy ordered Ebenezer to drive off quickly. He wished to get away as quickly as possible. It was irrational, he knew, but he wanted the carriage cleaned as soon as possible to remove all taint of Wickham's presence.

~~X~~

A heavy feeling of disgust settled over Darcy and even a whole hour's worth of fencing with Bingley did not clear it from his system, despite giving it his all.

"Stop!" cried Bingley, breathing heavily and wiping off his perspiration with a towel. "I hope you realize that giving me a thorough thrashing will not solve your problem with Wickham."

Darcy's lip curled. "Do not remind me of that slinking, villainous rat," he said, with feeling. "When I think of how my father welcomed that miserable toad into our house and gave him every advantage, I want to wring his neck."

Bingley burst into laughter. "He cannot be both a rat and a toad, Darcy."

"He can be those and a great many other things," he said, removing his wet shirt and slowly lathering himself with the wet towel his valet had provided. "I hope you are not defending him, Bingley, because—" He threw down the wet towel and went to the window, throwing it open.

"You know very well I am not defending him," said Bingley. "I do hope you realize, though, that you are standing at the window without your shirt, displaying yourself to all and sundry."

Darcy looked down and confirmed Bingley's words. "Where the devil is my shirt, Briggs?"

"Right here, sir."

"About time."

Bingley looked as if he wanted to say something but he refrained while Briggs expertly tied Darcy's starched cravat.

"Well then, now that you are dressed decently again, do you care for a night out? We could go to Vauxhall."

Darcy thought immediately of Wickham's actress-singer, Miss Woodruff. If she was to be believed, she was going to be performing there. "Not Vauxhall," he said. "Anything but Vauxhall."

"Dinner, then, followed by a card game?"

"Did anyone ever tell you that your jovial pig-headedness is really quite annoying?"

"Yes," said Bingley, cheerfully. "Many times. I take it you want to go home and sulk."

"Something like that," said Darcy.

"Then you will not mind if I join you. A good long sulk will do me a world of good. You do not have a monopoly on sulking, you know. I have plenty to sulk about as well."

It was really quite impossible to turn Bingley away. He was like a playful puppy. One did not speak harshly to a puppy, even if he followed you everywhere and made himself a general nuisance.

"Very well, Bingley," said Darcy. "I will invite you to dinner. I am sure Georgiana will welcome your company. And then we can sulk over a bottle of port."

"Capital," said Bingley, rubbing his hands and smiling as though Darcy had invited him to the rout of the Season.

Darcy suddenly felt a thick leaden lump settle into his stomach. He wished he had not suggested port, because it made him recall something he would have preferred to forget.

He had not yet called on Mrs. Fortin.

~~X~~

Georgiana was at Waithman & Sons looking at shawls and lace when Mrs. Annesley announced that she needed a new cap.

"I hope you do not mind, Georgiana," said Mrs. Annesley, "but I am going across the street to buy a ruffled cap at the milliners. You do not mind staying here for a few minutes alone, do you? I will be very quick, I promise, and I will leave Thomas outside the door."

Georgiana sent a quick look towards Thomas, who was chatting with the other waiting footmen. She wondered what Mrs. Annesley thought might happen to her if Thomas did not stand watch outside the door. Surely, she knew Georgiana was sensible enough not to stroll around Fleet Street by herself.

"Not at all, Mrs. Annesley," said Georgiana, who had no interest at all in looking at caps, ruffled or otherwise. She preferred lace. There were so many intricate patterns and it never ceased to amaze her how anyone could create something so refined and delicate. She had tried her hand at lacing and made a horrid tangle of it.

She had just found a piece that would complement one of her dresses very nicely when a shadow fell across the counter, blocking the already dim light inside. When she looked up, she had to stifle a gasp. It was none other than Mr. Wickham.

Georgiana trembled and prayed that he would not look in her direction. He was admiring his reflection in one of the mirrors and was too absorbed to notice her. She did not wish to talk to him. She began to move away slowly, edging towards a more hidden corner, trying not to be caught.

It was not to be, however. Raising his hand to straighten his hat as he viewed himself, he stopped abruptly as his gaze fell on her.

She shrank back, wishing she had had the presence of mind to leave while there was still time. Her heart was beating so fast she was convinced he would hear it if he approached. It was too late, however. He had seen her and was now moving towards her.

She drew a deep breath and tried to master herself. By the time he had reached her, she had controlled herself sufficiently to take up some lace and pretend to be fascinated by it.

"Miss Darcy! What an unexpected pleasure to see you in London. I did not know you were here." He cast a glance around her. "Surely you are not alone?"

Georgiana raised her chin defiantly, though she still did not look at him. Instead, she focused on a point just behind his shoulder. "I assure you, I am not. My companion has just stepped out for an errand and I am awaiting her here until the rain stops."

She reminded herself that she was perfectly safe from his persuasions. She was not afraid of him physically, but she was not sure that she trusted herself not to behave badly in his presence. It was some comfort that there were other ladies in the shop with them who were giving her some curious glances. It reminded her that she had nothing to fear.

"I am in possession of an umbrella, Miss Darcy. I would be happy to escort you to your carriage, if you would prefer to await your companion there."

She was tempted. For a moment, she wanted to throw caution to the winds and say yes. He reminded her of more innocent times – of the toss and turn of the waves at Ramsgate, of the sand squelching between her toes, of laughter and ices and sea breezes tossing her hair about. It had been her first time away from boarding school and she had felt free. Mrs. Younge had been very lenient with her, unlike her old governess who had been stiff as a rod and had watched every move Georgiana had made.

Then Mr. Wickham had shown up and for a few days, he had represented everything a young lady dreamt about in the privacy of her chambers. He was familiar, too, someone from her childhood and from the days when papa had been alive. She had trailed behind him and William whenever they came home for the holidays.

At Ramsgate, Mr. Wickham had paid her compliments and flattered her and made her feel as though she was the most beautiful young lady in the world. It accounted quite a lot for that heady feeling she had had of being happy and in love.

Then Darcy had appeared and everything had changed.

At first, she had thought Mr. Wickham's unwillingness to speak to her brother a lack of self-confidence. She had tried to give him the courage to speak to Darcy, but he would have none of it. Not only that, but he had insisted that they meet in secret. She had complied, at first puzzled and then worried.

If Mr. Wickham really wished to marry her, why did he not offer for her? Questions arose in her mind. By nature, she was honest and she disliked subterfuge. Lying to Darcy about where she was going with Mrs. Younge did not come easily to her. The easy companionship between her and Mr. Wickham had soon evolved into arguments in which she urged him to talk to Darcy directly and ask her brother's permission for her hand. She had been certain Darcy would never deny his childhood friend and his sister a chance at happiness.

Finally, she had taken matters into her own hands. She did not tell Mr. Wickham anything, but when Darcy asked her whether she wanted to go to London or to Derbyshire, she had finally confessed that she would be doing neither.

She had not seen Mr. Wickham since those miserable days when Darcy had told her the truth about Mr. Wickham. Part of her had always wanted to believe that it was cowardice rather than villainy that had prevented Mr. Wickham from standing up to Darcy and defending his love for her.

Even now, part of her hoped that Mr. Wickham would tell her that had all been a mistake, that he had been waiting for her since then and that his motives had been pure all along.

"Mrs. Annesley might be alarmed if she returned and did not find me here," said Georgiana.

"Still the obedient little girl, I see," said Mr. Wickham. "I thought by now you would have more independence of spirit."

Was that a sneer in his tone? She cringed at the harshness of his words. Had *she* been the one who had lacked courage? Had she failed to love him enough?

"There are rules," she said, apologizing. "There are things a young lady cannot do. Society does not permit it." She had let him down. He was disappointed in her. And all this time she had wondered if *he* had lacked the courage to fight for her.

It had never occurred to her that he might have blamed her.

"The rules are there for guidance, not to be followed blindly," said Mr. Wickham. He drew closer to her, close enough that his scent reached her – bringing with it myriad memories. "You could break them. You are older and wiser now. You understand the meaning of love as you did not a year ago. Surely, time had taught you not to throw away something so precious for the sake of what you call "rules.""

Had she really done that? All the certainty of the past year melted away. Was it possible that Mr. Wickham had cared for her after all?

She looked up from the lace she was examining into his smiling face. His eyes were warm and inviting. She stared at him uncertainly, confused.

"Are you planning to buy any of that lace, miss?" said the woman at the counter.

Georgiana discovered to her consternation that she was crushing the lace in her hand.

"Oh, I am very sorry, yes, I would like to buy some."

By the time she turned back to Mr. Wickham, she had recovered some of her equilibrium. More than that, she had remembered the consequences of believing what Mr. Wickham said.

"It is too late for all that, is it not?" she said. "It is my understanding that you are soon to marry Lydia Bennet."

The warmth in his eyes dissolved.

"Has your brother told you that? I assure you, he is very much mistaken. There is only one person I intend to marry, and that is you. Good day, Miss Darcy."

He bowed and in two strides had reached the door. The door clanged loudly as he slammed it behind him, drawing the attention of everyone in the shop towards it, then towards Georgiana. Her cheeks burned as she became the center of attention.

The door swung open again. She turned towards it anxiously, hoping that Mr. Wickham had not returned. Instead, she discovered Mrs. Annesley hurrying towards her.

"Sorry I took so long," said Mrs. Annesley. "It took me an age to finish with— my dear, what is the matter? You are shaking like a leaf. Are you unwell?"

It only made matters worse to reveal her reaction so openly. Oh, why was she not able to control herself like her brother did?

"It is just a slight headache," she said, pulling herself together, her voice coming from far away. She could sense all the listeners behind her, craning their necks for every word. "Are you finished with your shopping, Mrs. Annesley? Perhaps we can go to have some ices at Gunter's."

Mrs. Annesley brightened up. "Yes, that would be just the thing in this hot weather—." She hesitated. "But are you certain you are done with your shopping? Did you not say you wished to buy some of this ribbon?" She took up a spool and held it up.

Georgiana wanted nothing more than to leave the shop and run out into the fresh air. She wished she could take hold of Mrs. Annesley's hand like a child and pull her towards the door. Unfortunately, she could not, so she forced herself to be patient.

"Yes, I am quite done for the day, thank you." She wanted to run to the door, but she forced herself to walk to it quietly. Mrs. Annesley followed close behind and opened the door for her. Georgiana walked through it, her head held high, refusing to let the watching eyes intimidate her. Even when the door closed with a warning peal of the bell, she forced herself to walk slowly to the waiting carriage and stand around as boxes were brought to them.

It took forever, but to her surprise, once she entered the carriage, she began to feel less shaken. She always enjoyed the ices at Gunter's. She loved to exclaim over the elaborate shapes and flavors that were offered to her. They were the perfect distraction.

By the time Georgiana had returned home, she had recovered fully from the strange encounter with Mr. Wickham. It had given her a turn, to have him speak to her in that manner and had brought back memories she had thought she had buried long ago. She could only hope that the worst was over, and that she would be able to handle any future encounters that she may have far better. She was very glad that Mrs. Annesley had not chosen to make an appearance earlier; it would have led to a big fuss that might even have involved her brother.

To her surprise, however, as she took up her sewing, Mrs. Annesley asked her about the identity of the young man she had been speaking with.

"I would not have brought it up," said Mrs. Annesley, "only I noticed you were rather flushed after the encounter." She paused to look at a section of her embroidery she had finished and to cut off a thread with her teeth.

At least it gave Georgiana a few seconds to gather her thoughts. She had assumed, since Mrs. Annesley had not mentioned anything in the carriage, that she had noticed nothing.

Her thoughts tumbled over each other in chaos. Should she reveal Mr. Wickham's name, and risk making the matter seem more serious? Mrs. Annesley knew what had happened in Ramsgate and has been asked to be vigilant about anything to do with Mr. Wickham's presence. What if her companion thought that she had deliberately set up the encounter with him? Worse, even, what if she thought Georgiana's sudden return to London was because of him?

On the other hand, if she said nothing, supposing she ran into him again and was forced to introduce him? Then matters would look very serious indeed. Besides, she hated to conceal anything from Mrs. Annesley.

She felt a prick in her thigh. Startled, she jumped aside. Then reason was immediately apparent. In her nervousness, she had stitched straight through her embroidery frame. Her dress was now attached to her embroidery.

"Oh!" she exclaimed in distress. "I have made a mess of things."

Mrs. Annesley put down her embroidery and gave Georgiana her full attention. "I do sincerely hope not, Georgiana. I will have a difficult time justifying myself to my employer if you have."

Georgiana puzzled that out for a moment, then realized Mrs. Annesley had misunderstood.

"Mrs. Annesley," she said with a laugh, "I was referring to my needlework. I am afraid you will have to salvage the situation. If I try to do so myself I will tear my dress."

Mrs. Annesley rose with a laugh and the next few minutes were spent trying to untangle Georgiana's embroidery.

As Mrs. Annesley sat back down again, she took up her work and said calmly: "You have managed very effectively not to answer my question, Georgiana."

It was no use pretending she did not know what Mrs. Annesley was talking about.

She sighed.

"Promise you will not make up your mind about anything until you have heard all I have to say," said Georgiana. Her thoughts tumbled over each other in chaos. Hesitantly, she told her story to Mrs. Annesley. The older lady had to stop and ask her questions several times in order to comprehend her.

"I knew no good will come of coming to London," said Mrs. Annesley, looking anxious.
"What will Mr. Darcy say? He will put the blame on me for leaving you alone. I will be dismissed without a reference."

"Nonsense," said Georgiana, irritably. "My brother would not be so unfair as to do that. It was hardly your fault that Mr. Wickham showed

97

up in that particular moment. Besides, you need not say anything to my brother. It was a meaningless encounter – entirely a coincidence."

But how could it have been a coincidence? What would Mr. Wickham be doing in a lace shop? A niggling doubt arose in her mind. How was it, that in all London, Mr. Wickham had chosen to come into that shop just when she happened to be by herself? The coincidence was too striking.

She felt the hairs in her neck prickle. Now that she thought of it, she remembered a carriage waiting close to the townhouse when she had left the house. It had followed after them, but she had paid it no attention.

There was no question about it. She would have to tell her brother.

Chapter Ten

"Good morning, Miss Darcy," said Jenny as she drew back the curtains and let the light in. "It's a glum day today. Looks like rain."

Georgiana gazed at the slate sky outside the window and nodded. She was feeling unusually gloomy. As she strove to understand why, she remembered what she had been dreaming. The dream was about Mr. Wickham. The sensations related to the dream were still very strong in her mind and she shuddered, drawing the sheets around her as she sat up. She could not remember the whole dream, only the end. Wickham had been shouting angrily at her, shaking his fist and promising revenge.

Thank heavens it was only a dream! Unfortunately, the dream was in some ways an extension of reality and the bad feeling did not go away.

Jenny bustled about her, plumping up her pillow and straightening her cover.

"Shall I bring up a cup of chocolate and a sweet roll, Miss Darcy?"

Georgiana shook her head. She did not feel like eating just at the moment.

"No thank you, Jenny. I will go downstairs for breakfast. Is my brother about?"

"Mr. Briggs is attending to him, I believe."

"Very well," said Georgiana. "You may leave now. I will ring for you to help me dress in a few minutes."

"Is there anything wrong, miss? You look a bit pale this morning."

Georgiana managed a smile. "I am well enough. I just had a restless night."

"Well, then, I'll leave you to have a little snooze," said the maid, kindly. She curtseyed and left the room.

Georgiana had no intention of snoozing. There was an aching pain in the pit of her stomach. As she sought to work out where that feeling came from, more of the dream came to her. She had been leaning out of her window, staring at the silver slither of the new moon, when suddenly a hand had come out of the darkness beneath her and gripped her wrist. As she tried to pull it away, she had found herself entangled in vines. The more she struggled to free herself, the more the vines had held her tight. Then suddenly she had noticed that someone was using the vines to climb up towards her. She could not see clearly at first, but she had stayed absolutely still, pressing back against the curtains, hoping whoever it was would not notice her. Slowly the man had drawn closer and she recognized him as Mr. Wickham. He began to shout at her and accuse her of terrible things…

It was nothing but a ridiculous dream, Georgiana decided, shaking her head as if to rid herself of it. It was born out of her conviction yesterday that Mr. Wickham was trailing her. Now, in broad daylight, it seemed quite absurd. Why would he do that? What interest would pursuing her serve? She had foolishly caused her brother to worry by telling him last night about the encounter and suggesting that Mr. Wickham had been watching her, when she had no real reason to think so, not really. *She* had felt threatened because she had not expected to react so strongly to seeing him. That was all. There was nothing more to it.

She threw off the covers and tugged at the bell pull to call Jenny to help her dress. She needed to talk to her brother immediately.

~~x~~

She found Darcy in the breakfast room, pushing at the food in his plate, lost in reflection. From what Georgiana could see, whatever he was thinking about was not exactly pleasant.

Rather than waiting for William to broach the topic, Georgiana decided it would be far better to raise it herself.

"I have been thinking about things, Darcy, and I am sorry at my reaction to meeting Mr. Wickham yesterday, brother. Now that I have slept on it, I think perhaps I was too distraught to think straight. I have read too much meaning into Mr. Wickham's words. I do not believe him now to be a threat to me."

She carefully did not mention her nightmare. She had already done enough fear-mongering – enough that she had even frightened herself when there was no reason at all to do so.

Mr. Wickham had simply informed her he did not intend to give her up, which was exactly what a man in love would do. She did not comprehend why she had read anything sinister into his words. She had not seen him since Ramsgate. Naturally, he would be bound to play the role of one who was still in love with her, to reassure her that he still loved her, even if it were not true. He would not know that she was aware of Lydia Bennet's situation. After all, why would Darcy take her in his confidence when he had never done so in the past, and he would have every reason to maintain absolute discretion in this matter.

Georgiana had to smile inwardly at that thought. Mr. Wickham would, in fact, be quite right. Darcy had not taken her into his confidence this time either. If Caroline had not informed her, she might never have known. He had done everything he could to make sure she did not know.

In this context, Mr. Wickham's behavior was completely what one would expect. She did not understand now why she had been frightened. Perhaps it was because she was afraid of his influence on her, because she could not trust herself not to be charmed all over again by him.

At this moment, Mrs. Annesley walked into the breakfast room, looking flustered and not quite meeting anyone's eye.

"Good morning," she said, with a nervous curtsey.

"Ah, Mrs. Annesley," said Darcy, startling Georgiana's companion so much that she almost dropped the plate she had taken up. "You are just the person I wished to speak to. I have given consideration to Georgiana's situation and decided that, in view of the fact that Wickham has implicitly threatened to continue to pursue my sister, I will need to engage another companion for her."

Mrs. Annesley turned white and sank into the nearest chair. "You wish to turn me out? I know I have been remiss in my duties but pray reconsider—"

"Mrs. Annesley!" said Darcy in astonishment. "I have no complaints at all about you and have no intention of turning you out at all."

The color returned to poor Mrs. Annesley's face. Georgiana wanted to go over and put her arms around her, but knew she would be scolded for unladylike behavior.

Darcy wiped his mouth on his napkin and continued. "It would not serve my purpose at all. What I wish to do is hire an additional companion to make sure there is no danger of abduction. I worry that when he realizes he cannot cajole my sister into marrying him – Georgiana is older and wiser now, thank heavens! – he will resort to more extreme measures."

Surely not? It was Darcy now who was exaggerating the significance of the encounter. It was very kind of her brother to wish to protect her, but this was too much.

"William, I have been thinking about it, and I do not believe Mr. Wickham intended any malice. He merely wished to renew his attentions."

Darcy examined her closely. "You are defending him. I hope that does not mean you find his attentions acceptable."

Georgiana felt her face grow hot. She did not know what to answer. She did not yet know how she felt.

"I do not find his intentions acceptable," she said, looking anywhere but at Darcy. "You need not have any fears on that score."

That much was true. Beyond that, she did not know how she felt. Her emotions at seeing him again were too complicated to decipher in such short time.

Darcy came over to her and tilted her chin up.

"Tell me. Do you still have feelings for him?"

She could not bear it. How could she possibly have feelings for someone who had betrayed her so completely? If she felt anything for him, it meant she was an utter fool.

"No!" she cried. "I do not. Not after everything that happened. But seeing him again…"

Darcy released her and nodded.

"I can see that this is confusing for you. Wickham can be very persuasive. I have seen it so many times. I own I do not comprehend how he can exert such a hold on women, but the fact remains that he does. That is all the more reason that I must ensure that there is no possibility of an encounter. I must ask you, Georgiana, not to go anywhere without Mrs. Annesley, and to refrain from holding any conversations with Wickham. It is perhaps extreme, but your safety is paramount to me."

Georgiana felt a stab of pain as she considered how all that she had achieved in the last few months had been undone. William had learned to trust her, but now the trust was gone. She was once more a child to be watched over and guarded because she did not know her own mind.

Her spirit rebelled against being confined. Now Mrs. Annesley would feel justified to cosset her all the time, and if Darcy hired an additional companion she would not have a moment to herself. If only she had not been so muddle-headed!

She could not blame her brother, however. He meant it for the best, and perhaps she did need to be protected, not against Wickham, but against herself.

"I understand," she said.

But she felt her newfound confidence begin to crack, as if seeing Mr. Wickham was like looking at herself in the mirror; she had caused the glass to suddenly start cracking.

She would not give in to temptation. She would fight to stay strong. She would rise above this and prove that she was worthy of trust again.

~~x~~

Darcy did not know what to think of Georgiana's reaction to Wickham. Not for the first time since his father had died, he felt out of his depth. How was he supposed to gauge what a young girl thought or felt? Georgiana was in need of female council. Once again, he knew he was letting her down and it brought home to him the necessity for him to marry.

Not that he really required a reminder. The situation with Mrs. Fortin was never far from his thoughts, no matter how much he tried to avoid it. Like it or not, he had to deal with it. He had put it off long enough and could not in all conscience do it anymore.

It was time to call on Mrs. Fortin.

An hour later, he was in Bedford Square where Mrs. Fortin lived. His feet felt heavy and his heart heavier as he climbed up the steps. He rehearsed to himself the words he was going to say over and over. He did not wish to appear gauche, nor did he wish to appear indifferent. He had learned through bitter experience that proposals were not something to take lightly. If Mrs. Fortin was to be his wife, then he had to win her over or their marriage would start on the wrong footing. He had the feeling he *liked* Mrs. Fortin and that they could get along reasonably well. He had had Mr. Briggs make some enquiries about her, too, and discovered that she was well-regarded and from a good family. He would not be ashamed of her, certainly, but just as importantly, he hoped they would find some felicity in their marriage. Certainly, they seemed to have hit it off well right from the start. True, he had been in his cups, but it was very rare for him to trust a stranger with any of his secrets.

It would not be bad. Most couples did not marry for love. At least with Mrs. Fortin he would have companionship.

A tall butler opened the door for him.

"I would like to see Mrs. Fortin, if you please. It is a matter of some urgency," he said.

"I am afraid Mrs. Fortin is out of town, sir," said the butler. "She will be returning tomorrow afternoon. If you would care to leave her your card, I will make sure she receives it."

Darcy turned away, not quite sure if he was very disappointed not to have the whole matter settled, or whether he was delighted to be able to have one more day of freedom. Perhaps, he thought, he should take advantage of this small window of opportunity by calling on the Gardiners with Georgiana, as he had promised Elizabeth. It would give him a chance to say goodbye.

~~X~~

"Mr. Darcy," said the butler repressively. "There is a beggar downstairs by the name of David McKee. He says you know him and he has some information for you. Surely that is not the person you were expecting. He smells like the stables sir. Not clean stables, either."

"Young David is here?" said Darcy, springing up. "Send him up immediately. And have Cook prepare him a platter of cold meats and cakes for when I finish with him, if you please."

"He cannot be allowed to eat in the kitchen, surely, sir."

"Then have him eat on the steps outside," said Darcy, impatiently. "I have no particular preference as long as he is fed."

"As you wish, Mr. Darcy." As he left, Franklin's back radiated disapproval. He re-appeared later followed by the little street sweeper, who was peering into every corner of the house with intense curiosity.

"Well, David, I am pleasantly surprised to see you here."

"I told you I could be trusted, sir," said David.

"I am happy to hear it," said Darcy, gravely, hoping it was true.

"You are *not* to sit down on any of the chairs," said Franklin, at his most severe. "You must stand in the presence of the likes of Mr. Darcy. And do not think of touching the silver or you will be send straight to the hangman's noose."

"Why would I want to go stealing the silver, gov'nor?" said David, with a cheeky grin. "Mr. Darcy is *paying* for me to give information."

"You may leave now, Franklin," said Darcy.

"But Mr. Darcy, someone has to keep an eye on him—"

"David is too intelligent to ruin an opportunity to earn money by doing something foolish."

"If you say so, sir." The butler bowed, shot a warning glare at young David and retreated.

"Well, David, what do you have to tell me?"

"I watched the place as you asked me sir, and I heard Mr. Wickham and the young lady talking through the open window, on account of it being hot. Mr. Wickham said that he would be happy to drive the young lady back to Brighton, tomorrow, sir, on account of her having another singing engagement. "Only don't expect me to bring you back again. My leave is over," says Mr. Wickham. Soon as I heard that, I came over to tell you, sir."

The boy looked very pleased with himself.

Darcy considered the boy for a moment. Could the boy's report be trusted?

The boy's blue eyes met his squarely.

"Are you certain he said tomorrow?"

"Positive, sir."

"Did you by any chance overhear the young lady's name?"

"No, sir. He just called her "my little dove.""

That rang true. Wickham often used that term of endearment with his lady friends.

"And he didn't know you were listening?"

"How could he, sir? Nobody notices a street cleaner."

Darcy winced at the implications. Darcy took out a sixpence and handed it to the boy.

"If you find out anything more, I want to know, do you hear?"

The boy took the sixpence quickly. In an instant, it had disappeared somewhere within his clothes.

"Yes, sir. Though I was hoping for some'fing more."

106

So now, the road sweeper was bargaining with him?

Darcy regarded him warily. "Really?" said Darcy. "And what were you hoping for?"

"I work hard, sir, well and truly, 'cos I have ambitions, see."

"And what ambitions might those be?" asked Darcy, amused. If anyone told him he would be having a conversation about careers with a street sweeper, he would have considered them unhinged. Yet here he was.

"I want to open a gambling hell, like the ones the important coves go to. There's lots of money to be made there, on account of the bets being fixed."

"If you fix the betting," said Darcy, "you're more likely to swing from a rope than become rich."

"Then give me an honest job," said the urchin, with a cheeky smile.

The boy's answer took him so much by surprise that he threw back his head and laughed.

"Well, perhaps I might," said Darcy. "Not yet, because I want you watching that house, but since you're used to sweeping up, we might be able to use you in the stables."

The boy spat in his hand and held it out. "We've got ourselves a deal, sir," he said. "And given that I'll be in your future employment, I'll watch Mr. Wickham for you free of charge. Agreed?"

Darcy hesitated, then took the grubby hand. "Agreed," said Darcy. "Meanwhile, do not forget to stop and get some food from Cook. She will be expecting you."

"Not very likely I'd forget, is it now?" said the boy, with another impish grin. "It's not every day I get to eat in a grand house."

Darcy rang for Franklin, who was clearly standing guard outside the door since he appeared almost instantly.

When the boy was gone, Darcy washed his hands and considered the information. Perhaps he was wrong to rely on the boy, but in spite of appearances, there was something trustworthy about young David.

Assuming the information was correct, the question was, what was Darcy to do with it? Should he hurry over to Mrs. Carter's boarding house and try to surprise Wickham with Miss Lydia again? Should he lie in wait for the couple to leave tomorrow and catch Wickham red-handed?

Neither possibility seemed very practical. There was no knowing when Wickham planned to leave for Brighton. Darcy could wait all day to no avail, particularly if Wickham knew the house was being watched. As for trying to surprise Wickham with Miss Lydia, if he had not succeeded the first time, who was to say he would be any more successful the next?

Besides, if Miss Lydia were not in town but in Brighton, what good would it do in any case? Effectively, there were not many options, if Darcy wanted to find out the truth. Miss Lydia had not contacted the Gardiners, so one had to assume she was not in London, at least until something else came up. If she was not in London, then there was only one place she could be and that was, hiding somewhere in Brighton.

Darcy thought of Elizabeth. He had wished to say goodbye to her. Well, here was his opportunity. He needed to let the Bennets and the Gardiners know at once about Wickham's plans. A trip to Brighton was in order, not just to follow Wickham and find out if he was hiding Miss Lydia somewhere, but also to ask a few questions and see if he could discover anything new.

It was as good a reason as any to visit the Gardiners. His heart whispered that he would be seeing Elizabeth, and it sang.

Chapter Eleven

"Mr. Gardiner and Mr. Bennet are in the library, sir," said the steel-eyed butler. "If you'd care to follow me, Mr. Darcy?"

The butler led the way through the entrance hall and through a short corridor. As he passed the grand staircase, a voice floated down to him from upstairs. His heart recognized the voice before his mind did. It gave a little jerk then accelerated as Darcy strained to hear what Elizabeth was saying. Every instinct of his told him to run up the stairs towards her. Every instinct demanded that he throw himself at her feet and beg for forgiveness, for another chance, for a restoration of hope.

His rational mind, however, intervened. There could be no forgiveness, not after what he had said. Beside, even supposing she forgave him, what then? That did not change the fact that she felt nothing for him, that even under even the direst circumstances she still did not wish to marry him.

Nor did it change the fact that he now had other commitments, that he was obliged to offer marriage to someone else. He had had a respite, but that did not make the situation with Mrs. Fortin any different. Which was just as well, he supposed, because it would prevent him from making a fool of himself for the third time. There was no chance at all now that he would be ruled by impulse.

Accordingly, he kept moving onwards behind the butler, pretending he had not heard that voice. It was a siren call and he would do well to plug up his ears like Odysseus and resist it. He would conclude whatever he had to say and leave as quickly as he could. He hoped and prayed Elizabeth was too occupied to come downstairs. Then he hoped and prayed she would. He could not bear it to think she was within reach yet was unaware of his presence. He wanted to find a way to draw her attention – to cough loudly or to say something to the butler, but he could not think of anything that would not be too obvious.

The butler stopped in front of a cream-colored door, which a footman opened. Darcy delayed outside, hoping against hope that Elizabeth would appear, but nothing happened. He made a show of straightening his cravat. The steel-eyed butler announced him and waited. Finally, he could dither no longer. He stepped in and the door closed behind him. It was too late now. Elizabeth would not know that he had called.

Mr. Bennet looked up from a book he was reading and came to his feet. "Mr. Darcy! Are you here with news of my errant daughter?" he said, taking off his round spectacles.

"Good afternoon, sir," said Mr. Gardiner, with far more civility, rising from his desk and indicating a leather armchair. "Pray be seated."

Darcy bowed to the two gentlemen and sat down, trying to collect his scattered thoughts together. He was having difficulty remembering his reason for coming here. Too much of his attention was focused on listening for the sound of Elizabeth's footsteps.

"Have you heard anything new regarding Lydia's whereabouts?" said Mr. Gardiner.

Darcy forced himself to concentrate on the conversation at hand.

"I have no news of Miss Lydia, unfortunately. However, I have reason to believe Wickham is on his way to Brighton."

He said nothing about the offer he had made to Wickham. At this point, it was by no means certain that Wickham intended to follow up on it.

"Do you think Mr. Wickham has Lydia hidden away in Brighton?" said Mr. Bennet. "I find it hard to imagine Lydia being concealed anywhere. She is not known for her ability to keep a secret."

"It is possible that Wickham found lodgings in Brighton for her, with some promise of returning with a marriage license as long as she kept quiet about it," said Darcy.

Mr. Bennet paled visibly. "Are we down to this, then?"

Darcy had been determined not to involve himself emotionally in this matter, but he could not help pitying Mr. Bennet for the pain his words had caused.

"Whatever the case may be," said Darcy, more gently, "I believe I should travel to Brighton. There may be some clue there that no one has unearthed yet, something that Colonel Forster overlooked. Wickham is the only connection we have to Miss Lydia. I do not know what his game is, but I would prefer to keep an eye on him," said Darcy. "As it is, after so many days, the trail is cold. There is nothing further to be discovered in London."

"You, sir?" said Mr. Gardiner in surprise. "You have done more than enough for us already. One of us should go, surely? Besides, you are not as well acquainted with the Meryton militia as the Bennets are. It would be hard for you to gain their trust if you wish to ask questions."

"That is certainly true," said Mr. Bennet. "I will go."

Just then, the door opened and Elizabeth Bennet stepped into the room, with Mrs. Bennet in tow.

"Papa, please talk some sense into Mama—"

She stopped abruptly as she noticed Mr. Darcy and colored visibly.

"Oh, I am sorry, Mr. Darcy. I did not realize—that is, I was unaware—I—" She curtseyed, lost for words.

Darcy, who had had the advantage at least of knowing she was in the house, bowed gravely, his pulse hammering so insistently he was certain everyone in the room could hear it.

"Mr. Darcy," said Mrs. Bennet, with the briefest of curtsies. "Delighted to see you again, I am sure." Her expression suggested otherwise. "Did I hear you mention going to Brighton, Mr. Bennet? If we had gone to Brighton in the first place, none of this would have happened. I told Mr. Bennet that we should take the girls to Brighton, but he would not hear of it. Now see what has happened! Are we to go to Brighton, Mr. Bennet?"

"Since it appears Mr. Wickham has returned to Brighton, then *I* am to go to Brighton, Mrs. Bennet, though perhaps I should take you with me, in case Lydia is to be found in a bathing machine, dipping into the sea water," said Mr. Bennet. "However, if you decide to do sea-bathing, I hope you will stay under the awning to ensure none of the young men are watching you through their telescopes, eh, Lizzy?"

"How can you say such things, Mr. Bennet, when you know how distraught I am with Lydia's situation?" She sniffed into her handkerchief.

"I do not wish to mention such things, Mrs. Bennet," said Mr. Bennet in a loud whisper, "but lodgings in Brighton this time of the year are excessively expensive. Perhaps if you will wait another month, I shall contrive to arrange it."

"Another month? At that point, Lydia's situation will be helpless," said Mrs. Bennet. "Who knows what will have happened to her by then?"

"Let us remain optimistic that she will have contrived to marry someone else," said Mr. Bennet.

Darcy, seeing that the argument was unlikely to be settled for some time, stepped in. "I will write ahead and arrange for lodging at the Old Ship Inn. I would like to do whatever I can to help you under these difficult circumstances."

Mr. Bennet shot him a probing look. "It seems to me you have done us quite enough kindness already, Mr. Darcy, without taking on the expense of finding us lodging."

There was a question in Mr. Bennet's statement which Darcy could not quite answer. He was forced to resort to deception to cover his tracks. He did not wish Mr. or, worse, Mrs. Bennet to take hold of the wrong idea.

"I intended to travel to Brighton in any case with my sister Georgiana. It will be a simple matter to extend our lodgings further to include you." Then feeling that some explanation was still required. "I have known Wickham since childhood. I knew what he was like. I should have warned you, since he seemed to be spending time with your family, that he was not to be trusted. I knew what he was like, but I did not inform you. I feel partly responsible for the situation."

He felt awkward saying this but he was sincere. Mr. Bennet considered his statement gravely then nodded.

"Well then, it is settled. Mrs. Bennet, Lizzy, you need to have your trunks packed. We are departing tomorrow for Brighton. Mr. Darcy, you will let me know what I owe you for lodging of course."

"Certainly," said Darcy. He had no intention of doing so. Mr. Bennet was only mentioning it to save face.

He looked towards Elizabeth. She had not yet said anything. He could not leave without exchanging a single word with her.

"I hope the journey will not prove tiring for you, Miss Bennet. You have barely unpacked your trunks from your journey to town."

"We are here to find my sister, Mr. Darcy, and if travelling to the ends of the world will help, then I am prepared to do so."

"Your concern for your sister does you credit, Miss Bennet," said Darcy.

Then Mr. Bennet and Mr. Gardener wanted to discuss when best to set out and he was obliged to speak to them and forced to turn away from her.

He consoled himself with the knowledge that he had achieved far more than he could possibly have hoped. In fact, he could scarcely believe it. He was about to set out on a journey, and Elizabeth Bennet was to travel with him. He would be in her company for a few days at least. It would be painful, of course, and nothing would come of it. He would not paint castles in the sky. He knew she had not forgiven him for what had happened, but he would at least have a chance at some happiness.

He scarcely knew what he talked about with Mr. Bennet. As he took his leave, everything was in a blur. He hurried home, brimming with happiness, wondering how to explain to Georgiana that, far from trying to whisk her away from the danger of any encounter with Wickham, he was in fact taking her with him to Brighton and setting her in Wickham's path.

He did not dwell on it for long, however. He knew Georgiana would be pleased to spend time with Elizabeth Bennet and so would he. For now, that was all that mattered.

~~x~~

He need not have worried about Georgiana. She was in the parlor with Mrs. Annesley, looking at some fashion plates when he entered. No sooner had he explained to her what had happened than she clapped her hands enthusiastically and said she had always wanted to go to Brighton.

"I know we will have little opportunity to enjoy ourselves, since we are there on serious business," said Georgiana, "but it is always good to visit new places. Miss Marshall spoke of Brighton enthusiastically. They were to go there this summer but have been invited instead to a house party in Kent.

"I am glad the plan meets your approval," said Darcy.

"We shall make a big group. Is Mr. Bingley coming as well?"

Darcy felt a stab of guilt. Trust Georgiana to go straight to the root of the matter.

"Err, I have not yet asked him."

"He was not happy when I mentioned to him that you had found Mr. Wickham."

"I know. He told me so very clearly," said Darcy. "I will speak to him, never you mind."

"What about Mrs. Annesley?" she said, in a whisper.

Darcy looked towards the silent companion who was busy trimming a hat and humming a tune under her breath. "No," he said, in a conspiratorial whisper. "We are not taking lodgings. We will be staying at an inn. Just your lady's maid will suffice. Now I had better go and inform Bingley before he hears of it somehow and takes offence." He winked at Georgiana and she stared at him in shock. He grinned. "Bring one or two evening dresses, just in case."

He had his horse saddled and within minutes was at Berkeley Square. Some of his good humor diminished when he discovered Mr.

and Mrs. Hurst there as well as Caroline and Bingley. They immediately invited him to play a game and, given the awkwardness between him and Caroline, he was unable to refuse. He would far rather deal with Caroline over a card table than a dinner table. At the first opportunity, however, he asked to speak to Bingley privately.

Bingley listened to his explanation, then stood up and began to pace the room. Darcy watched him, puzzled, wondering what on earth he had to be displeased about this time.

"I do wish you would stop wearing out the carpet, Bingley, and tell me why you are so up in arms this time round," he said.

"Confound it, Darcy; if you continue to cut me out in this manner I will have no choice but to take a stand." He came and stood in front of Darcy. "I am sorry but I cannot continue to think of you as a friend when you seem determined to betray me at every turn."

Darcy was stunned by his words. Was Bingley really talking about betrayal? How could he, when he had told Bingley almost at once about taking the Bennets to Brighton? He could not help the delay caused by the card game.

"Bingley, you are talking nonsense. This whole business with Miss Jane Bennet is clouding your understanding."

"My understanding?" said Bingley, in exasperation. "What about your understanding? You are so eager to impress Miss Elizabeth that you allowed me no role in assisting you in finding her sister. I understand that you wish to play the hero, but I do not appreciate being kept out. I, too, would like to be a hero in Jane's eyes. You may think me a nonchalant, reckless type of person, but I do have my pride, nevertheless."

Darcy leaned back in his chair and closed his eyes, dismissing the impulse to defend himself against Bingley's accusations. Instead, he pondered the possible reasons for Bingley's anger. However, much as he tried, he was unable to come up a good reason.

Perhaps it was his attitude that was at fault. There was some truth in Bingley's accusations. Darcy did wish to prove to the Bennets that he was their savior, that he would be the one who would rescue them from their difficulties. Even though he no longer had any hope of any relationship with Elizabeth Bennet, he still wanted to impress them with his ability to accomplish things. Suddenly he knew what he had done wrong. He had not even thought to take Bingley with him to the Gardiners. He had been thinking only of himself and the opportunity to catch a glimpse of Elizabeth. Really, his selfishness had no bounds. He winced. No wonder Bingley was angry.

"I say, Darcy, are you unwell? Here I was ranting and raving at you and all the time you have not been feeling quite the thing. I am awfully sorry. I should not have lost my temper that way."

Darcy opened his eyes to find Bingley looking down at him in concern.

Was that what Bingley considered *losing his temper*? Darcy felt a strong and unfamiliar feeling of remorse. Bingley was such a kind, gentle person and did not deserve to be run roughshod over by his own friend. First, he had made him suffer by tearing him away from the woman he loved, for no reason at all and now he was excluding him when Bingley had already asked him not to.

Darcy shook his head. "I am not unwell. I am just undergoing a momentary feeling of guilt as I realize what a poor friend I have been. You deserve far better."

Bingley blinked, quite at a loss to understand the depth of Darcy's self-loathing at that particular moment.

"You are the best fellow in the world," said Bingley, shaking his head and smiling, his anger completely gone. "It was I who was being beastly by saying all those things. When I recall all the things you have done for me over the years – well, I could not wish for a better friend."

He put out his hand to Darcy. Darcy took it, and they shook hands. "Let us put this whole thing behind us and discuss instead how we are going to plan our trip to Brighton. You will need my carriage, no doubt. If you bring yours, we should all be able to fit. How many of that does it make? You should probably send word and Caroline and I will be travelling with them, though I do not imagine they will object."

"Wait," said Darcy. "There has been no mention of Caroline. I can understand why you would wish to come, but there is no reason for Caroline to come as well."

"If Georgiana is going, I will have a difficult time convincing Caroline to stay behind," said Bingley. "You know how she is."

Darcy groaned. "You are putting me in a very awkward position, Bingley. I explained to you why I was forced to use Georgiana as an excuse. I would not have taken her out of choice."

"Caroline has friends in Brighton. I cannot deny her the chance to go and visit them. Besides, she has been looking pale and wan lately. Some sea air or even sea bathing might do her good."

Darcy's spirits sank. He had envisioned spending as much time as possible with Elizabeth and Georgiana – showing them the sights, taking them for carriage rides, accompanying them along the Marine Parade. With Caroline there, it would be impossible to do these things.

"I am sorry, Bingley, but Caroline will have to wait to visit her friends for another time."

Bingley looked stubborn. "Then you had better tell her yourself," he said. "*I* will not do so."

It was a lost battle and Darcy knew it. When they were children, they had always allowed Caroline to tag along with them, even at times unwisely. If they refused her, she would wear them down until they gave in. Later, of course, they could always argue that it would be inappropriate for her as a young lady to join them.

However, in this situation, Darcy had no leg to stand on.

"Oh, devil take it, Bingley! You know I cannot tell her."

Bingley smiled.

"Then let us go and tell her, and we can discuss the arrangements together. I am looking forward to this journey."

~~x~~

Despite his capitulation, however, Darcy did make one last effort to prevent Caroline from going to Brighton with them.

"Caroline," he said. "It is a trip of at least five hours. I am sure you do not wish to share a carriage with Miss Elizabeth Bennet or any of the Bennets for that matter. I know you are not particularly fond of them. We will not be gone for long. We are only going to Brighton to see if we can discover anything new."

"Is Georgiana coming with you?" said Caroline.

"Yes," said Darcy, tightly. "But there is a reason for that."

"You surely do not intend to take her with you when you question the officers. I will accompany dear Georgiana while you do your tasks."

"Capital idea," said Bingley. "I think Caroline may prove very helpful, Darcy."

Caroline would not prove helpful at all. Could not Bingley see that having Elizabeth and Caroline together was bound to cause more problems than they already had?

He sighed. He should put his foot down and refuse to have her accompany them, but Bingley was giving him one of his hopeful smiles and Darcy did not have the heart to say no, especially since his friendship with Bingley had just suffered a setback.

"Very well," said Darcy, hoping he would think of a way out afterwards. "We will be setting out early tomorrow. Do you think you will be ready?"

"If you're asking me," said Bingley, "I can be away at the drop of a hat."

"As for me," said Caroline, "I have had experience of moving the whole household at one of my brother's whims. For a trip of short duration I assure you it is no trouble at all."

It appeared matters had been taken from his hands. Darcy was in for it.

Chapter Twelve

Darcy and Bingley arrived at Gracechurch Street promptly at seven o'clock in the morning. They were on horseback, accompanied by two carriages. Bingley was all smiles. He was looking forward to renewing his acquaintance with the Bennets, and hoping indirectly to enquire about the object of his affections. By contrast, Darcy was agitated and restless, spurred by a compulsion to explain why Caroline Bingley was joining them on what was, after all, a private undertaking. He had woken up with a jolt at night, worried that Elizabeth might think he had taken Caroline in his confidence and informed her about Miss Lydia's elopement. He could not allow her to continue under that misapprehension. He wanted to make sure she knew Caroline had received the information independently.

Standing at the bottom of the steps, he had the opportunity to follow Elizabeth with his gaze as she emerged from the elegant stucco house. She was wearing a pretty yellow bonnet with blue ribbons and a primrose spencer that hugged her body closely. Every instinct of his strained to run towards her, catch her, and draw her into his arms, and he required every ounce of control that he had, not to do so. He had to content himself with stepping forward quietly to intercept her.

"Miss Bennet—" he began but he was interrupted almost immediately.

"Mr. Bingley!" said Mrs. Bennet, coming quickly out of the house. As she passed Elizabeth, she gave her a nudge in the ribs with her elbow. "How very gratifying it is to see you again! Since you left Netherfield, we have been quite cast down. Things have been very quiet, especially after the militia left. I hope you are planning to take up residence again soon. If you are not, perhaps it would be better than to give it up, to give someone else an opportunity to move in." She turned to Mr. Bennet who was following at a more leisurely pace behind her. "Is it not quite like old times, Mr. Bennet, to be gathered together like this?"

"Hardly *old*, Mrs. Bennet. *I* may speak of old times, but *you* are not yet of an age to do so, my dear. Anyone who meets you for the first time might easily mistake you for Lizzy's older sister."

"You know very well I was not speaking of *being* old, Mr. Bennet," she relied. "Only we have not seen each other for so long and it is so agreeable to do so at last. It is a pity Jane is not here, for she would have been very happy, too. Well, Miss Bingley, you did not think it, but here we meet again."

"So it seems, and nothing at all has changed," said Miss Bingley, flashing Darcy a meaningful look. "Delighted to see you, too, Miss Bennet. It is an age since we were last together at Pemberley."

"On the contrary," said Elizabeth, "It seems like only yesterday to me. I have been preoccupied with so many matters lately I have scarcely noticed time passing."

"They say time passes quickly when you are in a crisis or when you are having fun. Which one applies to you, I wonder?"

At this juncture, Mr. Bennet intervened. "Since we will all have ample opportunity to continue this compelling conversation in the next several hours, I suggest we repair to our respective carriages and be on our way. There are rainclouds gathering and, the sooner we set out, the less chance we will have to encounter them."

"An excellent suggestion," said Bingley.

Darcy he recalled suddenly that he had neglected to introduce Georgiana to the Bennets. She was sitting quietly in the carriage, watching the scene through the open window.

"Before we go, may I introduce my sister to you? Georgiana: Mr. and Mrs. Bennet."

It was rather awkward, because Georgiana did not know whether to stay where she was or come out of the carriage. Darcy remedied the situation by saying he would introduce them more properly when they stopped in Sutton to break their fast.

"We shall have the opportunity to become better acquainted, Miss Darcy," said Mr. Bennet. "However, it would be better for us to be on our way. I dislike the Brighton road. I have one particularly bad recollection of becoming stuck in the mud after a period of rain."

"Mr. Bennet," said his worthy lady, "I did not know you had even been to Brighton. You are so very sly! You had me thinking you disliked it too much ever to visit it."

"Did I? Well I do not know where you had this impression. I have fond memories of Brighton."

"But then why did you refuse to go to Brighton with the girls when Colonel Forster first suggested it…"

They could be heard discussing the matter as they entered into Bingley's carriage. Darcy and Bingley had already settled that Mr. and Mrs. Bennet would ride in one carriage and the three ladies in the other. In case of rain, both Darcy and Bingley would take refuge with the Bennets. The servants, along with Mr. Darcy's valet, had already departed earlier.

The traffic in the commercial area of London was too busy for conversation, but as they left the crowded streets and approached the first turnpike, Bingley drew his horse to Darcy's side.

"I would have thought you would wish to ride with Miss Elizabeth," Bingley had said.

"You would have been entirely correct," said Darcy, feelingly, "However, now that you have foisted your sister on me, I cannot think of a more nightmarish situation than to be obliged to sit with both ladies in the same carriage for miles."

"Because they are rivals for your affection?"

"Hardly. Because both of them are offended and angered by me, and each of them dislikes the other for different reasons. I do not know why I agreed to such a madcap idea."

"It is too late now," said Bingley, cheerfully, "so you will just have to deal with it the best you can. You need not complain so much. You know this is a perfect opportunity for you."

"A perfect opportunity for what?"

"To prove yourself."

Darcy let out a disdainful snort.

"Then why are you doing it?"

"Bingley, a man is not always governed by self-interest."

"Agreed," said Bingley, cheerfully. "Jane Bennet may care nothing for me, but I still feel an obligation to assist her in her hour of need. I would do anything for her, Darcy, as you are clearly willing to do for her sister."

"I am not doing it for her sister," said Darcy. "I am doing it because I am a gentleman."

Bingley let out a guffaw. "You *do* know you sound entirely absurd, do you not?"

"I sound nothing of the sort," said Darcy. "It is you who have romantic notions."

"That is rich, coming from the man who spent hours polishing the speech for his proposal at Pemberley," said Bingley. "You seem to have forgotten that I was there."

"Well, the situation has changed since then," said Darcy.

Bingley frowned.

"How so?"

"I do not wish to discuss it," said Darcy. He spurred his horse on. "I will race you to the Kennington turnpike."

They broke their fast at the Cock Inn in Sutton, and dined at the King's Arms near Crawley.

After Crawley, the clouds unleashed their heavy burden upon the two horsemen, who were riding ahead. They had agreed to meet up at Patcham to take tea, once they had completed the ascent of Clayton Hill, but once the rain started they turned back to take refuge in the carriages. Darcy recalled that as they had left Crawley, the carriage in the rear was Mr. and Mrs. Bennet's. They stopped the carriages and hitched the horses to the rear, struggling in the pouring rain. Darcy's gloves grew wet and slippery in the attempt and as a bolt of lightning flashed across the sky, the horse skittered away, eyes flashing in fear. Bingley ran to the front carriage and disappeared inside. Pulling his greatcoat about him, and pressing down his top hat so it would remain on his head and shield his eyes from the slashing rain, Darcy ran to the rear one.

As he shut the door against the storm, he turned to apologize to Mr. and Mrs. Bennet. Instead, he found himself the object of sympathetic feminine attention. If he could have ran back out into the storm to the other carriage he would have, but it would have been uncivil.

"Darcy!" said Georgiana moving quickly out of his way, "you are all wet. Miss Bingley, if you will exchange places with me I can help my brother get out of his sodden coat."

"We will do it together," said Miss Bingley, "for I flatter myself that Mr. Darcy has known me long enough that I am not considered a stranger."

Darcy cursed the luck and the poor visibility that had brought him to the wrong carriage.

"There is no need for alarm, ladies," he said, conscious of Elizabeth's eyes on him. "I am sure the rain will stop very soon and I will be able to dry myself in the sun again."

His words had no discernible effect, however. Before he knew it, Georgiana had taken hold of one of his sleeves and Miss Bingley of the other. How they expected to remove the coat, he had no idea, since each of the two women were pulling in a different direction and seemed determined to accomplish the task separately, making no effort to coordinate their efforts.

"I thank you for your concern," he said, between clenched teeth. From the corner of his eye, he could see Elizabeth sitting in the corner and watching, her eyes brimming with laughter. What a miserable creature she must think him, having two young ladies fawning over him in that way. "I am perfectly capable of removing my own coat, if you will just sit back and grant me enough room."

Georgiana shifted immediately onto the other seat. Miss Bingley hesitated, then moved to the other seat as well. The three ladies now sat in a row,

Darcy struggled valiantly with the coat, but attempting to remove a wet article of clothing that was tailor-made for him, fitting snugly around the shoulders, while at that same time sitting on it proved to be more difficult than he had imagined. He wrestled with it for some time, almost wrenching his shoulder in his effort to try not to scatter water on his fellow-travelers or have a flaying arm strike one of the ladies.

A snort of derision met his efforts. Disbelieving, he looked to the corner and found that Elizabeth's eyes were dancing.

He had never known such acute embarrassment. That he, Mr. Fitzwilliam Darcy of Pemberley, Derbyshire should be turned into an object of mirth sat very ill with him indeed, particularly when it was in the eyes of a woman who had twice turned down his proposal.

He doubled his efforts to rid himself of the top-coat. The wretched thing fought him, as if trying deliberately to make him look as foolish as possible.

Then finally, he was free. He felt inordinately pleased with himself, as if he had passed some kind of test with flying colors.

"Bravo, Mr. Darcy!" said Miss Bingley, smiling and squeezing her gloved hands together. Georgiana was smiling at him, too.

Darcy felt very much like a child who had managed to button up his coat for the very first time. At least he had not humiliated himself further by requiring assistance.

He leaned his head against the squabs. "Well, ladies, please feel free to return to your conversation. I shall stay only until the rain stops. Meanwhile, I hope you do not consider me uncivil if I shut my eyes and go to sleep."

"By all means, take what rest you can," said Miss Bingley. "You must attend to your health. You do not wish to catch your death."

To hear her speak, one would think him an invalid.

"A little bit of rain will hardly be the death of me," he said. He did not want to give the appearance of being pampered and cossetted.

"He may be too proud to admit it, but do you not think he looks pale, Miss Darcy?" said Miss Bingley in a loud whisper.

Georgiana started to say something, only to be interrupted.

"I do not think him pale at all," said Elizabeth. "He looks exactly like a man who is hale and hearty but was caught in a rainstorm."

Darcy fought an impulse to jump out of the carriage and run away as far as possible. He kept his eyes resolutely closed and breathed slowly in an out to simulate sleep. Sleep! As if he could sleep for one second with Elizabeth sitting there within an arm's reach. Every sense of his strained towards her. With each deep breath he took the sweet scent of her perfume – roses – wafted towards him, though how could that be above the odor of damp clothing, of wet earth and of rain that infiltrated every last crack of the carriage? He fancied he could hear her breathing, but how could he, when the rain was beating against the window, the wheels squelching on the mud-spattered road and the horses clattering onwards. When she shifted position in her seat the movement sent ripples through him, though the seat hinges rattled and squeaked as the carriage swayed from one side to the other on the uneven road. He could feel her warmth beckoning to him, even though the draft in the carriage would make that impossible.

His whole being wanted to make his way towards her at the other end of the squabs – such a short distance, really – and feel her soft body against his. He was afraid to open his eyes because he was afraid he would not be able to stop himself if he turned his head and found her looking at him.

The carriage suddenly jerked to a standstill. Darcy opened the window to ask Ebenezer for an explanation.

"The axel is stuck, sir. We're going to have to push to get it moving."

Darcy looked around at his companions. "Well," he said with a grin. "It looks like I'm not the only one who is going to get wet after all."

Georgiana had been looking forward to the journey a great deal, but it seemed that everything was combining to make the journey as unpleasant as possible. In the first place, she had discovered at the last minute that Caroline Bingley was to travel with them. She knew that Bingley had a tendency to indulge his sister, and that Darcy had a difficult time saying no to her, but still. Of all the harebrained things to do! To have Caroline travel with them to Brighton! To make matters worse, somehow Caroline ended up in the same carriage as Elizabeth. The dislike the two had for each other was palpable. Georgiana had thought at least when Darcy came into the carriage matters would improve. Instead, the tension had only increased. Anyone could see things were not right between Darcy and Elizabeth, either. Georgiana did not like tension and she had had such high hopes for the journey that after four hours in the carriage, she had been on the verge of asking if she could move to the other carriage.

As if all that were not bad enough, now the carriage was stuck in the mud. Caroline, of course, was too particular to come out and push with them. As the rain poured down, they were drenched and knee-high in mud while Caroline remained inside, cool and collected as may be.

"Georgiana, you must put your shoulder to mudguard," said Darcy. "I will count to three," said Darcy. "On the count of three, we will all push as hard as we can." He called out to the man in front. "Postillion – prepare to handle the horses."

"Yes, sir."

"Ready?"

"What about at the count of four," said Elizabeth, "what do we do then?"

Darcy gave a grim smile. "I am sorry to say there will be no count of four," he said gravely.

Georgiana noted the tension between them and wondered at it. It had not been like this at Pemberley. Had there been some kind of a quarrel?

126

Unlikely. The two had scarcely seen each other since the Bennets had arrived in London, surely?

As Darcy counted three, everyone pushed as hard as they could. The rain was coming down in great streams and Georgiana's ringlets were flattened down, covering her eyes so that she could scarcely see what she was doing. She pushed but she felt self-conscious about it. She did not wish to appear unladylike. What if someone came by and saw them?

The carriage shuddered, jerked forward and then started to move backwards. For a terrified moment, Georgiana though it was going to roll back and knock her down, but in merely sank back into the mud with a resigned squelch.

"Let us keep at it," said Darcy.

Georgiana gave it all she could this time, grunting with effort as she anchored herself solidly in the road and leaned forward with all her might. For a second, she thought they had succeeded. The carriage moved forwards a couple of inches, but then got stuck again.

"Mr. Darcy," said Caroline, pulling down the window sash halfway and peering out at them. "You must come in from the rain. You will catch your death."

Georgiana felt a stab of resentment. Perhaps if they had one more person to push, they would be able to get the carriage out.

It seemed her brother had a similar thought.

"Miss Bingley, would you be good enough to step out for a moment? You need not push, but the lighter the carriage, the easier it will be to extract it from the mud."

He opened the door and offered her his hand with a bow. Since it was caked with mud, she hesitated, but decided she had no choice but to be gracious.

"Anything to help you, Mr. Darcy," she said, with a smile, tucking her parasol under her arm and putting her arms out to him. Darcy hesitated, then picked her up and swung her over to a rock on the side of the road where she erected her frilly parasol and stood sheltering under its flimsy protection.

"Very chivalrous of your brother, I must say," said Elizabeth, with a little smile.

"He is very amiable to those he is familiar with. He has known Caroline Bingley for years."

"Next you will tell me she is like a sister to him."

There was an ironic note to her statement.

Georgiana was glad to clear up *that* misapprehension at last. "Miss Bingley has been hoping to marry my brother for years, but William has been blind to it. We are so accustomed to having the Bingleys around they seem part of the family. It is only lately that he has become aware of her intentions, and he has discouraged them. However, as you will no doubt have noticed, it is nigh impossible to discourage Miss Bingley from anything."

She was prevented from saying more when Darcy returned to resume their attempt to extricate themselves.

This time, when they pushed, there was a loud whooshing sound and the wheel suddenly surged forwards. Unfortunately, great globs of mud flew out. One splotch landed on Elizabeth's chin, another on Georgiana's bonnet and the third splattered onto Darcy's face.

Elizabeth began to shake with laughter.

"His face!" she said, pointing at Darcy. "Did you see the expression on his face?"

Her brother's countenance held such a ridiculous mix of surprise and outrage that Georgiana could not help laughing too. William's first reaction was to look towards them in disapproval, but suddenly he, too, burst into laughter. The three of them squelched about in the mud, laughing away, while Caroline Bingley stood under her parasol and stared.

"How nice that you think the situation diverting," said Caroline, "but may I remind you that we still need to walk to the top of the hill."

The laughter died out as everyone contemplated the climb ahead of them. It was the general practice for carriages to go empty up Clayton hill, with the passengers walking on the footpath, but in the rain it was not an appealing prospect.

"At least we did not have to stay and wait for extra horses to extricate us," said Darcy, trying to make light of the matter.

"I was glad to have a little adventure," said Elizabeth, in the same spirit. "Now I can have something to talk about when I return to Meryton. I can amuse the neighbors with the tale for many months to come. That is, if nothing more exciting occurs to replace it."

Darcy rather thought the scandal of Miss Lydia's elopement would be far more exciting as a tale than their being stuck in the mud, but he refrained from comment.

The walk took half an hour. The ladies arrived faster than the coach, which required some assistance. Perhaps some time in the fresh air had improved their humor. They amused themselves cheering Darcy onwards as he pushed and shoved and turned red in an effort to keep the carriage from sliding back downwards.

Luckily, by the time they reached the top the rain had stopped and the sun was casting an eerie white aura over fields of harvested wheat. Everyone paused at the top to enjoy the view across the open space of the Downs and the picaresque windmills in the distance.

"Well, I must thank you both for your assistance," he said, as they all piled back into the coach. "Hopefully you will not suffer any dire consequences from the rain, but I am afraid we all look quite bedraggled."

"*You* certainly do, Mr. Darcy," said Elizabeth, laughing. "You have mud on your nose and on your cheek." He reached for his kerchief but he had already given it to Caroline, who was making a show of patting her turban dry with it. He could not imagine why she needed it, since she had used her parasol throughout.

To his astonishment, Elizabeth dug out her own kerchief from her reticule, leaned over and wiped Darcy's cheek with it. Her scent overwhelmed his senses, drowning out everything but the pleasure of her closeness. He shut his eyes, feeling her breath move over his cheek, as intimate as if she had brushed her lips against his skin. An exquisite joy shot through him. With his eyes shut, he could imagine her leaning over to kiss him. He wondered what would happen if he turned his face and let his lips skate across hers. Would the others notice? How would she react? He was sorely tempted to find out. If he moved just a quarter of an inch...

"You can have your kerchief back," said Caroline loudly, thrusting the kerchief into his hand and forcing him back to reality. What was he doing fantasizing about Elizabeth in a crowded carriage? "I have no further need of it. You may use it to wipe off the mud yourself."

Darcy shifted and sat up straight as Elizabeth drew away.

"The kerchief is soaking wet," said Darcy, frustrated no end by the interruption, "and no use to me at all. You may keep it."

He sulked in the corner while his unruly senses had the chance to return to normal. Once they had, he was overcome by remorse. He could scarcely believe that he was so far gone that he actually considered kissing Elizabeth in public. He had lost all sense of what was appropriate.

It was insanity – a sweet insanity, but that made it all the more dangerous.

~~X~~

They arrived in Brighton, mud-splattered and wet. Fortunately, Bingley had already procured their apartments at the Old Ship and was awaiting their arrival anxiously.

"Thank heavens you arrived. We decided to ride ahead of you when you did not meet us at Patcham. I was worried that you had met with an accident, and was just getting ready to set out to look for you."

"We were stuck in the mud, as you can probably tell," said Elizabeth, with a small laugh, looking down at her clothes. "I do not think they will allow us into the inn dressed like this."

"They are quite accustomed to it," said Mr. Bingley. "Everyone has to get out of the carriage at Clayton Hill and walk up in any case, so muddy and wet clothes are the common theme if it is raining. That was what the footman told me at any rate. You should come inside and have your clothes washed and dried."

Everyone was too tired to do much of anything beyond having food sent to their chambers and Darcy did not have any opportunity to speak to Elizabeth at all. Both mentally and physically exhausted, he fell asleep with the rhythm of the waves in his ears and the figure of Elizabeth Bennet filling his thoughts.

Chapter Thirteen

Darcy was unable to sleep. The pulsing rumble of the sea in the darkness disturbed his sleep and the unfamiliar bed felt hard and uncomfortable. The knowledge that Elizabeth was breathing softly on her bed just two walls away from him filled him with restless turmoil. The tangle of desire, yearning, self-reproach and despair tore into him with a torment that was both mental and physical. Finally, he could stand it no longer. Striking the flint, he lit a candle, dressed and, making his way out of the inn, he began to walk along the Marine Parade.

The Parade at this time of the night was very different from the daytime. The oil lamps that lined the terraced houses on his left were still lit, but to his right, total darkness stretched out as far as the eye could see, with only the lantern of a boat or a ship interrupting the expanse of inky black. Periodically, the lights of a passing carriage would flitter over the water, skimming the surface of the waves and turning them into little flames. Above the laughter and the voices, the sea could be heard, battering the coast in agitation. It flung itself onto the shingle beach then seethed as it withdrew to renew its onslaught. The unmistakable scent of salt and spray filled Darcy's nostrils and the wind whipped up his hair and clothes. He shivered as he realized he was growing cold, the damp spray seeping in under his clothes.

Who would have thought that love could bring such pain? Though he knew there could be no forgiveness for the harsh words he had uttered, he longed to throw himself onto his knees in front of Elizabeth and beg her to reconsider. He knew though that he had closed that door forever the moment the fatal words left his mouth. A loud groan of pain rumbled through his throat then a cry that joined the plaintive shriek of the herring gulls as they hovered overhead. He stood there for some time, surrendering himself to the moonless night, with the light breeze licking at his wet cheeks. He did not know if the salt droplets were spray from the sea or his own tears.

Eventually, he turned and began to stroll back towards the inn. He felt drained, as if the sea had sapped away his feelings. It was a peace of some sort, he supposed. At least the pain had diminished into a dull ache. Along the way, the oil lamps on the front of the houses began to go out, one by one. The clouds that had covered the moon were dispersing, separating into small dappled patches travelling across the sky. Slowly, a line of silver spread across the horizon, gradually changing color, flushing into a gold claret and reaching out across the waves. Fishermen's boats were gliding back towards the shore. Against the rising sun, their ship masts silhouetted the sky like a leafless forest.

By the time he had passed the Old Baths and was approaching The Steine, the fish market was beginning, the men hauling wooden boxes over the sides and the fisherwomen talking, arguing and laughing coarsely as they set up their wares. The smell of fish filled the air. It was an elemental world and he suddenly wished he belonged to it. His life had become so circumscribed by conventions that he had lost touch with himself.

As he approached the Old Ship Inn, he spied a familiar figure coming towards him with Jenny, Georgiana's maid. His heart lurched and his breath quickened. He feasted his eyes on her, knowing she was not aware of his presence. In the soft morning light, her visage seemed to glow. The sea breeze lifted up the curls around her face and swirled them gently. Her hand was raised to prevent her hat from being carried off, exhibiting the graceful curve of her arm. She walked with the subtle step of a dancer. Through the thin white muslin dress, he could see the shapely outline of her legs, the wind lapping delicately at her skirt like a sail, lifting it to reveal elegant ankles.

He knew the exact moment she saw him. Her arm came down and she pulled at her clothes as if to straighten them, her step became more hesitant.

133

Fearing that she would turn away and leave, Darcy advanced quickly towards her.

"I should have known I would meet you here," he said, forcing himself to speak, determined not to be an inarticulate fool. "You like to rise and walk out early."

He managed a trembling smile, or at least, that was what he hoped it was.

She smiled back, not quite meeting his eye.

"There is nothing like the freshness of the early morning. It brings with it the hope of a new beginning."

His heart quickened. Did she mean anything by those words? Did she wish for a new beginning between them?

For the first time in many days, a ray of hope lightened the dark corner of his heart.

"A new dawn and a new day," he murmured.

She smiled. "Yes," she said. "We have not been good friends lately, but perhaps we can lay the past at rest, with such a beautiful scene before us." His heart leapt up with joy. "It is certainly beautiful," he said, fixing his eyes on her face.

She laughed. "I do not have any claims to beauty," she said, "and you know very well I was referring to the sea." She leaned on the iron railing and stared out to the open horizon. "I am completely enchanted by the waves. How can they keep moving like that without ever stopping? Do they never tire and decide they would prefer to turn into a quiet lake instead of endlessly laboring?"

"I do not think they have any choice. They are drawn irresistibly to the shore, but are forced backwards by powers beyond their control."

"Such figurative language!" she said playfully. "What if they were not being forced back each time? Would they not grow bored, trapped unmoving on the shore?"

"It would be bliss," said Darcy. "A perfect communion of water and land. Peace at last."

She cast him a sidelong glance. "Or stagnation," she said. "Think of all the millions of tiny creatures that live beneath the waves. They would all die, if there was to be no renewal."

"They would adapt to living on land." His imagination failed him and he could sustain the metaphor no longer. He chuckled. "*Touché.* I surrender. Your rapier mind is too quick for me to match."

"To borrow your new metaphor – you seem to delight at crossing swords."

"Only with you."

Choosing to ignore his remark, she dusted her hands and began to walk. "Were you returning to the inn?" she asked.

"Not yet. I will walk with you for a while, if you have no objection."

"As long as you do not challenge me with more metaphors," she joked.

"Then we shall talk about something more serious. I have meant to ask you this question. You know your sister far better than I possibly could. Do you think it likely she would have been content to lie low for ten days, waiting for Wickham to return to Brighton from town?"

"No. I cannot imagine it. She is not the most patient of people."

"That is what I thought, but I did not wish to say anything to dash your parent's hopes."

"I see you have no objection to dashing mine."

"We have addressed each other with almost unbearable candor. I need not spare you now."

She nodded, a small acknowledgement of his statement, but said nothing further.

He took up position at her side, close enough to feel the air between them move with each step she took, but distant enough to be proper. He savored her, every nerve in his body tingling in response to every action of hers. He breathed in her presence – the scent of roses, the unique scent of her skin. He drank in the sight of her, covertly running his gaze over her sprig muslin walking dress down the length of her body. He could not touch her, but he could relish every aspect of her. He remembered how she was yesterday, her riding clothes plastered with mud and clinging tightly to her skin. She roused his senses like no other woman ever had. He was utterly enchanted.

"Oh, look, the fishermen are spreading their nets to dry along the Steine," she said, breaking the spell and bringing him back to the mundane world. It was a strange sight indeed. The nets covered the ground, a strange carpet of rope in front of the Prince Regent's Pavilion.

It was like a different world, and in this world, many things could happen.

The urge to take her hand and draw her to him was so strong he barely controlled it, but he could *not* resist reaching out for her and he found the perfect excuse. His fingers went to the ribbon on her bonnet and he tugged at it, his fingers brushing past her curls. They felt softer than the finest silk.

The touch invigorated him and made him feel more daring. After all, he had nothing to lose and everything to gain if only he could express some of his ardor and make her understand it.

"Your ribbon has gone askew, Miss Bennet," he said, with a small smile at her startled expression. He looked pointedly towards the servant walking behind her. "Though I admit I would use any excuse to draw nearer to you, my beautiful Elizabeth."

Elizabeth flushed. "Mr. Darcy, you are forgetting yourself," she said.

"I am forgetting nothing," he said. He did not know if he would get an opportunity to speak to her alone again. "You know my feelings. I have made no secret of them. I have not forgotten, either, that I said some very unpleasant things to you. I want you to know that they were spoken in the heat of anger and frustration and on no account reflect how I feel about you."

She turned away from him. Shading her eyes, she stood staring out to the sea. "There was a great deal of truth to them, nevertheless," she said. "I did not like them. I have thought hard about your words, and the cold reality is that my situation is as you described it. I acknowledge that, no matter how harsh, you were honest at least."

Harsh. Honest. These were hardly amorous words. His ardor cooled. Was honesty the only virtue she could ascribe to him? He searched her closely for some sign that she cared for him. There was pain on her face, nothing else. It made him desperate that, with all the love he held for her, all he had been able to do was cause her pain.

"If you would only see that I am offering to protect you, to save you from that same harsh reality you are speaking of! You would not have to worry about your future. It would not matter that your sister has caused a scandal. You will not have to answer to anyone."

"You say so now because you are in the first flush of love, but when that love cools, what then? You will be saddled with a wife for whose family you feel nothing but contempt, who only married you for practical reasons, whose vulgar origins will be a never-ending source of embarrassment at every occasion. I have seen enough in my own parents of what happens when a man falls foolishly in love and wakes up to find himself bound for a lifetime to the wrong partner. "

Her point came across forcibly. Of course. Mr. and Mrs. Bennet were one of the most ill-matched couples he had encountered. No wonder Elizabeth did not wish to enter into a marriage of convenience. Rationally, he understood her objections a little better now.

All the time his heart was slowly breaking as he stared the truth straight in the face. She was not saying it, but it was clear as that sun that had come rising above the horizon. There was no room in her heart for him. None at all. She would not consider marrying him for convenience even in the direst of circumstances. Nothing he said or did would make any difference to her. Not flowers. Not the most poetic speech in the world. Nothing.

She did not know it, but she had just tossed his heart by the wayside and, like what had happened to his hat, stood by and watched it get trampled. The worst of it is, she did it without even knowing.

"I understand," he said, turning away, crushed by the weight of her indifference. "Our conversation has been – enlightening. I must take my leave of you now."

Somehow, his legs managed to move and carry him away. As he started walking, he heard her cry out his name. When he turned round, however, she was walking away, her maid by her side, her back to him. It was only the cry of a gull.

~~x~~

Darcy withdrew to his room, and even when Georgiana called to him to ask if he wished to go down to breakfast, he pretended he was still asleep.

He could not skulk alone in his chamber all day, however. Besides, it was ridiculous for him to take the whole thing so much to heart when nothing new had transpired. He had known that the time for the parting of the ways had come, even if Mrs. Fortin was not involved.

The recollection of Mrs. Fortin's name served to have him sit bolt upright in his bed and strike his palm against his forehead. He had forgotten about the young widow entirely. He ought to have sent a note round to inform her he was out of town and would contact her when he returned. What would she think of him? He had left his card, promised to call when she returned and then disappeared. Such carelessness would not endear him in her eyes.

Forcing himself out of bed, Darcy rang for his valet and requested a bath.

"I beg your pardon, Mr. Darcy, but did you say a bath?"

"I did, yes, Briggs, and before you remark on it not being the usual time for a bath, I would like to explain that I was outdoors half the night and I smell distinctly of sea salt."

It was true. His skin felt tight and itchy.

Feeling distinctly better after the bath, Darcy was recovered enough to face the Bennets that, when they knocked on the door of his apartments to see if he wished to accompany them to see the Forsters, he was happy to oblige, though he scrupulously avoided looking at Elizabeth.

"We thought they might be billeted here with some of the other officers, but since they are militia and not regulars, it appears they have their own quarters at the camp."

"I believe the camp is some way out," said Darcy. "Allow me to hire a carriage to convey you there. Bingley and I will follow on horseback."

As they waited to procure a carriage, Mrs. Bennet expressed her gratitude to Mr. Bingley for their quarters.

"Oh, Mr. Bingley, you were very clever to find us such a pleasant inn to stay in! I am sure I have never had a better night's sleep in my life. The mattresses are so comfortable I could have been sleeping on air. I do not remember ever having such fine prawns as we had for breakfast. I am sure I could eat them every day for the rest of my life and never tire of them. And what a fine prospect of the sea we have from our window! There is nothing like the sea to raise the spirits. I am not at all surprised to hear that it has medicinal qualities. Just breathing in the salt air is enough to restore my spirits."

Bingley bowed and said he was very happy to hear that the inn was to her taste. "For it is far the best inn in Brighton, unless you count the Castle. However, I prefer the Old Ship for its location."

"And so you should. A finer location there could never be," said Mrs. Bennet.

By now, Darcy had managed to find them a carriage. Miss Bingley, fortunately, did not wish to accompany them, so there was room enough for Georgiana and the Bennets to ride together.

"We must leave no stone unturned," said Darcy, as he and Bingley rode together. "We must share any information we discover, however insignificant it may be. Who knows what we will discover?"

"I am certain we will find Miss Lydia," said Bingley, with the certainty of one who is an optimist by nature. "She cannot have fallen off the face of the earth. *Someone* must know where she is."

"Someone most definitely does. However, no one has come forward yet to reveal the information," said Darcy.

Nor did he expect any. He was pinning all his hopes on Wickham taking up his offer. If he did not, Darcy feared Miss Lydia may well be lost to her family forever.

Chapter Fourteen

Brighton was definitely nicer than Ramsgate, thought Georgiana, as they drove along the Marine Parade. Perhaps if Ramsgate had been as vibrant as Brighton was, Georgiana may not have fallen under Wickham's spell in the first place. She had been bored, and she had been lonely, and she had not cared at all for Mrs. Younge as a companion. Walking along the beach had been amusing the first three days, then, deprived of all company and with nothing to do, she had grown tired of it. Brighton, on the other hand, seemed like a smaller version of London, except that it had the added diversions of the bathing machines and the races. There were such throngs of fashionable people walking about on the Steine that one could never grow tired of observing them.

Still, she worried about meeting Wickham again, especially after the encounter in London. She fervently hoped she would not succumb to her attraction to Wickham again. As the camp came into view, Georgiana bit back an exclamation. She knew a number of militias from around the country had converged on Brighton to train in case of a French invasion, but from what she had seen so far of Brighton she had not thought the situation serious. However, the lines of white tents stretching into the distance, the sheer number of soldiers and officers and some of the drills she was witnessing brought home to her for the first time the fact that they were at war.

"Oh!" said Mrs. Bennet, "what a sight for sore eyes! Do look at that, Mr. Bennet. I declare I have never seen so many handsome officers in one place all at once."

"You must not become too distracted by the officers, Mrs. Bennet," said Mr. Bennet. "Remember why we are here. It is to find out more about Lydia's disappearance. You must promise me not to run away with an officer, Mrs. Bennet, for there is bound to be one who thinks you very handsome and the temptation may be too great."

Mr. Bennet smiled at Georgiana, who blushed in confusion, not certain quite what to make of Mr. Bennet's words.

"Fie, Mr. Bennet, what nonsense!" said Mrs. Bennet, laughing, straightening her cap. "With five grown up daughters I have given up all pretensions to beauty. But there was a time when the sight of a scarlet uniform would have my heart go pitter-patter."

Elizabeth put her hand out and patted Georgiana's hand reassuringly. "You must not let him put you to the blush," she said. "My father likes to tease, and if you give him half a chance he will tease you too. You must not allow it."

"I do not see how she can prevent me," said Mr. Bennet, "Miss Darcy is far too well bred to raise objections. Her brother, however, is another matter entirely. But on this score, I shall say no more. In any case, we have arrived at the camp. Are you looking forward to seeing the uniforms, Lizzy?"

"I care nothing for the uniforms," said Elizabeth. "As you know very well, papa."

Georgiana smiled at the way Mr. Bennet and Elizabeth joked with each other. She felt a sudden yearning for the father she had lost, though she remembered him as rather stern and forbidding.

Mrs. Bennet spotted one of the officers she knew from Meryton, a Mr. Carter, and asked for the carriage to be stopped to talk to him.

"Oh, it is just like old times, Lizzy, is it not?!" she exclaimed as they moved on again. "I knew it would be so. If only your father had agreed to bring us all to Brighton, then none of this would have happened."

"It is nothing like old times, mama, and you cannot blame Lydia's uncontrolled behavior on papa. We are in Brighton, but not for our own amusement. We are searching for Lydia."

"As if I could forget for one instant," said Mrs. Bennet. "I have been frightened out of my wits, and suffered such palpitations, it is a wonder I was not taken away. Mrs. Philips was very concerned. She told me if I carried on as I did, I would not last another week. You father heard her, did you not, Mr. Bennet? Lizzy, once we are finished with enquiring about poor Lydia, we shall go to the Ladies Cove. A little sea-bathing would set me up forever, I am certain. I am desperately in need of it, for with all this worry, I have become quite the invalid. I can scarcely stand on my own two feet. My heart is all aflutter and my knees shake like calves jelly."

"Let us hope, in that case," said Mr. Bennet, "that you will not dissolve in the water like jelly."

"Oh, Mr. Bennet," said Mrs. Bennet. "Must you vex me so? You cannot imagine what a dreadful state I am in."

"I assure you, my dear, my imagination is very active on that score," replied Mr. Bennet. "*You* cannot imagine how often I have regretted possessing that unfortunate faculty. The man who lacks imagination must be the most fortunate creature to walk the earth."

"I wonder if we will see Martha Gunn, the famous dipper," said Mrs. Bennet, ignoring his remarks. "I have heard she deals roughly with those who do not pay her enough. I cannot wait to tell Mrs. Philips all about it."

"I fear you will not be telling anyone about it," said Mr. Bennet, "for we shall be spending all our time at the officers' mess, inquiring about our missing daughter."

They had sent ahead to tell Colonel Forster to expect them. When they arrived, they found a soldier waiting to accompany them to where the Colonel was observing a drill. He came over to them, bowed deeply and withdrew with them into the empty mess.

"Mrs. Bennet, allow me to express my regret once again over what has happened," said the colonel, immediately. "I must be allowed to bear the full brunt of blame for such an unfortunate situation."

"Oh, Mr. Forster," said Mrs. Bennet, "you cannot imagine my feelings. My poor, poor child! What is to become of her? And we thought her so safe here with you in Brighton! We were sure you would look after her for us."

"Now, now, my dear," said Mr. Bennet, trying to soften his wife's harsh words. "You know Lydia is to blame fully. A sillier girl you could never imagine. We cannot blame her volatility and lack of propriety at the Colonel's door. Besides, he has already offered his apologies to you."

"No, indeed, Mr. Bennet. He is to be blamed for not finding her, however. Surely someone can tell us where Wickham has hidden her."

Colonel Forster looked chagrined. "Well, that is just it, madam. Mr. Wickham has just returned from his leave. I have questioned him most particularly, but he claims that he knows nothing of the matter at all. He cannot understand how such a letter came to be written."

"Surely you do not believe him, Colonel Forster," said Mrs. Bennet. "Lydia can have had no reason to write such a letter."

At that moment Mrs. Forster, a young lady of around seventeen, entered the room and went quickly to Mrs. Bennet to take hold of her hands.

"Dear Mrs. Bennet, you cannot imagine my embarrassment when I woke up to find dear Miss Lydia's letter. For I had no idea at all, you know. Miss Lydia was widely admired and she did not like to show any favoritism." She gave a little giggle. "In fact, I was telling her the very night she disappeared that she might need to settle on someone, since dear Colonel Forster was worried the officers would be dueling over her! Not that Miss Lydia would have cared. She would have thought it such a lark if one of them were to be wounded for her sake. *I* thought it exciting, but Colonel Forster assured me there could be serious consequences. 'Think of what would happen if someone was to be shot and killed,' he said. When he put it that way, it did sound very serious, which is why I told Miss Lydia about it. Now that I look back, perhaps she did listen to me after all, which could be why she ran off with Mr. Wickham. She did not really care about him, but it may as well have been him as anyone else. She thought him quite handsome." She giggled again.

Georgiana decided that Mrs. Forster was one of the silliest ladies she had ever encountered.

"I was saying before you came in, my dear," said the colonel. "That Mr. Wickham is back, and he claims he had nothing to do with it."

"Does he really?" said Mrs. Forster, her blue eyes widening in surprise. "Perhaps they changed their mind the last minute."

Mr. Bennet cleared his throat. "That does not explain why Lydia is still missing."

"No, it does not," said the colonel. "But I have no reason to doubt the word of one of my officers."

Georgiana stared. Did the colonel really believe this? She had heard rumors that the officers protected their own. Was this an example of such a situation?

"I beg to differ," said Darcy. "Mr. Wickham has a reputation of not honoring his debts. Surely that casts doubt on his word?"

Colonel Forster shrugged. "I will arrange for you to speak to Mr. Wickham yourselves. Perhaps it will be easier for you to get to the truth of the matter if you question him directly."

"Would it be possible to speak to some of the other officers as well?" said Darcy.

"Naturally," said Colonel Forster. "I will let them know that they are to be at your disposal."

At that point, a formidable looking, graceful lady in elegant clothing walked in. It was clear at once that she was accustomed to command attention. Mrs. Forster introduced her as Mrs. Sandra Hutchins, the wife of Major-General Hutchins.

She glanced curiously around at the visitors.

"Are we having some kind of an event I was unaware of?"

Mrs. Forster giggled. "No, not at all, Mrs. Hutchins," she said. "What a droll idea! These are the family of the missing young lady, Lydia Bennet."

"I see," said Mrs. Hutchins. "The young girl who foolishly ran away?"

"I will have you know that my girl did not run away," said Mrs. Bennet, bristling at the implication.

Darcy turned away, intent on getting the names of Miss Lydia's "admirers" from Mrs. Forster in the hope of finding some testimony there. Elizabeth soon joined in and began to ask questions of her own.

"Are you her sister?" Mrs. Hutchins enquired of Georgiana, seeing that she was standing alone. "You do not look at all like her."

"No," said Georgiana. "I am merely a friend."

Mrs. Hutchins sniffed. "If you ask me, I believe everyone is off target. From what I saw of her, I do not believe that Lydia Bennet had any special interest in Mr. Wickham."

At that moment, Mrs. Bennet could be heard declaring that she wished to be taken to Mr. Wickham at once and Mrs. Hutchins laughed.

"I believe they are wasting their time," she said. "However, since I cannot be entirely certain, I will not make a point of it."

Darcy, who had no intention of meeting with Wickham or of exposing Georgiana to him, excused himself at this point.

"Miss Bennet and I will interrogate some of the gentlemen suggested by Mrs. Forster. Would you like to come with us, Georgiana?"

"Yes, of course."

"Oh, Mrs. Bennet. I almost forget," said Mrs. Forster. "Before you go away I would like to invite you all to a dance at the Castle Inn tomorrow. Assemblies are held on Tuesdays and Thursdays. "

"Thank you, Mrs. Forster," said Mr. Bennet, "but I hardly think it appropriate to attend a dance when my daughter is missing."

"Nonsense, Mr. Bennet," said Mrs. Bennet. "You cannot mean that. Of course, we would be delighted to attend."

"May I speak to you, Mrs. Bennet?" said her husband. Mrs. Bennet looked like she would say no, but he drew her to the side by the elbow. He did not lower his voice, however, and Georgiana could hear every word.

"Mrs. Bennet," he said, "I may as well inform you that I will not allow Lizzy to go dancing as long as we have not found her sister."

"On the contrary, Mr. Bennet," said Mrs. Bennet. "It is all the more important for Lizzy to attend. With everything that has happened with her sister, Lizzy needs to marry quickly before word gets out or she will never find a husband. I have a soft spot for an officer myself. If I had not married you, Mr. Bennet, I am sure I would have married an officer, though I will admit that the militia make a dashing sight." She sighs. "I am sure Colonel Forster can be persuaded to introduce you to the Master of Ceremonies." Her gaze fell on Darcy and grew colder. "And Mr. Darcy as well, if he wishes to attend. Though I do believe Mr. Darcy dislikes provincial Assemblies and does not care to dance."

"Mama!" said Elizabeth, her cheeks turning a bright shade of scarlet.

"Do not say *mama* in that tone to me, Lizzy," said Mrs. Bennet. "I am only stating the truth of the matter. If at least one of you is married then there would be hope for the rest."

Georgiana wanted to giggle. Mrs. Bennet reminded her so much of her aunts. Perhaps if her own mother had survived she would have been similar. What was it about female relations and marriage? It seemed the moment they spotted a young unmarried relative they became single-mindedly obsessed with the subject. It was as if single females were an offence to the feminine race. She understood, of course, that for a female to remain single was to risk being dependent on the goodwill of her relations, but surely, there were more subtle ways to approach the subject.

Sometimes Georgiana wondered what would happen if she did not marry. She was independently wealthy – she did not need a husband to take care of her and she could not really envision herself caring for small babies. She knew nothing about them. In her lifetime, she had been exposed to very few, and those had been the children of the tenants on the estate. She had never looked at any of the mothers with envy. On the contrary, it seemed that children were more of a burden than a joy.

She blushed and looked around her guiltily, as if someone would read her thoughts and realize how little she cared for the married state. Very likely she would be perfectly content to play aunt to the nieces and nephews of her brother.

It had not always been so. When she had been in love with Wickham – another uncomfortable thought that made her glance about her uneasily – she had been not only willing to marry but she had even thought about what a son of hers would look like. She had wished him to resemble Wickham, whom she had thought the handsomest man in the world.

Perhaps she had been too hurt by Wickham's insincerity to wish to repeat the experience.

"You may scoff all you like, Lizzy, but with Lydia's situation looking more helpless every day that passes—" She brought a lace kerchief to her face and began to cry again. "Five unmarried daughters! Oh what will become of us?"

"Now, now," said Mr. Bennet. "I am sure Colonel Forster will oblige us by performing the necessary introductions, and if Lizzy succeeds in catching herself an officer in a red coat, then we will send after Mary and Kitty as well. 'Tis a pity Lydia did not succeed in doing so or we would not be in this situation, but then she lacks your wisdom, Mrs. Bennet."

"I would be happy to introduce you," said Colonel Forster, "though you can accomplish the same by signing your name in the book at the circulating library."

~~x~~

Nothing new was discovered about Miss Lydia that day, and Mrs. Bennet was able to indulge her desire to do some sea-bathing, dragging Elizabeth with her. She did not enjoy it as must as she expected, however. She complained about turning blue with the cold, and about being frightened by the rough waves that seemed set on knocking her off her feet. Elizabeth did not enjoy her experience, either, saying that she had been too distracted by her mother's protests to enjoy the bathing.

Mrs. Bennet had caused more trouble than she imagined when she had spoken of attending the dance at the Castle Inn. There were several objections made, the most crucial objection being that the only one in the party who had brought formal evening wear with them was Caroline, who had expected to be invited to visit her friends. Otherwise, no one had thought to do so when embarking on a journey not intended for pleasure. However, Mrs. Bennet would brook no argument. Having decided that the fate of the family depended somehow on attending the dance, she was adamant.

The door to the Bennets' rooms was open, and Darcy could hear Mrs. Bennet berating her daughter clearly.

"You are a selfish, selfish girl, Lizzy, if you do not consider your sisters! You may have the pick of the officers, and what do you choose to do? Not attend the assembly! How could you, Lizzy? You will be the death of me! You do not know what I suffer, with your sister gone and Jane—" She checked herself, aware that Bingley was in Darcy's apartments. "Well, the less said about *that* the better. You have no consideration for the dreadful state I am in! Such tremblings and flutterings, and it is all your fault! If you had agreed to marry Mr. Collins we would not be in such a situation."

Darcy winced at the shrill voice. Oh, so now Elizabeth was to scapegoated because she had refused to marry Mr. Collins? Little did Mrs. Bennet know that her daughter had turned down a far better opportunity! Darcy wondered what Mrs. Bennet would say if she discovered Lizzy's foolhardy rejection of one of the most eligible bachelors in England.

In vain did Lizzy protest. In vain did she give her reasons for not wishing to attend. Mrs. Bennet stood firm. She saw an opportunity for Elizabeth to make up for her sister's misstep, and she held onto it like a dog with a bone. Nothing would convince her that it was not practical, and all her thoughts now were on how to adapt one of Lizzy's dresses to turn it into an evening gown. Accordingly, they set out a little before noon and returned with several purchases that Darcy knew the Bennets could ill afford.

Caroline refused to attend at all, stating quite openly within Mrs. Bennet's hearing that she had never heard of such an ill-advised scheme.

"And what, pray, is to become of Miss Darcy? She is not yet out. Is she to be confined to her rooms for the whole evening? Who is to keep her company?"

"I am quite accustomed to keeping my own company," said Georgiana, embarrassed at being the center of everyone's attention. "I have several letters I wish to write and I will retire early. I am quite worn out by the sea air."

Bingley, however, would not hear of it.

"We cannot leave her to languish in her rooms alone," he said. "Oh, do let her come, Darcy. You need not be such a stickler. She does not have to dance, but she can derive some entertainment at least from watching everyone else."

"Well, I for one have no interest in an Assembly where I know no one," said Caroline. "I will call on my friends instead."

She did agree, however, to accompany Georgiana to a well-known Brighton *modiste* in the hope of finding some half-finished gown that could be completed by the next day.

It was obvious that Elizabeth was hugely embarrassed by the whole affair, and Darcy, in an attempt to relieve her embarrassment, tried to intercede on her behalf with Mr. Bennet, but found no sympathy in that quarter.

"Under other circumstances I would not impose such a thing on Lizzy, but for once I find myself in agreement with Mrs. Bennet. I fear things are bad enough that we cannot afford to indulge ourselves in this matter. We are looking disaster in the eye, and only an expedient marriage at this point could save the rest of the girls from being cast out by society and living their lives out in disgrace."

Darcy held his tongue. He teetered on the verge of saying that he would be happy to marry Lizzy if she would have him, but he checked himself. To say such a thing would force Elizabeth's hand. Her mother would hound her until Elizabeth agreed to marry him. He would achieve his heart's desire, true, but he did not wish it to happen that way.

He wanted Elizabeth to come to him of her own free will, or not at all, and he already knew the answer to that one.

~~x~~

The next morning, the group rose early to set up their carriages in a good spot to watch the review of the militia. Rumors were circulating that the Prince Regent himself was to take part in the review and Mrs. Bennet was eager to catch a glimpse of him. Accordingly, she woke everyone at an early hour, hoping to obtain good seats, but it soon became apparent that all of fashionable society had had the same idea, with some still in their evening clothes.

Georgiana also wanted a good seat, but for a different reason. Ever since she had seen Wickham in London, she had been worried about the effect he had had on her. Both Darcy and Mrs. Annesley had put it in her mind that she still harbored feelings for him. Georgiana wanted to see him at his most resplendent, in his regimentals. She wanted desperately to know, once and for all, how she felt and this was a perfect opportunity for her to observe him without drawing his notice.

She was more than a little nervous as she waited in the carriage and the band came into view, its martial beat tapping out the rhythm of her heart. She chastised herself for being so flustered. Perhaps it was all for nothing and he was not part of the review today.

Then she spotted him. She had never seen him in uniform. In the scarlet coat, shako and white trousers he looked like a different person. He was certainly elegant. Georgiana waited for her pulse to speed up, for her throat to constrict and for all the familiar sensations to take over. There was nothing. She felt nothing at all. Puzzled, she observed him closely. She noticed for the first time that his eyes were too close together, and that his chin was – well, it was very pointed. He had a false smile fixed on his lips that was unappealing and the way he marched was more of a boastful strutting than a proper march. His smug expression seemed to suggest that every woman in the audience had eyes only for him. There was something so insincere about him that she found herself repelled. How could she ever have found him attractive? She could only put it down to her inexperience. Thank heavens it was over.

She noticed the moment his gaze shifted past her and settled on the second carriage and onto Elizabeth, who was not paying him any attention at all and was looking out towards the sea. He nudged the man marching next to him and pointed her out. She could not see the other man – his face was hidden by a banner – but Georgiana was almost certain it must have had something to do with Miss Lydia.

Wickham was concealing something and they would need to find out what it was.

~~X~~

In the afternoon, Darcy and Bingley proclaimed they would once more question the officers. They refused to take the ladies this time, since they feared the men would be less likely to be open in their presence. Mr. and Mrs. Bennet also went to the camp, too, to ask questions. Thus, the young ladies found themselves left to their own devices.

"What are you planning to do, Miss Bennet?" said Georgiana. Then she realized Caroline was looking at her angrily and quickly added, "Did you have any plans, Miss Bingley?"

"I was planning to stroll along Old Steine to Mr. Donaldson's Circulating Library," replied Elizabeth.

"Are you going there to appear fashionable, or do you wish to go to the lending library? You have not yet seen the sights," said Caroline. "Ah, but now I do recall. You prefer reading to playing cards, so naturally you would prefer books to shopping expeditions. Are you a bluestocking, Miss Bennet?"

"If I were, I would not be ashamed of it; however, you very much mistake the matter. I am far from being so erudite. I like to read before I sleep and, having left quite suddenly to come to Brighton, I forgot to bring something to read."

"Perhaps you should ask Mr. Darcy if he has a book to lend you," said Caroline with a titter.

"Perhaps I will," said Elizabeth, cheerfully. "If he has one to spare, which is unlikely. However, my main reason for visiting the library is to sign the Master of Ceremonies' Book in order to be introduced at the dance."

"I see," said Miss Bingley. "I have no need of that, since my friends would introduce me, if I chose to attend, however, I do not. I find dances a bore."

Even Georgiana could tell that Miss Bingley was goading Elizabeth.

"I would hardly think the dances at Brighton qualify as provincial, Miss Bingley," she said. "Considering that they are attended by the Prince Regent himself as well as many of his staff."

"That may be. However, since the Prince Regent is not in attendance, then it can be of no consequence. For the time being, therefore, I would prefer to visit the Lanes. I am told that they have merchandise available nowhere else."

"So I have heard, Miss Bingley – if you hold with buying smuggled goods," said Elizabeth.

"Everyone buys smuggled goods. There is not a gentleman's house in England that does not have brandy. Where do you think that came from? You did not think it was made in England, surely?"

Elizabeth did not answer.

Miss Bingley took up her reticule and began to walk to the door.

"Would you like to come with me, Miss Darcy?" said Miss Bingley.

Georgiana was torn. She did not wish to offend Miss Bingley, but she sensed that if she went with Miss Bingley she would be pressured to buy things she did not particularly wish to.

"I would like to see what the lending library has to offer," said Georgiana, in a soft voice. "I have heard it is quite a crush."

Caroline gave her a piercing look then turned away. Georgiana felt that she had betrayed Caroline and wished she had not turned down her offer. However, it was too late now.

"As you wish," said Miss Bingley, looking down her nose. "I cannot conceive of a more dull way to spend the afternoon."

Once Caroline had gone, Elizabeth turned to her. "You need not be polite for my sake, you know. Truth be told, I have a great deal on my mind and I cannot fully enjoy what Brighton has to offer."

Georgiana smiled. "No, I assure you, I am not being polite," she said, blushing, "I do not mind confessing to you that unlike many young ladies my age, I am not particularly fond of shopping. Perhaps it is because I do not know what to buy and must rely on the guidance of others, which makes it tedious. I was glad of an excuse to avoid it."

Elizabeth hooked her arm through Georgiana's. "I am sure you will grow to like it once you are more confident of your likes and dislikes," said Elizabeth. "It must be difficult for you without a Mama to direct you."

Georgiana considered that point. "I did not think of that, but perhaps you are right."

"Who chooses your clothes for you?"

"So far it has been my companions or governesses, and occasionally my brother will surprise me with a new bonnet or lace."

"Does he, indeed? It is kind of him to show an interest in such feminine matters."

Georgiana saw a good opportunity to sing her brothers' praise. "I could not have wished for a better brother. He is so remarkably considerate and caring."

"Then you are very fortunate indeed," said Elizabeth, her voice more distant.

Georgiana knew better than to pursue the topic. They walked silently down the road for some time, until they reached the library, where they paid the subscription, signed their names in the Master of Ceremony's book and each managed to find a novel to please them. The more serious aspect of their business concluded, they now took a look at some of the stalls, where there were such pretty gifts on display that Georgiana was sorely tempted to buy something, even though they were mostly pretty nothings. Finally, on impulse, she bought some paper with colored edges and gave half to Elizabeth. Afterwards, they walked about the library, and discovered to their delight that there was a small rotunda where musicians were playing, with chairs laid out for people to sit and listen.

When the musical entertainment finished, the two ladies emerged again into bright sunshine and began the stroll back. Georgiana was very pleased with the visit and could not understand why Miss Bingley was so disdainful of the library. It was as much a social place as a repository of books. She did not dwell on the matter, however. She was simply glad that she had decided to go there with Elizabeth.

A couple of cavalry officers passed them by.

"Good afternoon, ladies," said one of them, bowing and smiling. Georgiana blushed and shrank behind Elizabeth, but her companion merely gave them a quick curtsey and a smile and continued on her way. Georgiana felt a sense of envy at the easy manner in which her friend had dealt with them. While she was all flustered and nervous, Elizabeth had promptly forgotten them.

"I wish I could be more like you," said Georgiana, the words bursting from her unexpectedly. The moment she said them she wished them unsaid. Her face burned, and she dared not look at Elizabeth for fear she would be laughing at her.

"Miss Darcy," said Elizabeth, stepping closer and tilting up Georgiana's chin with a finger, "it is all a matter of practice. You spend far more time practicing the piano than I do. You are alone in a great big house without friends of your age to talk to, while I am constantly surrounded by people, from my sisters to their equally silly friends. If you had been dragged so many times to see the officers in Meryton, you would find talk and smiling with officers as natural as I do."

There was something calm and soothing about Elizabeth. Her ability to make light of things reassured Georgiana that there was every possibility that she, too, would be able to behave casually in such situations.

"Do not forget," added Elizabeth, "that I have four sisters. I have seen each of them grow and develop. You are lacking experience because you have not come out. Wait a few months and you will feel entirely different."

At that moment, a blast of wind from the sea sent a ribbon from Georgiana's hat flying. Georgiana tried to grip it as it sailed by but she was unable to do so. A group of officers were walking behind them and one of them put out his hand in time to catch it.

"Here it is, Miss," he said.

Georgiana blushed and took it from him with a quick word of thanks, uncertain what to do since they had not been introduced. To her surprise, instead of leaving them, the officer peered more closely at Elizabeth.

"Miss Bennet! What a pleasure to see you here!"

"It is you!" said Elizabeth. "I scarcely recognized you, after all these years. How is your sister? I hope she is in good health."

"She is in excellent health," said the officer. "I cannot stop and talk now," he added, "as I am on my way to a meet at the camp, but if you give me your direction I will call on you in the evening."

"We are staying at the Old Ship," said Elizabeth. "However, I am planning to attend the Assembly there tonight."

"Are you indeed?" said the man. "Then I shall most certainly be in attendance. However, I will call for you earlier. You must know that in Brighton the fashionable thing to do is to drive along the promenade in the evening. The dance does not start until much later. I hope you will do me the honor of coming driving with me?"

"It would be a pleasure, sir," said Elizabeth.

He bowed and rejoined the other officers who were urging him on.

"Well, Miss Darcy, I am very pleased that I have at least one acquaintance now in Brighton," she said, looking rather pleased with herself. "Though the other side of the coin is that now I will have to appear at the ball without looking like a complete drab. Let us go back to the Inn to make sure we have something to wear."

Chapter Fifteen

Georgiana was writing a letter to Mrs. Annesley, as she had promised, describing the sights and sounds of Brighton, when Darcy stepped into the room, looking completely out of countenance.

"Has anything new been discovered, brother?" said Georgiana, with a frown.

"Nothing at all," said Darcy, striding over to the desk and looking down at what she was doing. "Are you writing to your companion?"

"Yes," said Georgiana.

"Please give her my greetings."

"I will. She was very disappointed she could not come with us," said Georgiana.

There was a long silence in which Darcy went to the window and leaned his forehead against it as if to cool it.

"Do you like the sea?" he asked, abruptly.

She put down her quill and gave him her full attention.

"It is very beautiful on a fine day," she said, "but I do not like it when it is stormy." She had had her share of storms at Ramsgate and she had come to dread them.

"I think there is something majestic about the sea in all its power and fury," said Darcy.

"Perhaps," said Georgiana, "but I do not like to hear of shipwrecks and people being swept up to the beach the next day."

Darcy came and put a hand to her shoulder. "You are a sensitive soul, Georgiana. It is a wonderful quality to have."

She smiled. "So are you, brother, under that arrogant exterior of yours."

His expression changed. "You think me arrogant as well?" he said. "Is that how I appear to you?"

Her brother's mercurial mood changes were growing more pronounced. "*I* do not think you arrogant, because you are not arrogant to me. But you give the impression of being arrogant when you are among strangers."

Her answer seemed to have appeased him because he did not answer. He disappeared into his room and came back a few minutes later with a book. He dragged a chair to place it by the window and settled down to read.

Georgiana went back to her writing.

> *We have had good weather so far, which is fortunate. It is neither hot nor cold, so we can walk about very comfortably.*

"Do you know where I can find Miss Bennet?" said Darcy, abruptly. "She is not with Miss Bingley, and she is not in her chambers, either. I expected to find her making preparations for the dance tonight. Has she gone out?"

So now she knew what was bothering him. The explanation for his strange mood was apparent.

"Why, yes," said Georgiana. "An old acquaintance of hers called on her. They have gone on a carriage ride along the promenade to reminisce about old times."

"A female acquaintance?" said Darcy.

Georgiana hid a smile by pretending to cough. "No. It was a gentleman."

Darcy frowned. "She went on a carriage ride with a gentleman, without a chaperon? How could you let her do such a thing when you know the reputation of the whole Bennet family hangs by a thread?"

"William, be reasonable. How could I possibly have prevented her? I have no influence over her at all. However, you need not worry in any case. Jenny has gone with her."

This should have had the effect of appeasing her brother, but it did not.

"And how, pray, are you supposed to do without Jenny? This shows a lack of consideration—"

"I have no need of Jenny at the moment, William. Would you have preferred Miss Bennet to be without a chaperon?" interrupted Georgiana, mildly.

Another silence.

"I do not wish to be cooped up inside," said Darcy. "We must take advantage of the good weather. Shall we go for a drive as well, Georgiana?"

Georgiana would have been happier if Darcy had offered to take her out before he knew what Elizabeth was doing. No doubt Darcy was hoping to catch a glimpse of Elizabeth's friend and discover who he was. However, she did not really mind, since she had been hoping to be invited for a drive anyway. She agreed at once, hoping William's mood would improve amongst the revelers.

It was a most pleasant day. White clouds outlined the horizon, appearing like snow-topped mountains from afar, and the white-tipped sailing boats completed the illusion. The blue of the sky and the blue-green of the sea complemented each other, like a well-chosen bonnet matching a pelisse. Darcy had dismissed the coachman, deciding to handle the ribbons himself, and he had taken Georgiana up in the front with him. Although the sea breeze prevented her from feeling hot, the sun was warm. Georgiana put up her parasol to protect her face. She did not wish to turn red as a lobster before her first dance.

"I am excited about attending the dance tonight," she said.

Her brother said nothing, concentrating on handling the ribbons as a carriage with four noisy Corinthians dashed through the crowd, causing havoc all around them.

As the traffic settled into a more sedate pace again, she felt her brother's gaze on her.

"Are you not worried you will encounter Wickham at the dance? It is very likely he will be there. You must be prepared."

The question was unexpected and Georgiana was flustered by it at first. However, she composed herself quickly. If her reaction at the parade was anything to judge by, she did not feel herself likely to be ill at ease.

"It no longer matters," she replied. "I know now that I do not care for him at all."

Darcy reached out and gave her hand a squeeze. "You do not know how relieved I am to hear it, Georgiana. I will not conceal from you that I have been very worried that you would succumb to him once again."

She shook her head vigorously. "Never!"

"You have removed a huge burden off my shoulders."

A gentle breeze came up from the sea. It was fresh and wet and carried with it the scent of a great salty expanse, teaming with millions of fellow creatures. It felt good to be alive – and free. At this instant in time, she loved the sea, and the way the waves danced as they crawled merrily onto the shingle and she loved the way the horizon seemed to stretch on forever, like her own future.

Just then, a carriage came into view, coming in their direction, with Elizabeth and her acquaintance talking animatedly and Jenny smiling at something they were saying.

"Oh, there they are!" she exclaimed. She waved and Elizabeth grinned and waved back.

Darcy turned his head sharply to inspect the gentleman in the other carriage.

"Look out!" said Georgiana as their carriage veered to the right.

By the time Darcy had straightened the horses, Elizabeth and her companion had passed them by.

"I have seen him before," said Darcy. "I feel I ought to recognize him. I seem to remember something unpleasant about him. Do you know his name?"

"Miss Bennet introduced me, but you know how easily I forget names. I am sorry.

"How did you say they were acquainted?"

"I believe he is the brother of an old friend of Miss Bennet's who moved away from Meryton. They have known each other for years."

She had expected her statement to be reassuring. After all, what could be more harmless than a childhood acquaintance?

William was grinding his teeth. He was not at all reassured.

Georgian smothered a giggle. There was nothing to laugh about, and certainly, she did not want to laugh at her brother's pain. It was only that – love did such awful things to people. Her normally sensible brother had been driven to complete irrationality. She hoped she would never fall in love again. Once was more than enough.

She felt very guilty suddenly that she had laughed.

"Brother, you cannot take it so much to heart. All she did was go riding with him. It means nothing. Your prospects are not at all threatened by this gentleman. You are far superior in every possible way."

"You think me more handsome than him?"

"Much more handsome, William."

He seemed to be appeased by this, and Georgiana hoped she had heard the last of it.

~~x~~

The dance at the Castle Inn Assembly Rooms was a crush, as these events were apt to be. Bingley waved at him from across the room as soon as Darcy's name was announced. There were a great many people Darcy knew from London and Darcy found himself obliged to nod and bow the moment he stepped into the large room, but his gaze was immediately drawn to Elizabeth, who was already there, her mother in

160

tow. She was resplendent in a simple ball gown that showed off her trim curves beautifully. Mr. Bennet was nowhere to be seen. He had already announced his intention to put his time to better use with his friend the book and despite Mrs. Bennet's protests, he must have stuck to his word.

There was no one there he particularly cared for, and thankfully only two ladies who would have any expectation of being asked by him to dance. That meant he would have ample opportunity to dance with Elizabeth. He intended to request her hand for the waltz. He knew he danced it well, and it would be an opportunity for a little more intimacy than the other dances.

Bingley had undertaken to get drinks and now he appeared, handing Darcy a glass of madeira.

"Do you remember the ball at Netherfield?" remarked Bingley, nostalgia filling his voice. "It seems an age since it happened. How happy we were then, and how unhappy we have been since!"

Darcy did not wish to be reminded of that ball, nor of his infernal stupidity since that day.

The memories came nonetheless, unbidden. Elizabeth at the Netherfield ball, her eyes sparkling with laughter, the highlights in her brown ringlets capturing the candlelight and his heart. The heat that had swept through him as their hands touched and parted. The graceful, inviting arch of her neck as she circled him in the steps of the dance. The delight he had felt even when she teased him. The temptation he had felt to lead her outdoors into the darkness and cover every inch of her with kisses. He recalled every detail of what she had been wearing that night, each smile, each glance she had given in his direction.

That evening was branded into his mind. His heart clenched inside him. As if, he could ever forget!

"Come, Darcy. I hate to see you standing about by yourself in this stupid manner," said Bingley. "There is only one woman I would wish to dance with and she is not present, but that is hardly true of you. Invite her to dance, Darcy."

There was no need to wonder who *she* was. There was only one possibility.

Nevertheless, Darcy held back. "What if she says no?"

"Then she will be punished by being forced to sit out the dance," said Bingley, giving Darcy a prod between the shoulder blades.

Taking a deep breath, Darcy began to move in Elizabeth's direction, trembling at the thought of once again holding her in his arms. However, just before he reached her, Mr. William Forth, the Master of Ceremonies, came up to her and introduced her to a young officer who claimed her hand immediately.

Not wanting to look like a fool, just in case she was glancing in his direction, Darcy sought out one of the ladies he knew and led the young lady into the dance. He soon regretted the impulse, however, because by the time he had returned his partner to her hovering chaperon, the next dance had started up again and Elizabeth was engaged to dance with someone else.

By now, Georgiana had arrived and was keeping company with Bingley and a lady they had met at the militia camp, Mrs. Hutchins. As soon as Darcy approached, Bingley, who had thrown off his pensive mood, announced that he was prepared to dance with anyone and set out to procure introductions. Darcy offered to obtain refreshments for the two ladies, but returned to find Mrs. Hutchins had been invited to dance. Spying an empty sofa, Darcy led Georgiana to it and they sat there for some time, engaging in conversation, watching those around them and observing the dance floor from time to time. Darcy suffered the pangs of seeing Elizabeth flit in and out of his sight dancing with someone else.

Clearly, *he* was not the only gentleman enticed by Elizabeth. From then on, every one of her next dances was claimed. Her popularity brought to him powerfully his own folly at their first encounter during the Meryton Ball. How had he thought at the time that no one wished to dance with her? It appeared a whole regiment of officers wished to do just that. He would have to beg for a place on her dance card and very probably find that there was none.

I am in no humor at present to give consequence to young ladies who are slighted by other men. Had he really said such a thing? How could he have done so?

A vast feeling of shame came over him. He finally understood the mistake he had been making at every turn and discovered the real reason why Elizabeth Bennet would never marry him.

He had claimed that he loved her, but on every one of those crucial encounters, he had disparaged and belittled her. At the Meryton Assembly – he had implied that no one found her attractive. In his first proposal, he had made it clear that both she and her sister were from backgrounds inferior to his. In his second proposal, he had practically informed her that no other man could possibly want her because of the scandal in the family. He shuddered. In retrospect, he could see that his last proposal was even worse – if possible – than the one at Hunsford. He had suggested that she had no choice but to marry him. In his eagerness to have her, he did not consider that he was demeaning her by presenting himself as her only possible candidate.

However, that was so far from being the case, it was laughable.

With this insight into his own character came another one, one that was even more fundamental. As she danced and laughed and spoke to others, it struck him that the answer to the question he had been asking himself was very simple. *Why did she not want to marry him?* He had hypothesized, conjectured, and ruminated on it for months now. The answer came to him like a thunderbolt. Miss Elizabeth Bennet did not need him. Even now with all that was happening with Miss Lydia, she still did not feel desperate enough to turn to him. He, on the other hand, needed her. He needed her so deeply he could hardly live without her. The problem was, she could live very well without *him*.

As if to drive the last nail into the coffin, he saw Elizabeth's face brighten up with a welcoming smile. He did not have to look to guess whom the smile was meant for. It was her old acquaintance from Meryton, decked out in scarlet, smiling in an equally tantalizing way.

"Oh," said Georgiana. "I have found out from Miss Bennet the name of her old acquaintance. His name is Mr. Drabble. Now do you know why he seems familiar?"

Drabble. The name was not uncommon. It did seem familiar but he could not think why.

"No," said Darcy. "However, if you would not mind it very much, I would prefer not to stay on much longer. The next dance is the waltz. It is the supper dance, after which everyone will go in for supper." Darcy had hoped to dance the waltz with Elizabeth. "Do you wish to partake of supper, sister?"

"I have no particular preference, William. I have enjoyed watching, but as I do not know anyone, I cannot but help feeling a little of an outsider."

"Then let us go."

He could not resist a last look at Elizabeth, however. She had taken her place on the dance floor and as the first chords of the waltz sounded, she stepped forward gracefully and arched her arms above her head. She did not even realize Darcy was leaving.

So she would prefer someone like Drabble to him. Well, he wished her good fortune.

~~x~~

Later, however, as Georgiana parted from Darcy to go to bed, Darcy brought up the subject of Mr. Drabble again.

"Do you really think there is nothing to Miss Bennet's attention to this gentleman?"

"How could there be," said Georgiana, "when you are infinitely more appealing than he could ever hope to be? Your status in society alone is far beyond his reach."

Darcy shook his head. "It is not as simple as that, Georgiana. This gentleman is from a similar background as Miss Bennet's. He is handsome. He is charming." Darcy threw himself down onto an armchair and drummed loudly with his fingers against the wooden arms. "Besides, you heard her mother. She is pushing Miss Bennet to contract a quick marriage, before the scandal strikes their family in full force."

Darcy was dwelling far too much on this one encounter.

"Surely one cannot contract a marriage so quickly. Sleep on it, brother. Tomorrow you will be more yourself and you will realize that things are not as dark as you are painting them."

"If only I could remember where I last saw him," said Darcy. "I am sure I have seen him somewhere before."

It was no use trying to inject any logic into the conversation when William was in this state. It would be better to leave him be and hope he would be more reasonable after a few hours' sleep.

"I will leave you to it, then, William," said Georgiana. "I will retire. Let me know in the morning what you discovered."

She did not think he would remember anything. It was all a figment of his imagination. She knew exactly why William was disturbed by Mr. Drabble. It had less to do with a former encounter than with something else entirely, something that went by the name of jealousy.

Chapter Sixteen

It was mid-morning on the day after the dance. Georgiana and Elizabeth were quietly writing letters in the Darcys' sitting room at the inn when a messenger arrived with a note for Elizabeth.

"For me?" she said, looking surprised and rather pleased. "How very peculiar! I do not know anyone in Brighton."

She opened it and began to read.

Georgiana had been unaware that she had taken her brother's words about Mr. Drabble to heart, but she found herself instantly remarking that there was something rather duplicitous about the way Elizabeth was reading the letter. She held it in such a way that nobody could possibly see the contents, and there was an unfamiliar expression on her face.

Since she did not wish to alert Elizabeth to the fact that she was being watched, Georgiana pretended to be engrossed in her writing in order to observe her covertly. Just in time. Elizabeth looked up from the note to see if Georgiana had noticed anything, re-read it again, then folded it into very small segments and rose to her feet.

"Anyone you know?" said Georgiana, looking up from her writing with a smile, hoping not to reveal that she had noticed anything amiss.

"Yes, in fact it is from an old acquaintance of mine. I did not know she lived in Brighton. It is an invitation to meet. The Forsters mentioned my name and she was immediately eager to see me. I must set out at once."

"How exciting to be able to renew an old friendship!" said Georgiana. "Would you like me to accompany you?"

"No," said Elizabeth, more forcefully than usual. "That is to say, as it is an old friend, it is more than likely we will wish to exchange confidences."

While Elizabeth's story might be plausible, her behavior was not. Why was she in such a hurry? Why did she not tell Georgiana the woman's name? There was definitely something furtive about the way Elizabeth was behaving and it was all the more striking since she was generally in the habit of being open. Georgiana recalled strongly William's disquiet about Mr. Drabble. Was it possible the note had been from him? It was all very puzzling.

A prickling of unease seized her as Elizabeth placed it in her reticule and, without saying goodbye, hurried nervously from the room. Without giving herself a moment to think, Georgiana sent the footman outside their chambers for Briggs and ran to the window to see which direction Elizabeth would take.

Very probably, there was nothing to the whole thing, and she would soon laugh at herself for allowing William to unnerve her, but at the moment, she could not shake the worry from her mind.

Briggs seemed to take forever to arrive. The moment he stepped in, she asked him to run after Miss Bennet at once.

"You must not lose sight of her. There is something amiss, and I want you to be at hand in case you are needed."

It was a credit to his training that he did not look at all surprised.

"Very well, Miss Darcy," he said.

A few minutes later, Georgiana was relieved to see him in the street, walking up Ship Street in the same direction as Elizabeth, towards the Lanes. There was something very reassuring about that sight and the sense of urgency that had gripped Georgiana disappeared. It was quite absurd, really, to think that anything untoward would happen. She was reading too many Gothic romances. Mrs. Annesley did not approve of them. She claimed they led to an overactive imagination and for once Georgiana had to agree.

She felt embarrassed now that she had sent Briggs on such a fool's errand and hoped Elizabeth would not see him and ask him why he was following her.

When Miss Bingley arrived a few minutes later to ask her if she would like to accompany her to the Lanes, Georgiana jumped up eagerly. She was in need of something to occupy her and she might well come across Elizabeth in the Lanes, although from what she heard they were such a warren of narrow streets it might be difficult.

"Yes, if you will give me time to change into a walking dress," said Georgiana.

"I hope I am not keeping you away from the library," said Miss Bingley with a sneer.

"Not at all," replied Georgiana. "I am sure there is more than enough to entertain us in the Lanes."

Miss Bingley seemed pleased. "I will take you to a milliner's shop. You will absolutely love the hats they have," remarked Miss Bingley enthusiastically.

Georgiana groaned inwardly. To have to spend hours looking at clothes and hats was not her idea of entertainment, but having offended Caroline by refusing to go with her to the Lanes the other day, and having doubted Elizabeth and sent someone to spy on her, Georgiana decided she deserved to suffer a dull afternoon. It was, she decided, a kind of penance.

The outing was not as bad as she had expected, however. The Lanes were more amusing than the London shops. No doubt some of the goods were smuggled from France. Georgiana was particularly pleased with the Valenciennes lace, which was hard to come by in London. By the time the two of them returned to the Inn, Georgiana was hungry. They ate some cold meats then parted ways when two of her friends called upon Miss Bingley and took her away in their carriage. Georgiana went upstairs to continue her interrupted correspondence.

She found Darcy there, reading. He smiled at her when she came in and she wondered if she should tell him about the note Elizabeth had received or not. In the end, she decided that it was Elizabeth's concern if she had something private to hide, and it was not up to her to feed her brother's jealousy. Instead, she broached the topic of Miss Lydia again.

"Did you and Mr. Bingley discover anything new?" she asked.

"Nothing in particular. We wished to speak with Captain Denny, who knows Wickham quite well, but unfortunately, he is on leave. However, we did speak to one officer who says he does not believe Wickham had much interest in Miss Lydia. He did not have any particularly useful information, but he gave us the names of two officers who may know more. We have agreed to be introduced to them later in the day."

"What about the Bennets?" she asked.

He gave a crooked smile. "Mr. Bennet asks a great number of questions but he does not stay to hear the answers. I hate to admit it, but I have come to the conclusion that Mrs. Bennet is far more resolute, and she does, in fact, ask some probing questions."

"Heavens, brother! You will soon be telling me that you are beginning to like her."

"I would not go so far," said Darcy, chuckling, "but I agree there may be more to her than meets the eye."

Georgiana was delighted to hear this. If William were to marry Elizabeth, it would be far better for him to like his new relatives than to despise them.

Just then, there was a scratch on the door and a footman came in with a letter.

As he opened it, Georgiana considered once again whether she should mention Elizabeth's letter. She had quite decided to do so – after all, Elizabeth had not asked her to keep it a secret – when William gave a groan, dropped the letter to the ground and slumped back in his seat.

"What is it, brother?" cried Georgiana. "Are you ill?"

"No," he said, staring right through her with glazed eyes. "I am not ill. I have received bad news."

Her stomach twisted. Had someone close to them died? Had there been an accident? Who could it be?

"What has happened, William? You look as though you have seen a ghost. Tell me!"

Darcy made a listless gesture towards the letter. "You may read it for yourself."

Dear Darcy,

When you receive this note, I will be far away. I have finally found a way of making you pay for all the times you have humiliated me and rubbed my nose in the dust. I have seen you and Miss Bennet together and have realized the extent of the affection between you. What a pleasure it shall be to thwart you both!!

I have in my possession your dearest and most cherished belonging. For once, it is in my power to take something that you own and make it mine. Think about this, and while doing so think what it felt for me to be raised by your side, seeing the vast properties that you own while having absolutely nothing myself, and with no resources but my own wits to depend upon.

Why should I be shackled to a girl such as Lydia when I can get the woman of your dreams? But I digress. Tempting as it may be to destroy Elizabeth Bennet's reputation and to take her away from you by marrying her myself; it is not in my interest to do so. I will not cut off my nose only to spite my face. I would far prefer to gain something useful from the situation. I notice your precious little sister wore your mother's diamond set at the ball. As I recall, the set is not only very old but also very valuable. Now it is time to discover exactly how valuable Miss Bennet is to you. If you would like to pay the diamonds as ransom for Miss Bennet then I would be happy to receive them in exchange for her person.

Meet me at four o'clock at the abandoned mill next to the chalk quarry near Jevington. Come in a hired carriage, not your own. If anyone comes with you or follows you, I will leave immediately and there will be no exchange.

Most sincerely, your most devoted friend, GW

Georgiana looked at Darcy, trying to assimilate the meaning of those words.

"He hates you," said Georgiana. "Why does he hate you so much?"

It was not a real question. She knew the answer, though she could scarcely credit it. Darcy did not trouble himself to reply.

"I suppose it did not help that you thwarted his plans to marry me and take over my property."

Darcy's gaze shifted. "No, it did not."

"And now he has abducted Miss Bennet."

The desolation on Darcy's face tore at her. She had never seen such emotion on her brother's face and it terrified her.

She stood up and went immediately to the safe behind the picture where their valuables had been placed, produced the key from her reticule and brought out the jewels.

"Take them," she said. "Please."

"But they're yours," said Darcy. "I cannot deprive you of your inheritance."

"They are nothing more than pretty stones, William. If they will save Miss Bennet – then what are you waiting for? Go!"

Her words seemed to awaken him from the stupor into which he had fallen. He sprung up, took the jewels and, emptying out her reticule, stuffed them inside. Giving Georgiana a quick peck on the cheek, he ran out of the room and down the stairs.

~~x~~

Darcy stopped two hackney carriages. They were willing enough to take up a customer until he told them the address. Then each of them shook his head and said it was too far out of town, and they were more than likely to lose their way. The third coachman gave Darcy a careful examination up and down and seemed satisfied by what he saw. He then named an exorbitant fee and asked for half of it in advance.

At this point Darcy was willing to be transported by the devil himself, as long as he could reach his destination in time.

The place Wickham had named turned out to be quite a way out of Brighton. The road was well maintained at first, and then became increasingly more uncomfortable. The carriage jolted and rattled until

171

Darcy felt his teeth were ready to fall out. He could understand now why the previous two hackney cabs had refused to bring him this way. The only advantage of all this jostling about was that it prevented him from thinking, which was a mercy as his thoughts were all reprehensible and involved various unpleasant ways to beat Wickham to a pulp.

It seemed like hours before Darcy finally caught sight of the chalk quarry and the abandoned mill Wickham had described in his letter.

Darcy knocked on the roof with his walking stick and the driver stopped and let down the steps.

Darcy lowered the window and, putting his head out, looked around.

"Doesn't seem to be anyone around, sir," said the hackney driver.

"That is the general idea," said Darcy.

Presently, they heard the sound of a carriage coming from the other side of the quarry. It stopped across from them. Darcy realized the meeting place had been carefully thought out – there was no road from where they stood to where the other carriage stood – only a narrow path along the hillside.

"Must have come from Jevington, sir," said the hackney driver, nervously.

Darcy had never heard of Jevington, but from the driver's tone, he assumed it had an unsavory reputation, no doubt involved in smuggling brandy and French lace as some of the villages around tended to do.

A masked man jumped from the carriage and stood across the gap, pointing a pistol.

"Mr. Darcy, if you would kindly step out of the carriage."

Darcy hesitated. He had expected to see Wickham, but clearly, there was a more organized criminal element involved. He had already recognized the masked man from his voice. He had heard it just yesterday, when Mr. Drabble had stolen Elizabeth away to dance. He was not likely to forget him.

Now, of course, he understood why he had remembered the man in the first place. He had been at Oxford with Wickham and had been sent down after being accused of robbing one of the Dons.

He tried to think through his situation. Why should he step out? He did not know even if Elizabeth was in the other carriage.

"How do I know you have Miss Bennet here?"

"Show her to the gentleman, Cole."

The door of the other carriage was opened, revealing a large man in rough clothes who pushed forward a bound woman's figure with a sackcloth bag covering her head.

"Say something, sweetheart," said Mr. Drabble. "Tell him who you are."

Elizabeth struggled and kicked out. He felt a sense of pride. She was not one to go quietly. That was his girl – that was Elizabeth. She would never give up without a battle. She was trying to make sounds but it was clear that her mouth was tied as well.

"What is the matter? Did the cat get your tongue?" said Mr. Drabble. "Oh, I remember now. I stuffed a rag in your mouth because you were complaining too much."

Rage coursed through Darcy at the thought that someone could have done this to her. He wanted to throw himself somehow across that gap and bring the man to the ground. But it would not do. Mr. Drabble had the pistol and he did not. He had not thought he might need it, believing as he did that he was meeting Wickham.

If the two of them were to get out of this safely, Darcy had to keep his head and not doing anything rash.

Of course, it was possible the man would take the jewels, then kill him, or both of them. Robbers routinely killed for far less. But then, why would he do that? The man was not a petty criminal who would swing from the end of the rope for stealing a loaf of bread. He was clearly a member of the privileged classes. He would not kill lightly, not for a set of jewels, surely?

At least, that is what Darcy hoped.

What if he refused to step out of the carriage and Mr. Drabble simply shot him? He reasoned that the man had no reason to kill him. In the end, Darcy stepped out of the carriage because he had no choice. He wanted Elizabeth back and this was his only hope.

173

Mr. Drabble now pointed the pistol at the hackney driver.

"Go back to Brighton," he ordered, "And don't come back, if you value your life."

The hackney coachman did not wait to be told twice. He did not know Darcy – he owed him nothing, and he had already been paid half the fare. He turned the coach and took off as fast as the poorly maintained road would allow.

Darcy felt a momentary panic. He was in the middle of nowhere. No one would know if he was shot. He could be left to rot here.

Take hold of yourself, Darcy and think. This is no time to lose your head.

"Come, bring the jewels and set them on the ground over there."

Darcy shook his head.

"I came for Miss Bennet. How do I know you will honor your part of the bargain? I will not hand over the jewels unless you make the exchange."

"Very well. Place the jewels where I told you and I will leave you Miss Bennet."

"Take her out of the carriage," said Darcy.

Mr. Drabble stared at him for a long time through the mask. Darcy stared back, refusing to back down. For a moment, Darcy thought he was going to refuse. Then he turned to his accomplice.

"Set her down on the ground," he ordered.

The ruffian pulled her out and pushed her to the ground none too gently. Elizabeth squirmed and twisted at the ruffian's touch. Darcy stepped forward in outrage.

"The jewels," said the man in the domino mask. "Take them out of the bag and put them on the ground."

Darcy wished he had thought to ask Briggs to follow him – and to come armed, but he had done neither, so there was nothing he could do but submit to whatever Mr. Drabble required.

"The diamond set," said Darcy, walking to the place on the path where the man had indicated. He opened the reticule and poured the jewels onto the ground, wincing as he thought of the damage it would do to the setting. The diamonds glistened in the sunlight like tears.

"Now go back to where you left the carriage," said Mr. Drabble.

Darcy returned slowly, wondering if he could risk running over to the other side and trying to grab Elizabeth. He dismissed the idea at once. He could not risk getting Elizabeth shot.

The masked man nodded to the ruffian, who ran over and seized the diamonds.

"Bite them," said Mr. Drabble.

The ruffian bit into them and nodded. "Seems like they're real enough."

Darcy groaned at this ridiculous manner of authenticating a jewel. All he wanted was to get Elizabeth back.

Mr. Drabble put out his hand for them. He then shut the door of the carriage, leapt onto the box and flicked his whip. The carriage took off as the ruffian ran alongside it and then jumped in. The carriage disappeared down the road, leaving Elizabeth behind on the ground.

Darcy rushed to her, his heart thudding, and frantically tried to unravel the rope. His job was rendered all the more difficult because she was struggling to get loose.

"My sweetest Elizabeth," he said, with great tenderness. "I am doing what I can to untie you, but you must stay still."

In response, she twisted and turned even more frantically.

He tore off his gloves and tossed them to the ground in an attempt to grip the rope better and untie the knots. They were clearly tied by someone who knew about knots – a navy man or a fisherman.

"Try to stay still," he repeated. She continued to struggle. Darcy began to worry. Why was she struggling so hard? Was she having trouble breathing? Was she suffocating in there? He was gripped with terror.

Darcy looked around for help, but there was no one around. He considered his options. Could he carry her all the way back to Brighton without untying her? Not if she continued to struggle, certainly, and even then, how would he do it? He was in the midst of the Downs and there was no sign of habitation in sight.

There was no way around it. He was going to have to stop her from squirming by sitting on her.

He hesitated, but there was really no choice.

"I am very sorry to do this, Elizabeth, but it is for your own good."

There was no time to think about what he was doing. His body weight helped, but Elizabeth kept kicking at his legs. He swore as he used a sharp rock to cut the rope, which was impossibly thick. He seemed to cut himself more than he was cutting the rope, but eventually he was able to do it. Smiling with relief, he pulled at it and it began to fall away. As the ropes loosened, Elizabeth flayed out with her arms, breaking loose. The burlap sack covering her fell to the floor.

The smile on Darcy's face died. The woman he had just untied was not Elizabeth Bennet.

Which could only mean one thing. Elizabeth was still with Wickham.

Chapter Seventeen

The woman screamed at the top of her voice and began to run away as fast as she could. Darcy chased after her. Why the deuce was she running from *him*? He had been the one to untie her. Besides, where did she think she was going? There was nothing around here on the South Downs but grassland and sheep. He would have let her get away, only he needed to question her. She might be able to reveal a few things about Elizabeth's abductor.

He caught up with her soon enough. Her long dress hindered her and her delicate slippers were no match for his leather Hessians.

"You are going nowhere, madam, until you have answered my questions," he said. "How did you come to be involved in this despicable scheme? Are you another of Wickham's lightskirts?"

She was on the verge of tears, but she rallied, raising her chin and looking defiant. "I will have you know, I am a respectable lady, even if I work on stage. I am certainly not anyone's lightskirt. I did not even know the man's name. All I know is that a handsome gentleman – not the same one who took your jewels – came backstage at the Royal Theatre just after rehearsals and offered me a good sum of money for a bit of acting. He said he wanted to play a trick on an old friend – just for a lark, he said. I saw no harm in it. He told me I was going to be trussed up and I was to kick and scream as much as possible. Well, I kicked and screamed in earnest, I can tell you." She took out a lace-bordered kerchief from inside her sleeve and wiped the tears from her eyes. "What is to become of me? I heard them selling me to you for some jewels."

It had never occurred to Darcy that she might consider him a criminal. He noticed her for the first time. With large blue eyes and light brown curls, she looked the picture of innocence. Surely, she was no older than sixteen. She was trying hard to stay strong, but he could see she was terrified. No wonder she had kicked and struggled. Her fate lay completely in his hands.

"You have nothing to be afraid of, not from me," said Darcy, gently. "I did not pay the jewels for you. I paid them as ransom money for someone else entirely. They paid you to impersonate her."

Hope rose up in her eyes and she gave Darcy an uncertain smile. "So I am free to go?" she said, a wobble in her voice.

"Yes," said Darcy, wondering how being free to go would help her when she was in the middle of nowhere, in an area known for some rather rough smuggling groups.

Then the devastating truth sunk in. Wickham and his accomplice had taken off with both the jewels and Elizabeth. Darcy's stomach clenched. He tried to reason the whole situation through. He could not imagine why Wickham had chosen to keep Elizabeth, unless it was to taunt him. It was doubtful she would come to any harm at his hands. That was not Wickham's style. The other man, however – Mr. Drabble – he did not trust at all. What if he decided to kill her because she was a witness? His hands went clammy at the idea. Surely, Mr. Drabble would not stoop so low.

He dismissed the notion because he could not bear to think of it. He refused to believe it. The worst-case situation he would entertain was that, if Mr. Drabble was to be believed, the two men planned to escape to the Continent, never mind that there was a war raging there. They would keep Elizabeth as hostage for safe passage and release her once they had boarded a vessel.

By then, of course, Elizabeth's reputation would have been ruined beyond repair.

He clenched his fists in futile anger. How was he supposed to do anything about it when he was marooned in this backwater with no means of transportation? It would take him hours to return to Brighton, by which time Wickham and his accomplice would have had ample time to make their escape. He wished he had had the foresight to scout the area around them on their way here, but he had foolishly assumed it would be a simple exchange and he would be returning by carriage – with Elizabeth. These were the Downs – they were grazing lands, not farms, and settlements were few and far between. It was going to be a long walk; their only hope of relief would be if they came across a rider along the way, or if they were lucky enough to find a farm that kept horses. Wickham's accomplice had planned things well. Wickham himself was too lazy for such an elaborate plan, so clearly there was someone else with the brains to concoct it.

He considered the actress. How far would she be able to walk? Not very far, probably. The girl had brought this on herself – she should never have agreed to such a scheme, no matter what the incentive. A quick glance at her face, however, and at the red mark branded into her cheek where the villain had tied a cloth to hold the rags in, changed his opinion. She was as much a victim of Mr. Drabble's schemes as anyone else, and she did not deserve what had happened.

He let out a frustrated breath. His instincts cried out for him to forget the girl and hurry to Brighton. She would slow him down, and every moment he wasted would be a gain for Wickham. His conscience, however, would not allow it. Suppose something were to happen to her?

"It is going to be a long walk," said Darcy. "I want to help you, but I'm not sure what the best way to do that is. You have one of two options. You can wait here, near the quarry, and I will send my coachman to pick you up. That may take several hours, depending when I arrive in Brighton, but with the days being so long it should still be daytime. You must promise, though, not to move or he will never find you."

She looked around and swallowed.

"What is the second option, sir?"

"You can walk with me as far as the next village. However, I warn you, I cannot hold back for you. I need to get back to Brighton with the utmost urgency. You do realize that the lady I paid the ransom money for is still in their hands?"

Her eyes widened. "Yes, yes. I understand. I will walk as far as I can, and I promise not to slow you down. I just do not wish to be left alone here." She took a pin from her bonnet and, taking up the edge of her skirt, she pinned it so she could walk more easily. "Oh, if only I never agreed to do this. I feel terrible for being part of it."

Darcy began to walk.

"You were not to know," said Darcy, "and you are not the first girl to fall under Wickham's spell." The scoundrel seemed to favor sixteen-year-olds. "Did you bed him?"

His voice sounded harsh, even to his own ears.

"No!" she said. "I told you already. I may be an actress but that does not mean I have no scruples. I only ever met him once. He came backstage at the Theatre Royal. I only have a small role in the farce," she said, shyly, "so gentlemen don't often come to see me." She shrugged. "When he offered me the chance to earn extra by playing a trick on one of his friends, I did not think there could be any harm in it."

"As you see, there was a great deal of harm in it."

"Yes, sir," she said, starting to cry again, "but I did not think so at the time."

Darcy nodded. "It could have gone a great deal worse for you," he said. "With someone unscrupulous." He did not want to be harsh, but she needed to learn a lesson from it. "Meanwhile, let us save our breath to cool our porridge and try to move as quickly as we can."

They walked in silence for some three miles or so, though it was difficult to judge distance in an area where the land rippled with small knolls. All around them, sheep grazed in blissful ignorance of the turmoil that filled Darcy's soul. If only one could ride sheep, he reflected, it would have made his life much easier.

"Can we stop for a moment?" said the young girl abruptly. "I have a stitch in my side."

She was looking worried and guilty – as if she expected him to walk on and abandon her.

"I am sorry to hear it," he said. "Please take your time and catch your breath." As he said that, he shifted his weight from foot to foot, impatient to get going. He turned and looked around him, hoping to spy some signs of civilization, but in vain.

Now that he stopped to think, it occurred to him that it would save him time if he knew where they were keeping Elizabeth.

"Do you happen to know where either of those scoundrels lives?"

"No, sir," she said. "They took me straight to the carriage and trussed me up. I never saw anything."

It had all been too well planned, thought Darcy. They had left no loose ends.

"I am feeling better now," she said. "We can start walking." She took off again, walking with a very fast, smooth and easy stride. She reminded him of his Elizabeth. Clearly, she was not city bred.

"What is your name?"

"Hester Cannon, sir."

"Pleased to meet you, Hester. I am Mr. Darcy."

She curtseyed shyly. She was a well-mannered young woman, obviously. It was really unfortunate she had fallen into Wickham's hands.

"I take it you were not born in Brighton?"

"No. I come from a village near Steyning. My father was a parson, that was, until he died and left us with no one to take care of us. I tried to find work but since I was not used to the drudgery of being a maid no one would take me on. I always used to put on plays at the parsonage, and everyone said I was good at acting, so I thought perhaps I could become an actress. Luckily, I found a manager to take me on and I can send money to my mother and younger sister. I should have known better than to be tempted by this man's – offer."

It was a common enough story. There were not many choices for a girl of her upbringing. She was too young to be a governess, and besides, she was too young, but not trained to do anything else.

They had been walking more than an hour further when the sight of a donkey cart on a dirt road in the distance set Darcy running. He had never seen a more welcome sight in his life. The girl ran behind him, and they both shouted and waved. The cart driver continued on his way, oblivious. Darcy told the girl to wait and sprinted forward as fast as he could.

Luckily, the cart was going very slowly indeed or he would never have caught up with it. When Darcy reached it, his lungs were hurting so much he could not speak. He had to bend over double and wait for the breath to return to him before he could explain their situation.

However, it was no easy task to convince the farmer, who had just come from delivering vegetables at Burgess Hill, to turn around and return whence he had come.

"It be an hour at least," said the man, who had lost most of his teeth and was hard of hearing. However, his hearing was good enough to hear the rattle of coins in Mr. Darcy's hand, which seemed to exercise an extraordinarily persuasive power.

He agreed to turn back the cart, provided Darcy managed the obstinate donkey. "I've half a mind to sell him for meat, but then how would I get to market? I've never seen such a slowcoach in my life."

The words did not inspire confidence, certainly, particularly when Darcy was in a tearing hurry, but there did not appear to be any choice.

"Come on up, then," said the farmer, offering his hand to the girl. "What are you waiting for? There's room for all of us in the front, unless you would prefer to sit on the cart in the hay, young lady."

She looked doubtfully at the hay then took the offered hand and climbed up beside the two men.

Darcy, who had never driven a donkey cart or a hay cart either, rapidly developed an appreciation for the patience of those who did. His thoughts turned to Mr. Coulter, with his old horse and his hay cart. Immediately, he remembered the overturned cart and that terrifying moment when he had thought Elizabeth was injured in the accident. His anxiety then was nothing to the turmoil he was feeling at the idea that Elizabeth was at Mr. Drabble's mercy.

"Be this pretty young thing your wife?" he asked.

The girl giggled and began to explain who she was, but Darcy shook his head at her. He did not wish his tale to be bandied about. One never knew who would hear of it.

"No," said Darcy. "She is my niece and I was taking her to town for some new clothes. Our carriage overturned and our horse was lamed. I need to go for help. I wonder if you would be kind enough to take us to the nearest inn where I can obtain a horse."

It was a highly unlikely tale, but it seemed to satisfy the old man, particularly after Darcy had handed him some coins.

"It weren't worth laming a good horse just to get some new clothes," he said, chewing on a stick of hay. "That's what women are about. Always wanting something or the other to wear." He shook his head. "My wife was always nagging for a new bonnet or some ribbons for the girls, God rest her soul." He fell into a glum silence, whether reminiscing about his wife, considering the vicissitudes of fate, or regretting some bonnet he had purchased, Darcy could not determine.

The journey to the village was excruciatingly slow. The donkey moved at a snail's pace. Darcy ground his teeth and endured it, but his patience was wearing thin.

Fortunately, when he reached the village of Burgess Hill he discovered that there was a posting inn, albeit a shabby one, and he was able to obtain a horse. The farmer, rather than deciding to turn back again, settled in the taproom.

"I think I deserve a mug of ale, after all that hard work," said the farmer, to some fellow farmers who had just come in from the market. "Driving that donkey back all the way quite drained the life out of me."

Restraining himself from pointing out that it was he who had driven the cart, not the farmer; Darcy bought him a large mug of ale.

"You're a right good one, sir," said the farmer, raising his mug to him in salute.

As his horse was saddled. Darcy saw to it that Hester was set up in a private parlor.

"I will send my coachman for you. He will return you to the theatre," he said. "I am sorry you were put in such a situation."

"It was hardly your fault, Mr. Darcy," said Hester. "I should not have trusted a stranger."

183

He ordered food for the girl and left her at the inn to be picked up, then set out as fast as he could for Brighton.

~~X~~

Darcy pushed his way recklessly through the squeeze of carriages that thronged Marine Parade. He operated on blind instinct alone, managing miraculously to avoid a collision with a high-perch phaeton with only inches to spare. He could abide no delay, not if every moment might count towards being able to rescue Elizabeth.

The part of him capable of thought told him it was lunacy to rush so fast when he had no idea where to look for Elizabeth. As he passed the militia camp, he briefly considered going in to look for Wickham, but it would simply be a waste of time. Wickham would not be foolish enough to sit there and await his arrival.

He decided to stop off briefly at the Old Ship, to determine whether there had been any further ransom notes. Perhaps they intended to make him pay through his teeth to have her back.

He would happily do it.

Tossing the reins to a standing footman outside the Inn, and asking him to keep the horse exercised until he came back down, he took the stairs two at a time and threw open the door of his apartment.

His heart came to a standstill at the sight before him. For a moment, his mind refused to believe what his eyes could see. He was sure it was an illusion born of his desperate need, like a mirage to a thirsty man.

There, before him, was the most wonderful sight he had ever been fortunate enough to behold. It was none other than Elizabeth Bennet, his Elizabeth, who was there before him, seated on a chair, safe and sound, not a hair on her body harmed.

Darcy wanted to go down on his knees to give thanks. Instead, he stood leaning against the doorjamb, his legs having suddenly lost their ability to move, and stared at the heavenly apparition before him.

She was the first to see him. "Mr. Darcy!" she cried.

Suddenly there were faces all around him, voices were asking him questions. Someone – he thought it must be Bingley – took his arm and led him to a chair. There was a lump in his throat the size of an apple and it hurt. His eyes burned.

"Mr. Darcy!" exclaimed Caroline Bingley. "We have been so anxious about you. When you did not come back for hours, we feared you had met with some accident."

He cared not in the least what Caroline feared. He wanted only to keep his gaze fixed on Elizabeth Bennet to make sure she did not simply vanish but there was something in his eyes and he could not see clearly. Brandy appeared in his hand and he tossed it down in one short gulp. The brandy burned into his throat. It cleared the lump enough for him to get a word out.

"How?" he said, his voice little more than a croak.

"More, sir?" asked Briggs, his little valet, and Darcy nodded.

Bingley gave him a bone-shaking slap on the shoulder. "Glad to see you are recovering," he said. "We are all waiting to hear what happened to you."

Darcy had no intention of telling them anything until he had heard what had happened to Elizabeth. He cleared his throat and more of the lump went away.

"I want to hear Miss Bennet's story first."

"The others have heard it," said Elizabeth, "but if there is no objection, I'll tell it again."

"Before Miss Bennet starts, brother," said Georgiana, "shall I order some refreshments? You look as if you've been through an ordeal."

He wanted nothing except to hear Elizabeth speak. That was the food of his soul. He shook his head at Georgiana with a grateful smile.

Slowly everyone drifted away. Caroline went and stood by the window, staring out as if longing to leave. Elizabeth sat on the green damask chaise, draping her arm along the back. Georgiana sat on an Egyptian-style stool with lion's feet. Bingley balanced on the arm of another chair swung his leg back and forth in a distracting manner.

"Very well, Mr. Darcy. I will try to keep this brief in order not to bore the others," said Elizabeth, with a faint smile. "You will have guessed, of course, that I received a letter from Mr. Drabble and that I very foolishly trusted him enough to agree to meet him. You must understand, I have known the family since childhood, and I have corresponded with his sister now for several years. It never occurred to me that his situation was so different as to keep company with some unsavory characters, but from what I gather, gambling debts have forced him into desperate measures. I never thought of wondering why my friend's family left the neighborhood, but now that I look back on it, it is possible that they were forced to rent out their estate because of the son's debts. I suppose I was too young to know the details at the time."

She took a deep breath. Darcy thought how beautiful she looked, even now when she was deeply distressed. He had feared so much for her safety he did not care how she managed to escape – only that the dearest thing to him on earth was unscathed and sat before him. He drank in the sight of her, eternally grateful that she had been restored to him and was not somehow in the unscrupulous hands of Mr. Drabble and his uncouth assistant.

"I am not so improper as to have agreed to an assignation with Mr. Drabble," she said, her cheeks flushed. "I am certain some of you will have already thought so. The reason I was foolhardy enough to believe him was because the letter said that Mr. Wickham had revealed my sister Lydia's hiding place to him. According to the letter, Mr. Wickham had been in his cups and Mr. Drabble had boasted of the fact that she was hidden right under our very noses. I believed him because he had said he knew Mr. Wickham and promised to see what he could discover from him.

The note made it sound urgent – something about Mr. Wickham planning to move her that very night. I do not recall the exact wording of the note but he asked me not to bring anyone."

Elizabeth stopped and covered her face with her hands. Darcy wanted to peel her hands back and cover that face with kisses. He could not bear to see her suffer.

"I should have known better, of course. I should never have agreed to go alone. But I was thinking only of Lydia. By the time I realized there was something wrong, a sackcloth covered my head and someone was winding rope around me. Then I heard Mr. Drabble and Mr. Wickham argue what to do with the jewels once they got them, and I realized the kind of a trap I had fallen into."

She paused, overpowered by the moment. Darcy was shaken to the core to see how uncertain she sounded. All traces of the playful, laughing Elizabeth he knew was gone. Her hands were unsteady. He was seized with an overwhelming need to shield her from harm, to make sure nothing like this ever happened again. He clenched his fists at his side at the thought that it was Wickham who had done this thing to her.

"They carried me into a carriage and left me there, tied up, with a man to guard me. I tried to loosen the rope that was binding me, but whoever had done it knew what they were doing." She gave a wry smile. "That was when Briggs appeared magically on the scene." She looked in the direction of the little man, who grinned at being at the center of attention. "I don't know how he slipped by the guard, but I have never felt as happy as when I heard the sound of his voice telling me not to be afraid!"

"Bravo!" said Bingley, clapping his hands. Everybody joined in the applause while Briggs bowed and looked very pleased with himself. "Now we want to hear your side of the story, Mr. Darcy".

Darcy told the tale quickly. He tried his best to gloss over the fact that he had been cheated of Georgiana's diamonds by dwelling instead on the young actress and her plight. However, when he was finished, Elizabeth looked around the room with a stricken expression.

"I will never forgive myself for my folly," she said. "Georgiana has lost her family heirloom diamonds because of my stupidity, and I have caused you all untold anxiety."

She looked so forlorn; Darcy was unable to control himself any longer. He stood, went to the chaise, took up Elizabeth's hand, and kissed it.

"You must not blame yourself, Miss Bennet," he said. "It was a mistake easily made. Mr. Drabble knew your weakness was your sister and he exploited it to the full. You have been through an ordeal," he said, tenderly. "Once you have had some rest, you will feel better."

Was it his imagination, or did she tighten her grip on his hand? No doubt she was only doing it out of gratitude, but he cherished the gesture, wanting it to last forever.

At that moment, Mrs. Bennet came into the room.

"What is the meaning of this, sir?" she said. "Let go of Lizzie at once!"

Elizabeth drew back her hand quickly and signaled with a look that she did not wish her mother to know anything about her abduction.

"Explain yourself, Lizzy."

"It is nothing, Mama. I felt I was about to faint and Mr. Darcy was assisting me."

"Nonsense, Lizzy, you have never fainted in your life. You have the constitution of a horse."

"Even horses occasionally show signs of weakness," said Elizabeth. "Thank you, Mr. Darcy; you cannot imagine how much I appreciate your assistance."

Mrs. Bennet gave Darcy a hard glance then took Lizzy's arm, pulling her away.

Elizabeth, too fatigued to resist her mother for once, excused herself and left. Mrs. Bennet's voice could be plainly heard in the hallway.

"I hope you have met Mr. Drabble again. Remember, we will not be staying in Brighton very long, and you need to secure his affections quickly."

"I have met Mr. Drabble," said Elizabeth, "and I do not wish to meet him ever again. A more odious person I have yet to encounter."

Mrs. Bennet gave out a cry. "Have you not understood a word I told you, Lizzie? I quite despair of your folly!! Must you be so obstinate? You cannot expect to marry to please yourself."

Their voices faded as the door to the Bennet chambers closed.

The love shining in William's eyes as he watched Miss Bennet leave made Georgiana's heart ache for him. Surely, he deserved some happiness. For the rest of her life she would never forget the expression on his face when he had burst into the room and found her there unharmed.

"You were very wise to send Darcy's man to look after Miss Bennet, Georgiana," said Caroline. "The members of the Bennet family have a rather unfortunate tendency to get themselves into bad situations, do they not? Consider what would have happened if you had not been around to send someone to rescue her."

This was so blatantly unfair that Georgiana opened her mouth to object. However, she was beaten to it by Mr. Bingley.

"How can you lay the blame on the members of the Bennet family for Wickham's perfidy? Wickham would not have dreamt of doing such a thing if it were not for the fact that Darcy—"

"—refused to give him more money after he went through his share," interrupted Darcy, noting that his friend was about to be indiscreet and mention his love for Elizabeth. "Wickham is intent on avenging himself – though the root problem is jealousy rather than any deed I committed – and he considers harming the Bennets a way to inflict harm on me."

"I am aware of that," said Miss Bingley, "but he would hardly have been able to accomplish it if the Bennet girls had not been so foolhardy and so easily led astray. One could be almost ready to excuse the younger girl for being caught in his wiles. One could make a case that she is too young to know any better. But to have the older sister repeat that folly! You said so yourself, Mr. Darcy. She knew nothing of that gentleman she was so adamant on meeting. You tried to warn her, but she obstinately refused to listen. She is little better than her sister. She is headstrong and foolish and her head is easily turned by a handsome face."

Georgiana knew it was jealously that was prompting

"You need not be holier than thou, Miss Bingley," said Georgiana hotly, aware that she, like the Bennet girls, had failed in this, "The only reason you are not susceptible to a handsome face is because you have been in love with my brother for years and have eyes for no one else. That does not make you more virtuous than anyone else, merely more foolish."

A tense silence followed her words and she regretted them at once, particularly since Miss Bingley looked stricken. How could she have said such a horrible thing?

"Oh," she said. "I am sorry. I did not mean that. It has been such a strange day. I do not know what came over me."

"Well," said Bingley, with an obvious attempt at cheerfulness. "It *has* been a difficult day, but all's well that ends well and I for one am ready to retire. How about you, Darcy?"

"I am aching and sore from having walked the Downs," said Darcy. "I would certainly welcome a good night's sleep. I am just waiting to hear from the coachman that the young actress has been brought home safely. I cannot rest without being certain."

As the Bingleys retired to their own chambers, Darcy came towards Georgiana. She waited nervously for him to berate her for her rudeness. Instead, he took both her hands, squeezed them tightly, and kissed her on the cheek.

"I have not thanked you yet for what you did, Georgiana. Briggs is the hero of the day, but it is you who deserves the most credit, little sister," said Darcy. "I shudder to think what would have happened if you had not sent Briggs to follow Miss Bennet."

Georgiana smiled widely. She was delighted that her brother's faith in her had been restored. She would never have wanted such a thing to happen, but she hoped this incident had proved once and for all to her brother that she was not a child to be pushed aside and forgotten.

"It is because you said you did not trust him that I thought of doing so – your words stayed with me and I felt there was something not quite right about the situation. Who could have known that Mr. Drabble was in league with Wickham?"

"Wickham has gone too far this time. I will leave no stone unturned to bring him to justice. Abduction is a serious crime, and he will have to answer to it. I will not allow something like this to happen ever again, to anyone."

Georgiana nodded. She still looked back in dismay at how deceived she had been by Wickham's charms, but she now felt that, by participating in Elizabeth's rescue, she had managed to atone somehow for that moment of weakness. It was as if she had spent the last year under a shadow and was only just emerging. She had not realized how much the near-disaster with Wickham had affected her.

It was finally behind her, however. She could now look forward to her Season with a slate wiped completely clean.

Chapter Eighteen

It was now Saturday, and the London party assembled for breakfast in a glum mood. The appeal of Brighton had faded and the reality of Lydia's situation was now felt strongly. There was no sign that Wickham was hiding Miss Lydia, and Darcy could not imagine that someone so high-spirited would have had the patience to remain concealed for so long.

"I see no purpose in staying longer in Brighton," said Mr. Bennet, setting aside his breakfast plate with a clang. "Mrs. Bennet has accomplished what she came here to do, which was to bathe in the sea and eat as many prawns as possible. Lizzy has proved that even outside Meryton, gentlemen will flock around her. I have gone sea fishing. Apart from the fact that we have not found Lydia, I would call our outing an outstanding success. I am now quite ready to return to the comforts of home, to sit in my old armchair and ruminate over the happy times we have had. "

"How can you say such a heartless thing, Mr. Bennet?" said Mrs. Bennet. "You know how utterly downcast I am! I only wished to distract myself while we waited for word of Lydia's whereabouts. How can we possibly abandon my poor child and go home?"

"We can and we must, since we have no evidence that she is here at all. We may well have been barking up the wrong tree, Mrs. Bennet, and it has been a rather small tree in a very large forest. Lydia could be anywhere. Nothing points to her being here and we have learned nothing new since we arrived."

To Darcy's surprise, Georgiana suddenly entered the conversation.

"Unless you consider what Mrs. Hutchins said," she replied.

Everyone turned to her at once. "Mrs. Sandra Hutchins? The lady we met at the officers' quarters?" said Elizabeth.

"Yes. She was also at the assembly the other night."

"Miss Darcy, if you have new information, I hope you will tell us," said Mr. Bennet, putting down his napkin and looking towards Georgiana expectantly.

Georgiana flushed at finding herself the center of attention. "I thought everyone had heard and had discarded the idea, which was why I said nothing. It is not much to go on, in any case." She looked apologetic. "According to Mrs. Hutchins, Miss Lydia could not have run off with Wickham. Although she flirted with him, she did not like him. There was another officer who fixed her interest. I do not recall his name, but Mrs. Hutchins seemed to think him a much more likely contender for her affections."

"Nonsense!" said Mrs. Bennet. "Why would Lydia write one thing and do another? I never heard anything more ridiculous."

"For once Mrs. Bennet and I are in accord. I do not believe we can give this account any credit," said Mr. Bennet. "It is far more likely this Mrs. Hutchins is a gossip with nothing better to do than spread false reports."

Darcy thought cynically that the Bennets would soon be claiming that Miss Lydia never lied.

"Lydia never told a lie in her life," said Mrs. Bennet.

Darcy smiled. "Nevertheless," said Darcy, "I think it is worth pursuing, if only to be absolutely certain there is nothing to it. Do you know where we can find your Mrs. Hutchins, Georgiana?"

"She is the wife of one of the officers," said Georgiana.

Darcy tossed down his napkin and rose from the table.

"Then I think we ought to find her without delay, though perhaps only I and Mr. Bennet—"

"And I," said Bingley, still quite determined not to be left out.

"You cannot prevent me from discovering the fate of my own daughter," said Mrs. Bennet.

"Very well," said Darcy. "Let us go and find Mrs. Hutchins."

Mrs. Hutchins was an elegant lady with an air of education and refinement. She did not appear to be the type of person who enjoyed gossip. Certainly, her response to their questions was very measured.

She did not have much to add to what Georgiana had reported, beyond giving them the name of the officer she believed Miss Lydia liked.

"She seemed quite taken with Lieutenant Denny. I was surprised that he had captured her attention as he was rather shy and unassuming."

Bingley laughed. "Not her type at all, I would have thought."

"Lydia is the sweetest girl," said Mrs. Bennet, giving him a wounded look. "Perhaps he was in love with her and she took pity on him. Why, when I first met Mr. Bennet—"

"—now, my dear," said Mr. Bennet. "Perhaps the story of our whirlwind romance can wait until after we have spoken to Colonel Forster and the other officers."

The mention of the officers was enough to make Mrs. Bennet forget the story and hurry from the room.

Privately, Darcy thought they were on a wild-goose chase, but he wished to leave no stone unturned. "Thank you, Mrs. Hutchins," he said, since the Bennets had already left. "I really hope you are right and we can find Miss Lydia through Mr. Denny."

"I wish you luck," said Mrs. Hutchins. "By the by, I wanted to tell you that your sister is perfectly charming. I hope we will have an opportunity to become better acquainted."

His heart swelled with pride. Shy, quiet Georgiana was beginning to come out of her shell. "I appreciate your kind words," he said.

Bowing, he took his leave. He found Colonel Forster completing a training exercise with some new recruits. The colonel waved to Darcy but continued with the training.

"He said he would be finishing soon," said Mrs. Bennet, in a loud whisper, "but 'tis such a pleasure to watch, I am loathe to see it come to an end. How do they manage to bring their legs up so high when they march? They are such high steppers. They put me in mind of hackney horses."

"I never thought of it quite that way," remarked Bingley.

The exercise ended and Colonel Forster strode over to where they were standing.

Mr. Bennet explained the situation to him. "We would like to know the whereabouts of Lieutenant Denny."

"Funny that you mention it," said the colonel. "I was wondering the same. Lieutenant Denny requested permission to go on leave about a fortnight ago to visit his aunt who lives in Mickelham. He said his aunt was gravely ill. His leave ended three days ago but he has not yet returned."

"If you can think back, sir," said Mr. Bennet, "did his leave begin before or after Lydia's disappearance?"

"I did not think to connect the two, but I now realize that Denny's leave began the day before Miss Lydia's disappearance was discovered."

"So it is likely Miss Lydia is with Mr. Denny," said Bingley.

Darcy responded quickly as an expression of alarm appeared on Mrs. Bennet's countenance.

"Even if the dates coincide, it may mean nothing at all," he said. "I suppose the next step is to find Mr. Denny's aunt. It should not be difficult to locate her in a small village like that. Do you know her name, Colonel Forster?"

"I believe it is Mrs. Gillespie," said Colonel Forster, "In any case I do have her address. She was Mr. Denny's guardian before he came of age."

Armed with the aunt's address, the party took their leave of Colonel Forster. It soon became apparent that Mr. Denny's delay in returning to Brighton, coupled with Miss Lydia's disappearance, had given the whole matter an ominous undertone. For the first time since they had arrived in Brighton, Mr. Bennet abandoned his usual amused stance and became business-like.

"We need to visit Mr. Denny's aunt at once," said Mr. Bennet, "Though I hardly think it worthwhile to ride all the way to Mickelham and return the same day," said Mr. Bennet, as they left the camp behind them. "We may as well set out for London. Mickelham is not far off the London-Brighton road. We can take rooms at an inn if we find we have been delayed by our visit."

Darcy understood Mr. Bennet's sense of urgency very well. Tomorrow was Sunday, and one did not travel on a Sunday, which meant another day's delay. Moreover, even though no one was saying it, there was a sense now that matters had taken a more unpleasant direction. Denny's disappearance along with Miss Lydia's did not bode well.

"Then let us be on our way as soon as possible," said Darcy.

~~X~~

It had been agreed by everyone that, under the circumstances, Elizabeth Bennet's parents would not be told about her ordeal with Mr. Drabble. This went against the grain for Darcy, who did not like the subterfuge. He was of the belief that keeping a secret like this could only cause complications later if anything surfaced, but Elizabeth was adamant, and he was in no position to deny Elizabeth anything.

"My parents have enough to worry about," she argued. "My mother may not show it, Mr. Darcy, but she worries a great deal."

Not show it? Darcy tried to puzzle that remark out. Did Elizabeth really have such a deluded perception of her mother, or was she merely so accustomed to tantrums and nervous fits that she did not even notice them?

"You may look surprised, Mr. Darcy, but you may as well admit that you have thought her indifferent to Lydia's plight more than a few times."

He gave a twisted smile. "It is true enough."

Now, returning from the visit to the officer's camp, he was grateful Mrs. Bennet knew nothing of Elizabeth's ordeal. Already Mrs. Bennet's imagination had run riot, and she had spent the whole distance from the camp to the inn bemoaning her daughter's fate.

"She is dead, I am certain of it, or we would have heard from her by now. My poor beautiful baby, killed by a madman! Oh, I do not know how I will endure it!"

"Mrs. Bennet, I can imagine the horror you must feel at such a prospect," said Darcy, sincerely. "However, do not despair just yet. It is still very likely that there is a rational explanation for Miss Lydia's disappearance. Let us not assume the worst."

His words fell on deaf ears. She continued to speak of palpitations and flutterings and to wave her kerchief about. As they drew closer to The Old Ship, however, Darcy thought of another way to help her recover her composure.

"We will have to inform the young ladies of what we have discovered, Mrs. Bennet. Perhaps it would be best if you speak to them. They will be alarmed by the unexpected turn of events, I am sure, and I am worried about their delicate sensibilities. May I appeal to you to help me calm their fears? Being imminently sensible, I am sure you will be able to do so."

Mr. Bennet, who had been making a concerted effort not to react to his wife's agitation, snorted loudly in disbelief.

Mrs. Bennet had been hesitating, torn between giving vent to her own feelings and proving to Darcy that she was as sensible as he had painted her. Her husband's remark made the decision for her.

"There is no cause to be impolite, Mr. Bennet," she said, sweeping regally off the carriage. "I can certainly help Mr. Darcy handle the girls."

Darcy repressed a smile. It was no laughing matter, but he was pleased that he had managed to avert a public scene. His nature prevented him from being comfortable as the center of attention, and having Mrs. Bennet fall into a fit of anxiety in a public inn could prove very unpleasant. He was more in sympathy with her than ever before, and could not help feeling that she had displayed more strength of character by repressing her own fears to help the others than he had could ever have given her credit for.

The journey from Brighton back to Town was very different from their journey to the coast a few days ago. They had started out with a feeling of expectation. Now a heavy cloud of anxiety had settled over everyone. There was a great deal less certainty; the situation had become more critical. Each person's imagination supplied a different interpretation of Mr. Denny's absence, none of them positive. Darcy's theory was that Miss Lydia might have been forced to pen the letter saying she was running away with Wickham before someone carried her off, possibly Denny. However, Darcy preferred not to dwell on that possibility.

Fortunately, for their peace of mind, nothing happened on the way to hinder their progress and they reached their destination in good time. The village of Mickelham was situated in the Mole valley, and was reached through a narrow, winding road. They pulled up in front of a large brick house. Two footmen in livery appeared at once to open the door and let down the steps, prompted no doubt by the crest on Darcy's carriage.

"I will not be too long," said Darcy, passing by the carriage that held the Bennets. They had agreed that it would be best for Darcy to conduct the enquiry. It was a delicate matter. One did not wish to accuse Mr. Denny of anything without having enough information, nor was it wise to put Mrs. Gillespie on the defensive. It would be best to have a single person handling the interview. Initially, Darcy had suggested Mr. Bennet, but Elizabeth's father had refused, saying Darcy would do a far better job than he could.

Darcy strolled up to the door self-consciously, aware of several pairs of eyes watching him. He handed his card to the butler and asked to speak to Mrs. Gillespie.

He was led presently into a small drawing room where a tall, imposing woman in a purple turban with three ostrich feathers stood looking out of the window.

One thing at least was immediately evident. Lieutenant Denny's aunt was not suffering from a grave illness.

Darcy bowed.

"A pleasure to meet you, Mr. Darcy," said Mrs. Gillespie, graciously. "To what do I owe this visit? We are not acquainted, are we? I meet so many people when I am in town I fear I cannot keep track."

"I am here to inquire after your nephew, Lieutenant Denny."

Mrs. Gillespie looked surprised. "My nephew? But why? He is not in some kind of trouble, I hope?"

If he told her Denny was in trouble, would she deny having seen him? Darcy could not chance it.

"Not as far as I know," he said. "His commanding officer was concerned that he had not returned from his leave. We were travelling this way and promised to stop and remind him of his duty."

"He was on leave and he did not visit me? Well, I will have a few words with him when I see him next, I assure you! He invariably pays me a visit of a day or two when he has time off. I am like a mother to him, you know. I raised him."

"He did not come here at all in the last two weeks?"

"No. I *had* realized he has been away longer than usual. He usually comes to visit at least once a month when he can get away." She frowned. "That is certainly odd. I hope nothing untoward has happened to him."

She was genuinely concerned.

"This is a very impertinent question, Mrs. Gillespie, and you may choose not to answer it, but having raised Lieutenant Denny, would you say he lost his temper easily or tended towards provoking fights?"

"Are you trying to say Denny may have been involved in a brawl?" She laughed softly. "Now I know you are funning me!! Denny is the best tempered boy you can imagine. Of course, like all young men he gets into minor scrapes – the kind any healthy young man may get into. I have seen him come home with a bloody nose once or twice. But a proper brawl? Not Denny!"

"I am relieved to hear it, Mrs. Gillespie."

He was at a loss how to proceed from here.

"Do you know of any place we could find him? Some friend of his or another relative he might have visited?"

"I have the address of a friend of his in London. You can enquire with him. Oh, I do hope Denny has come to no harm!" She went to the escritoire and, looking through a tattered notebook, found the address and wrote it out in a neat hand.

Darcy stood up.

"Thank you very much for the information. I hope I did not inconvenience you."

"Not at all," said Mrs. Gillespie. "Would you care for refreshments? Cook made some delightful almond rout cakes this morning.

"I am afraid I have others waiting for me in the carriage. We must continue on our way. Thank you, Mrs. Gillespie. You have been very helpful."

~~x~~

Outside, Mrs. Bennet was standing outside the carriage, waiting anxiously for him. As he approached, Mr. Bennet stepped out and joined her, followed by Elizabeth.

"I am ready to die of suspense, Mr. Darcy," said Mrs. Bennet as he approached. "Have you seen Mr. Denny? Is he here? Does he know anything about dear Lydia? Please tell me at once!"

Darcy waited until everyone had gathered around him and explained what little he had discovered.

"What a despicable young man, to be sure, to have lied to his superior officer about visiting his bedridden aunt!" she said. "He is up to no good, you mark my words. What I want to know is where has he gone with Lydia?"

"But, mama, we cannot be certain that it *is* lieutenant Denny who is responsible for Lydia's disappearance," said Elizabeth.

Mrs. Bennet ignored her. "What if they have disappeared without a trace? What if they were both murdered by footpaths while walking along the Parade in Brighton? Did you see some of the riff-raff there? Anything could have happened. Anything." Her voice rose a notch. "There are those who favor Brighton, but I tell you, I did not like it at all. The sea is cold even on the warmest day and one can never feel safe there." She took her kerchief out and began to cry. "Oh, what am I to do? I will never see my baby again."

"Now, now," said Mr. Bennet. "Let us resume our journey. We can sit comfortably in the carriage and discuss this possibility calmly instead of standing about where we can be overheard."

Elizabeth shook her head. "I do not know how you can be so calm about it, papa."

"It will do me no good to indulge in a fit of hysterics," said Mr. Bennet. "Though at this moment I wish I could do so. I fear the worst."

The last statement provoked Mrs. Bennet into giving a loud cry and darting into the carriage, where she flung herself onto the seat.

"Papa!" remonstrated Elizabeth.

Mr. Bennet had the grace to appear contrite. He followed Mrs. Bennet inside and sat patting her awkwardly on the shoulder.

"There, there," he said. "It is not as bad as all that. Even if we lose one daughter, we still have four more. That is more than enough."

This had the effect of making Mrs. Bennet cry even harder.

Elizabeth closed her eyes and put her hand instinctively on Darcy's arm. Darcy covered it with his hand and pressed it warmly. She drew it quickly away as Mr. Bennet leaned out of the window.

"Go, Lizzy, to the other carriage and inform the others of what has happened. They must be rather anxious to hear what has been discovered. I will deal with your mother. And for heaven's sake, let us be on our way."

"Do you think it likely we will ever recover Lydia?" asked Elizabeth painfully, as she and Darcy walked to the second carriage.

Darcy wanted to crush her to him and take away all her pain, but he could only stand by helplessly. He would do anything to bring about a different outcome.

"I think we should remain optimistic. Something else may surface that could take us in an entirely different direction."

He fervently hoped that was the case.

As they entered the carriage, Georgiana looked at him expectantly. He shook his head gently, and by her crestfallen expression, he could tell she had been hopeful. Georgiana immediately reached over and took both Elizabeth's hands in hers.

"I see our journey has been in vain," said Caroline. "What do you propose to do now, Darcy?"

"We will continue to London, asking at the inns along the way. Some information is bound to surface, especially since we will be providing a different description. We have been asking for someone dark with brown eyes and curly hair. Denny has flaxen straight hair and blue eyes. That will make a difference, I am sure. "

"How very clever of you, Mr. Darcy," said Miss Bingley.

"I would think it was rather obvious," said Elizabeth.

The tension in the carriage suddenly grew oppressive. Darcy sought for something to say that would relieve it, but drew a blank. He hoped their journey would end peacefully. Nerves were frayed but it was important for Bingley's sake that a quarrel should not erupt between Caroline and Elizabeth.

"I find this area of Surrey enchanting," said Darcy finally, breaking into the heavy silence. "Have you ever come picnicking on Box Hill, Miss Bennet?"

He cursed himself for directing the question to her. He could see her hesitate, on the verge of some remark that reminded him that they did not have the finances to travel so far for a mere picnic.

She checked herself however, simply shaking her head. "Never. I live too far away."

"You must try it, Miss Bennet," said Caroline. "The view from above is quite entrancing and the air remarkably sweet."

"I would love to go one day, William," remarked Georgiana wistfully. "I have heard about it from one of my friends at finishing school. Lady Helena Goodwin. Perhaps you know her, Miss Bingley?"

Georgiana chattered on for a while about what her friend had told her about Box Hill.

Darcy gave her an encouraging smile. He was happy to see that Georgiana was employing her conversational skills to try and ease the situation. It was remarkable how she had changed in the last few months. He was especially relieved that Elizabeth, who was leaning against the squabs in the corner, was apparently listening to Georgiana. Her beautiful, intelligent eyes had lost some of their haunted expression as they fixed on his sister's face.

As if feeling him watching her, Elizabeth looked towards him. Their gazes met. Darcy exhaled sharply as something unidentifiable leapt into her eyes. It was as if she was seeing him for the first time. He sat motionless, his heart racing, afraid to stir, afraid even to blink in case he lost the connection between them. He felt naked in front of her, stripped of all pretenses. She was delving into him, learning all his secrets. She saw him without his pride, without any armor. She saw him as he was and he felt at once terrified and exhilarated.

Then Elizabeth flushed and looked away, deliberately breaking the contact. Darcy felt bereft, as if the bright candle that had lit his way through the dark had been snuffed out. He turned away, shaken, and gazed blindly out of the window, stunned by the intensity of his reaction. He had experienced nothing like this before. He had believed himself in love when he was at Hunsford, but it was nothing to the depth of passion he felt for her now, having lost her once and again.

"Look," said Georgiana, suddenly. "A lavender field. May I open the window please? I love the scent of lavender."

As she let down the sash, the sweet scene of lavender burst in. It brought back to him that day when he had stood staring across the lavender at Netherfield. He had been so carefree then, almost a boy. Now the scent invaded his senses, bringing with it the sharp pain of his loss.

His gaze turned to Elizabeth, searching for hope. Her face was turned away from him. She had shut him out of her world again.

He was building castles in the air and he had to stop.

Chapter Nineteen

Darcy took up the invitation from the mantel place and stared at it, though why he was doing so was unclear as he had already memorized the contents. It was an invitation from Mrs. Deborah Fortin to a musical soiree at her town house for later that night.

He dipped his quill in the inkpot and penned a missive telling her he was delighted to accept. As he put his seal on it, he reflected that he was, in effect, sealing his fate. His life would look very different from now on.

He did not regret it, not really. The interlude with Elizabeth in Brighton had taught him many things, but there had been so much pain and so little pleasure that he was now ready to settle for a more serene existence. It was actually a relief that he was committed to marrying Mrs. Fortin. It certainly saved him the trouble of searching for a wife all over again.

Now all that was left was to say goodbye to Elizabeth. An invitation had arrived that morning from Mr. and Mrs. Gardiner for dinner. He would dine with them before going to see Mrs. Fortin. It was a perfect opportunity for a last farewell. The Bennets would be returning to Longbourn the next day and he would not see them again for some time.

With any luck, if all went well, at his next encounter with the Bennets, the new Mrs. Darcy – Mrs. Fortin – would be at his side.

~~x~~

He had never had much luck with courting Elizabeth and his last evening with her was no exception. Dinner was almost never conducive to intimacy and on this occasion the seating arrangement seemed deliberately set up to thwart him. She may as well be as far away as the moon. Placed on the opposite side of the table and two people removed from him, Elizabeth was too far for anything but a shouting exchange, even if Darcy broke all the rules of etiquette.

He longed for her with every part of him, body and soul. It was an impossible longing, doomed to die without fulfillment, but for now he cherished being in the same room with her, breathing the same air. He sank into the alluring timbre of her voice and bathed in the laugher that made her eyes flare up like firelight.

As if feeling his gaze on her, she turned towards him. The laughter died down to an ember that scorched his very soul and brought an involuntary groan to his throat.

"Mr. Darcy? Are you well?"

Startled by the sound of his name, he turned to find Mrs. Gardiner speaking to him.

"I beg your pardon? I am afraid I missed your last words."

A knowing smile appeared on Mrs. Gardiner's lips as her eyes flicked towards Elizabeth, but she did not remark on it.

"'Tis no matter," she said. "I hope you are enjoying your soup."

"Very much so," he said. However, when he looked down he found that all his silverware was lined up on the white tablecloth, untouched. Acute embarrassment followed.

"I was distracted," he said.

"I believe you were, sir," said Mrs. Gardiner with a little laugh that reminded him of Elizabeth. "I have no objection at all to such a distraction."

Was Mrs. Gardiner giving him her blessing? Her words brought to him all the agony of his situation. He sank into dejection. Even if the whole world gave its blessing, it would do him no good.

Just then a hubbub rose up outside the townhouse as a carriage drew up and the bell clanged loudly three times. Everyone looked up from their food and conversation ceased. Voices were heard downstairs and the sound of altercation, then the door of the dining hall was flung open.

"I will announce myself, thank you. You will not know what to say," said a familiar voice. "Mrs. Percy Denny."

Mrs. Bennet screamed and dropped her spoon in her soup. Mr. Bennet sprang to his feet. Chaos reigned as Lydia flounced into the room, laughing and pointing to Lieutenant Denny who was hovering in the doorway. She looked round at the astonished looks surrounding her with evident delight.

"Did I not tell you they would be dumbfounded, Denny? No one ever guessed! Oh, this is much better than I could ever have imagined!"

She made a dramatic gesture towards her husband. "This is my darling Mr. Denny. We were married in Scotland. Oh, and look at the ring he gave me. Is it not beautiful? It used to belong to his mama. We had to elope because his aunt would never have approved, you know, she was forcing him to marry a horrid heiress. Oh, Lizzy, did you read my letter? It was such a lark. I wrote it to spite you, you know. Denny said I ought not to, but you were so self-important thinking Wickham liked you that I could not help wanting to tease you. You went on and on about Wickham and I was quite sick of it. I wish I had seen your face when you heard!" She grinned. "Come Lizzy, you need not scowl so. It was not as if you really cared about Wickham. Was it not a fabulous joke? I had such a laugh as I wrote it. Besides, you know, we were obliged to keep the elopement a secret, since Denny's aunt might have sent someone after us. It served very well to confuse everybody by saying I had gone away with Wickham. As if I would run away with someone who owed money to half the officers in Brighton! Though I will admit, Wickham is quite handsome. Nothing to my dear Denny, though."

"We meant to be back a long time ago but Denny developed a putrid sore throat and we could not travel. Denny said we should send an express to let you know but I would not hear of it. 'What, and spoil the surprise?' I said. I wanted to see how you would take it. I knew you would be falling off your chairs with astonishment."

Darcy was torn between wishing to box the brat's ears and embracing her in delight. Things had turned out so much better than he had hoped. Not only was she happily married, but there would be no

Wickham in the family to make her life a misery. He felt weak with relief. At the back of his mind, some little elf was whispering that now he would not have Wickham as a brother.

"Oh! My dear, dear Lydia!" said Mrs. Bennet, "Oh, it is the most *wonderful* surprise, is it not, Mr. Bennet? Well! I am so happy! We were all cast down terribly, thinking we would never find you, but now here you are, and married, too! I can't wait to tell Mrs. Philips! She will be green with envy, for after all her daughter married a very ordinary man, nowhere as distinguished as Mr. Denny."

"La! Wait until I show her my ring. I am going to Longbourn until Denny has broken the news to his aunt, so I will have a chance to do so." She waved it around and looked around the table to see the impact. "And here we have Mr. Bingley and Miss Bingley. Are you acquainted with my husband? Of course you are. He was at the ball in Netherfield. Well, I did not expect to see Mr. Darcy of all people here, dining with you, uncle. Are you his sister? I imagine you must be, for there is a resemblance. Do you like my ring? It is very old, Denny tells me, but you would never know since the diamonds sparkle so nicely in the sun. Well, papa, you have said nothing. Is this not a good surprise?"

There were tears in Mr. Bennet's eyes. "You cannot imagine what a good surprise it is. When we reach Longbourn, I shall scold you for putting us through so much worry, but for now, I am simply delighted to discover that I have a new son-in-law. May I congratulate you, Mr. Denny? I hope you do not live to regret your choice."

"Not at all. Lydia is the best girl in the world," said Mr. Denny, handsomely.

"Only a fool or a man very much in love would say such a thing. I am looking forward to discovering which one you are," said Mr. Bennet.

"Are you going to congratulate me, Lizzy?" said Lydia. "You have not said a word."

Elizabeth gave her sister a tight embrace. "I have two opposite feelings in my heart at the moment: a deep inclination to be happy for you and a strong desire to strangle you. Fortunately for you, I believe the happiness is winning."

"Oh, now you are funning me, Lizzy! Why would you wish to strangle me? You must not tease me anymore, you know, for now that I am a married woman I will take it upon me to find all of you husbands. Denny has so many friends in the militia I am sure we can find you an officer each, though I cannot promise that they will be near as handsome as my dear Denny. Perhaps not for Mary, though, because she is so tiresome and says such gloomy things, but for you and Jane and Kitty."

Denny gave Lydia a besotted smile and bowed to Elizabeth. "It would give me great pleasure to be at your service."

Elizabeth bowed gravely. "I am looking forward to becoming better acquainted, Mr. Denny."

"Have you eaten on the way? Would you like to join us for dinner?" said Mrs. Gardiner.

"I am so hungry I could eat a horse. It has been *ages* since we ate," said Lydia, "but you will have to change the seating arrangements. Now that I am married I have precedence and need to be seated higher up than you, Lizzy."

The little hussy! Darcy could scarcely believe her audacity. No one objected, however, since no one was willing to cast a pall on this happy occasion. Mrs. Gardiner gave the signal for the table to be rearranged and there was a great deal of clatter as the footmen stepped forward to move plates, silverware and glasses.

Since everyone was obliged to stand to change seats, Darcy took it as a good opportunity to take his leave.

"Georgiana, I think we ought to withdraw and allow the Bennets and Gardiners some privacy to enjoy this happy occasion," said Darcy. "What do you think, Bingley?"

"Oh, yes, delighted at the news," said Bingley, smoothly, "but I regret to say we have another engagement."

Caroline agreed readily, a forced smile pasted on her face. She looked as though the carpet had been pulled from under her feet. Darcy thought he understood the source of her unhappiness. Bingley would undoubtedly soon be proposing to Jane, and Caroline would have the Bennets as in-laws.

He understood her distress but could not fully approve it. He was only too relieved that Lydia was no longer dishonored and that the reputation of the family remained more or less intact. The scandal of the elopement would soon be forgotten, though there was bound to be gossip about the fact that she had eloped with a different person. However, her marriage would be rendered all the more respectable because she had married someone both handsome and well connected, particularly since he stood to inherit a generous-sized estate, though Darcy did not think the new Mrs. Denny would wish to spend much time in Mickelham.

"You cannot leave," said Mr. Gardiner. "You must celebrate with us. After all the assistance you rendered us, no one better deserves to be here than you."

It did not take much persuasion for Bingley to take his seat. Caroline tried to catch her brother's eye but he was already engaging Mr. Denny in conversation.

"Do we stay, brother?" said Georgiana.

Darcy nodded. He preferred to delay the inevitable.

All too soon, dinner was over, and the harrowing moment had come. Darcy congratulated the Bennets and the Gardiners and said everything he ought. Then, waiting until the others were distracted, he bowed to Elizabeth, grasped her hand and ran his lips across her knuckles. He turned her hand over and planted a kiss in the center of her palm, then kissed the soft pulse at her wrist. He could feel the blood beating rapidly under her silky skin. If they were alone, he would have showered her with kisses, but they were not and he could not do anything more.

"Goodbye, dearest, sweetest Elizabeth," he whispered fervently. "I wish you all the happiness in the world."

She was blushing furiously and he thought she had never seemed more desirable to him than now, when he had to walk away and leave it all behind.

He bowed again and released her hand. The feeling of emptiness slammed into him, leaving him winded.

"I hope we will see each other soon," said Elizabeth, faintly, her eyes fixed on his face. "Mr. Bingley says he intends to return to Netherfield."

Darcy looked away. "I will not be visiting Netherfield," he said, needing to hear the finality in the words.

She was displeased, but he did not allow himself to dwell on that. It was irrelevant. He needed to get his life in order and there was no room in it for regrets.

He bowed.

"Goodbye, Miss Bennet," he said and, before he could say any more, he turned and walked away.

As he and Georgiana climbed into the carriage to return home, he felt numb.

"All's well that ends well, Darcy, eh?" said Bingley, grinning at him. "What a wonderful surprise."

Bingley was looking deliriously happy. All impediments to his marriage had now been removed, Darcy had no doubt that he would ride over to Netherfield at the earliest opportunity.

"I am sorry, Bingley, but I really am engaged elsewhere and cannot linger," said Darcy. He knocked on the roof for young Ebenezer to get going.

Darcy felt the sharp prick of envy as the carriage moved away. If he had not ruined everything by humiliating Elizabeth at the very moment when she was most vulnerable, he would have been able to accompany him to Netherfield.

Darcy dismissed the thought. It was really far too late for all that. There was a time for self-indulgence, and a time for duty. He had indulged himself in ridiculous fantasies long enough. In real life, there were no knights in shining armor or ladies waiting for the victor to come home to bestow their kiss. In real life, romance meant misunderstandings, pain and sleepless nights. Pretending otherwise was self-indulgent, and he had had more than enough of it.

It was time to do his duty. Within a few days, he, too, would be engaged, and that would be that.

~~x~~

"Well, that was a surprising turn of events," said Georgiana, cheerfully, as the carriage left Gracechurch Street and made its way to the more fashionable area of town. "How wonderful that Miss Lydia is not only safe but married! You could have knocked me down with a feather when she came in with Lieutenant Denny."

"Hmm," said Darcy, his head bent, staring intently at his fingers.

"He is certainly a far better choice than Wickham."

There was still no response from Darcy. She was not even certain he had heard her. She could hardly blame him, knowing exactly what it was that occupied his attention. They could not have been more obvious if the two of them had been proclaiming it from the rooftops. The smoldering looks he and Elizabeth had exchanged had been apparent to everyone. Elizabeth was not as indifferent to William as her brother thought. Georgiana was hardly an expert on these things, but she had noticed a definite change in Elizabeth's attitude towards him, small things like covert looks, blushing when William looked at her, seeking his attention more often, watching him when his attention was elsewhere. It warmed Georgiana's heart to see that. William had been through so much apprehension and soul-searching, surely he deserved a taste of happiness.

"So, when are you going to propose?" she said, with a laugh, just to tease him.

Darcy's head shot up, his gaze narrowed. "Propose? To whom?"

"Who else?" said Georgiana, puzzled. "Miss Bennet, of course."

There was a long silence. The clip-clopping of the horses' hooves sounded like heartbeats in the dark narrow space of the carriage.

"I—. It is impossible," he said, in a chocked voice. He covered his face with his hands.

Georgiana stared at him, dumbfounded.

"But— how? Why do you say it's impossible?"

Darcy shifted in his seat and leaned his head back. Even in the dark, she could see the grimace that marred his handsome face.

"Because I am promised to someone else."

Georgiana turned cold. If that controlling, self-serving arrogant *wench* had tricked William into marrying him, she would rue the day.

"To Miss Marshall?"

"Miss Marshall?" he said, with a snort. "Certainly not."

There was no "certainly" to the conversation at all. None of it made sense. Unless something had happened in the interval between leaving Pemberley and arriving in London. *Oh, William, how could you?*

"Do you mind my asking the name of the lady who is to become your wife? After all, you can hardly keep your engagement secret, especially if you plan to announce the bans."

"Her name is Mrs. Fortin."

A *widow*? Well that was unexpected. Why had she never heard of this paragon before?

"Does she live here in London?"

"Yes," said Darcy.

She waited for him to say something else, but he did not. Georgiana did not ask. Oddly enough, she did not wish to know, not now. It did not bode well that her brother was so unhappy, but if he was already engaged to this widow, there was not much point in questioning it. As a gentleman, he could not break the engagement. They were as good as married.

Georgiana wanted to cry. She had really dreamt of having Elizabeth Bennet as her sister. She just hoped this Mrs. Fortin was a kind woman and that William had not made a terrible mistake he would regret for the rest of his life.

Darcy made his way to the musical soiree with a persistent ache in the pit of his stomach. He did not have the slightest notion how he would react to seeing Mrs. Fortin. The invitation was a godsend. He welcomed the opportunity to meet her when she was surrounded by others, and a musical soiree was perfect because it would not require a great deal of conversation. It would give him time to accommodate himself to being at her house and time, too, to discover a little more about Mrs. Fortin without having to reveal anything of his feelings.

He had given the situation a great deal of thought since they had returned to London, and he was determined to approach the whole matter intelligently. He did not want to make a hash of things. If his experience with Elizabeth had taught him something, it was that one should never take anyone for granted, and that there was a right way and a wrong way to propose. He would do it the right way because he owed it to Mrs. Fortin to do so. It would not do at all to make his future wife *feel* that the only reason he was marrying her was to atone for his guilt, even if that was the truth of the matter. He knew better than to make the mistake of thinking honesty was a great virtue when the truth could be insulting.

Fortunately, he was no longer arrogant enough to think that proposing to a lady was an act of great condescension on his part. He would be forever grateful to Elizabeth because she had cured him of that overbearing pride.

As he stepped into Mrs. Fortin's house, he was struck with fear that he would not recognize her. Did he even remember what she looked like? It would be horridly embarrassing if he could not pick her out of the crowd. He had a vague memory of a beautiful young lady with brown hair and enormous honey-brown eyes, but that was all.

He need not have worried. He had no sooner been announced than Mrs. Fortin came hurrying towards him. He recognized her instantly. She had a broad welcoming smile on her face and her eyes sparkled with intelligence. She was as pretty as he remembered, and better still, she was very amiable.

If he had to make a list of the qualities required in a wife all over again, he thought those qualities were good enough. Luckily, he did not.

"Mr. Darcy, I am exceedingly glad you were able to come. The music is about to start, so do allow me to show you to your seat." She led the way through the weave of people to a chair in the front. "When you sent the note to say you were coming, I saved you a seat next to mine. Not that I expect more than two dozen people. I am in half-mourning and it will be frowned upon if I entertain. My guests are family and some close friends."

It was alarming to be thought one of Mrs. Fortin's close friends. It only confirmed what he had feared all along.

She was expecting something from him.

He bowed. "I am honored you think of me that way."

"I rather thought our last encounter entitled you to that claim," she said, her eyes twinkling.

Darcy's cravat felt suddenly very tight. He pulled at it to loosen it a little. He would have to have a word with Briggs not to tie his cravats quite as closely.

Luckily, the music struck up at that moment and Darcy was spared the embarrassment of having to reply, but as he listened to the familiar strains of Haydn, he had to remind himself to breathe.

No matter how many amiable qualities he found in Mrs. Fortin, there was not avoiding the fact that he felt trapped. He wanted to turn and run.

But running would earn him nothing. Only a guilty conscience.

Chapter Twenty

It was the most excruciating visit in his life.

He had told Mrs. Fortin before he left the soiree that he would be calling on her in the morning, and now here he was, seated on an armchair in Mrs. Fortin's dainty salon, sipping tea, and doing everything he could to postpone the inevitable.

"You said there was something particular you wished to speak to me about?"

Darcy took a deep breath and put his teacup slowly and carefully on the table. How on earth was he supposed to go through with this? There was no way to approach the matter delicately. Going on his knee seemed hypocritical, given that his feelings were not engaged. However, simply bursting out with the question seemed woefully inadequate.

In the end, he decided that the simplest approach was perhaps the best. "Mrs. Fortin, I am here to request the honor of your hand in marriage."

In the silence that followed, he heard the sharp input of breath from Mrs. Fortin's maid who was stitching quietly in the corner. He did not dare look at Mrs. Fortin herself.

"Mr. Darcy," said Mrs. Fortin. "Are you certain that you wish to propose to me?" She sounded genuinely puzzled.

He looked towards her sharply. Was she toying with him?

"Of course I wish to propose to you, madam," he said, taking refuge in arrogance because he was out of his depth.

"We have met only once, sir, apart from last night," she said, in a gentle voice. "I do not understand why you feel compelled to do so."

Darcy rose, too agitated to be able to stay seated. Confound it! Was she going to make him spell it out? The whole situation was as clear as day.

"Yes, it is true that we have met only once. However, you will admit that our first encounter was rather – eventful." He ran his fingers nervously through his hair, wishing he could be anywhere but here.

"It certainly was," said Mrs. Fortin, with a little laugh.

He gave her another piercing look, trying to read something into that laugh. He was entirely at a disadvantage. *She* remembered exactly what had happened. *He* did not. He was coming into it blind.

"I cannot help feeling that on that occasion our interaction was rather more intimate than is usually the case with complete strangers."

"I certainly agree, Mr. Darcy," she said, which gave him no clue at all.

Perhaps he was coming at it the wrong way. He ought to start with what he himself knew. He needed to explain that, even though he had given the impression that he was a widower, he in fact had lost the love of his life because of his own folly.

"I owe you an explanation. I am not a widower. I believe I may have suggested that I was."

"Mr. Darcy, you do not owe me any explanation. I am perfectly aware of what your circumstances entailed."

"You are?" Good heavens! Had he spilled out his heart to a perfect stranger?

"Yes. You told me all."

"All?" said Darcy.

"A great deal, at least about Miss Elizabeth Bennet. I know the color of her eyes, the way her face lights up when she laughs. I know she does not mince words and that she stood up to your Aunt Catherine, who, I gather, is rather formidable."

He was flabbergasted. She knew all this, yet she had been willing to bed him?

"Then why—?" How on earth could he ask this question delicately? "The chambermaid seemed to imply that we shared a bed."

She frowned. "I wonder why she did that. What did she say?"

"That I was rather wild, and that you – brought me to my chamber."

She laughed out loud. "You have come to the wrong conclusion, sir. No, Mr. Darcy, we did not – share a bed. I helped you upstairs because you would not allow any of the servants near you. You were – challenging them all to duels. You insisted you did not need their help even though you could scarcely stand, but you had no objection to mine. I had no choice but to accompany you upstairs. I then coaxed you into allowing one of the boys to help you undress. That was the extent of my embarrassment. That, and the fact that you kept telling me about Elizabeth's luscious lips and how much you wanted to kiss them."

He had not thought he could possibly be more embarrassed, but he was. He blushed to the very roots of his hair.

Mrs. Fortin gave a lopsided smile.

"Is that why you proposed to me? How very noble of you, Mr. Darcy, but I must decline your kind offer." She smiled kindly. "I am very sorry. You must have really agonized over this. I regret that I was a source of unhappiness, even unintentionally."

She came and put her hand out to him.

"However, one thing I do not regret is the resumption of our friendship. I am glad you called on me and even more glad to know that you are a true gentleman. We started as friends and I hope we can continue to be friends. I would love to meet your Elizabeth."

His Elizabeth. How wonderful those words sounded. If only it were true.

The interview was over. Darcy stood up, bowed and kissed her hand in gratitude for her understanding and generosity. She had managed to clarify the situation without drawing it out and making it unpleasant. More importantly, she had said no.

"I would love to have my sister Georgiana meet you, if you will permit it," said Darcy, enthusiastically.

"Most certainly, Mr. Darcy."

Darcy could no longer hold back his relief. He grinned at Mrs. Fortin and thanked her profusely, promising to invite her for dinner at the Darcy townhouse. He then took his leave as quickly as politeness would allow.

He bounded down the stairs and into the street. He was free. He could scarcely believe it. That night at the inn had been like a thundercloud threatening rain for so many days now he could scarcely believe that it had dispersed.

Outside, it was a beautiful day. The weather was turning cooler, heralding a change in seasons. The crisp blue sky reflected a brisk sharpness in the wind that lifted away the oppressive heat. As he settled into his carriage, Darcy began to whistle.

~~X~~

His mood lasted all the way to the Darcy townhouse. The new sense of energy he was feeling reminded him that he had been neglecting his fencing practice. He ran upstairs to change into clothing more suitable for exercise and rang for his valet.

"Good news, sir?" asked Briggs. "Anything I should know about?"

"Certainly not," said Darcy. "Curiosity killed the cat, Briggs."

"As I am not a cat, sir," said Briggs, cheerfully. "I do not need to worry about that. Besides, I remember an occasion not so long ago when you were very grateful about my curiosity, very grateful indeed."

"I was grateful *then*. My gratitude does not discount the possibility of getting rid of you for interfering in my affairs *now*."

"You would not sir. I'd wager all I have on it," said the little man, with a wide grin.

Darcy paused and gave him a searching look. "Would you really, Briggs? Are you so certain you can trust my judgment?"

The valet turned serious, recognizing at once that Darcy's mood had changed.

"I would trust you with my life, sir. You are the most honorable gentleman I have had the privilege to valet, Mr. Darcy."

Darcy laughed. "I am the only gentleman you have had the privilege to valet," he said, "since you inherited this position from your father."

"I meant it most sincerely, Mr. Darcy."

Darcy nodded. "I know you did." He paused, hesitating. "For the record, though I will probably never say this again, I trust you with my life, too."

"You do, sir. All the time," said the valet, breezily. "Do not forget the blade I hold to your throat each day."

"Ah, but I have the upper hand, Briggs. I provide the blade," said Darcy.

It was a long-standing joke between them. However, Darcy's response was so devoid of enthusiasm that the little man frowned.

"If you don't mind me saying so, sir, you seem suddenly in a very pensive mood. Is there something wrong, Mr. Darcy? Have you discovered you are in ill health?"

"You ask too many questions, Briggs. And just in case you are inclined to spread rumors that I am on my deathbed, I assure you that, as far as I know, I am in perfect health.

"Well, that *is* a relief, sir."

But as Briggs bustled around taking care of Darcy's clothing, Darcy wondered at the reason for his glumness. He had been in buoyant mood when he had left Mrs. Fortin, but a heavy melancholy seemed to have settled over him since then.

It did not take him much reflection to discover the source. He had pushed it to the back of his mind, since he had taken his commitment to Mrs. Fortin for granted. While he was bound to Mrs. Fortin, he had not had to face the reality of his situation. Now, however, the truth could no longer be denied. He may be free, but that did not matter one iota. Elizabeth Bennet would not have him, and there was nothing he could do about it.

He was back to his original dilemma. How on earth was he going to find a wife?

~~x~~

"So, brother," said Georgiana, when he joined her for dinner later. "Am I to congratulate you?"

"No," said Darcy. He could not help wincing as he remembered his interview with Mrs. Fortin. She had been perfectly charming, but now that the initial relief was over, he could not forget how awkward it all had been.

Georgiana clapped her hands.

"Excellent news, brother! That is – I do not know Mrs. Fortin. Perhaps she is very agreeable, but there *are* other claims to your affection."

He wished he had not come down to dinner. He was still squirming with embarrassment at having confessed his debacle at the inn to his own sister. He had always wanted Georgiana to look up to him, to see him as a model for her own behavior. No doubt she had lost all respect for him and for his authority. He should have kept his own council. It was too late to repent, however. He had been desperate enough to express his misery and now he had to pay the price by answering uncomfortable questions.

"I have set my mind at rest. It appears nothing at all occurred that night in the inn. The only impropriety was that Mrs. Fortin was obliged to take me to my bedchamber since I was fighting with the male servants and refused to allow them close."

Georgiana beamed. "Then there is no longer any obstacle to your marrying Miss Elizabeth Bennet, since you have been let off the hook."

At the sound of Elizabeth's name, Darcy's defiant heart gave a leap. He suppressed it quickly. Yes, he was off the hook, but he already knew in his heart that he would not propose. He would not go through any more humiliation. He had had enough.

"Georgiana, I am sorry to say that it is out of the question."

"But William—"

"Enough!" he said. "I know I have confided in you, but that does not give you the right to intervene in matters you know nothing about. It is out of the question for me to propose, not unless Miss Bennet gives me clear signs of welcoming it. I have humbled myself enough. I do not intend to do so ever again."

Just then, the butler, looking disapproving of anyone who would interrupt his master's dinner, announced that Mr. Bingley was here.

"Shall I have him wait in the library until you finish dining, sir?"

"Of course not, Franklin," said Bingley, walking through the door. "I have come to dine with my friend. Have an extra place set, there's a good fellow."

Franklin looked towards Darcy, who gave a quick nod.

"Very well, sir." He bowed stiffly and retreated.

"Mr. Bingley, you have come at the right moment. You are just the person I needed," said Georgiana.

"I am delighted to receive such a welcome!" he said. "Though I can only suppose there must be some reason for it. Has Darcy been giving you trouble?"

"He most certainly has," said Georgiana. "You must help me convince him of something. "

"I should warn you that your faith in me is misplaced. I have never been able to convince Darcy of anything. He is as obstinate as a mule."

"Perhaps in this you will be successful." Georgiana took a deep breath. "I am trying to encourage William to propose again to Elizabeth Bennet. He will not."

Bingley darted a quick glance at Darcy, who was stabbing into a piece of meat with his fork.

"Do you have good reason to refuse, Darcy?" said Bingley. "I thought you were planning to do so anyway. We even rehearsed your speech at Pemberley. What could have changed your mind? You are not developing cold feet, are you, my friend?"

Would he never have any peace? It was bad enough having to sort out his own emotions without being constantly badgered by everyone around him. Suddenly he could stand it no longer. He had had enough.

He pushed back his chair angrily, rose to his feet and slammed his fist on the table. A plate that was precariously balanced skidded to the side and fell off. Georgiana stared at him in shock.

"Neither of you has *any right* to advise me," he said. "Or to tell me what I should or should not do. I will not have my feelings be the subject of discussion by all and sundry. You will do well to keep out of it, Bingley. You know *nothing* of what has happened."

"Clearly something has happened, since you are behaving like a bear who is being baited," said Bingley, quite unimpressed by Darcy's display. "You really cannot go around breaking plates, Darcy, no matter what the provocation." Then understanding dawned on Bingley's face. "I see what it is now. You *have* proposed to Miss Elizabeth a second time. I would conclude, given your ill-temper, that she turned you down a second time."

The cat was out of the bag now. He would never hear the end of it.

~~X~~

"Is this true, brother? She turned you down? When? Today?" Georgiana frowned. He must have gone straight to Gracechurch Street after he had visited Mrs. Fortin. It was puzzling, since she was certain the Bennets had said they intended to depart for Longbourn early in the morning. They were very eager to announce the good news in Meryton, and to have everyone meet Miss Lydia's new husband.

"Yes, it is true that I proposed again," he said, running his fingers through his hair, "and yes, she refused me. However, it did not happen today. It happened before I arrived in London."

So that was what had taken Darcy away from Pemberley so suddenly. Elizabeth had left before hearing his proposal, so he had followed her to deliver it. Poor William – to have been turned down after he had ridden all the way to Meryton!

Darcy paced around the room for a moment then stopped.

"I did not intend to propose. In fact, I said nothing of the things we planned together, Bingley. I—" He stopped.

"And?" prompted Georgiana, when it appeared he was lost in remembering that moment.

"And I insulted her even worse than the first time."

222

"Ah," said Bingley. "Now, that is certainly a problem."

Georgiana frowned. "But you have dealt together very well since then."

Darcy looked grim. "Hardly. Have you forgotten that how quickly she grew attached to Mr. Drabble?"

Georgiana felt the fight go out of her. "I suppose so." Then she thought of how Elizabeth had looked when Darcy had returned from his rescue attempt. "Though I believe her feelings may have undergone a metamorphosis since." She turned to Bingley. "Have you not noticed? Do you not think my brother should approach Miss Bennet again?"

Bingley shook his head. "I have to agree with Darcy. I do not think it will serve any purpose to do so."

"Now you see that I am right, sister," said Darcy, his face grim. "I have had enough of this conversation. Bingley understands these matters far better than you do and he agrees with me."

Georgiana let out an impatient breath. "That is because Bingley cannot naysay you. If you were to insist this very minute that the sky is green then he would find a way to see it as green to oblige you. I am as fond of Mr. Bingley as anyone, but you know very well that he does not like to contradict you."

"That is unfair of you, Georgiana," said Bingley.

"That remark is quite uncalled for," said Darcy, in a forbidding tone. "Bingley is a friend. Just because he is agreeable does not mean he has no opinion to offer. We will speak no more of this matter. As a young lady with scarcely any experience of life, you cannot claim that you know any better."

Georgiana looked at the two men in frustration. They were looking at her with identical expression of masculine superiority.

"Oh, it is no use talking sense to you," she said. "Very well. I wash my hands off the matter. If you choose to stay miserable, brother, then I will say nothing further."

Smarting with the injustice of being born a female and being the younger sibling, she swung round and left the room.

Chapter Twenty One

Darcy returned from a hard and fast morning ride in Hyde Park and was about to settle down to a book when Franklin appeared, looking even more disapproving than usual. Darcy would not have thought it possible.

"What is it, Franklin? It seems you have something to tell me."

"That beggar boy has been here again, asking for you, Mr. Darcy."

"The beggar boy? David?" said Darcy. "Did you say '*again*'?"

The butler looked straight ahead of him, avoiding eye contact. "He came two days ago, sir."

"And you did not think it appropriate to tell me."

"I do not approve of beggars roaming around the place whenever they wish, sir. If you do not mind me saying so, Mr. Darcy—"

"I *do* mind you saying so, Franklin, very much. I will discuss this matter with you later, after I have seen David. Bring me my hat and cane."

Darcy set out immediately for Mrs. Carter's house. He had not given Wickham much thought since he came from Brighton. The burning sense of revenge he had felt when he was on the Downs had dissipated when he had found Elizabeth was safe, and after that he had been too preoccupied with other matters. However, he had promised himself to bring both Wickham and his accomplice to justice and he would. If the young urchin had some revelation for him about Wickham, then it might enable Darcy to set the wheels of justice in motion.

He found David in his usual place, sweeping up the street behind the horses. The boy grinned when he saw Darcy and came up to him at once.

"About time you came looking for me, gov'ner. I've been keeping an eye on this house as you told me to, and I have news for you. Mr. Wickham has upped and gone off. Came here in a tearing hurry, he did, bundled all his belongings together, and jumped onto a hackney carriage."

"Did he say where he was going?"

"I had to come up real close to hear him. I tell you, I was that worried he would see me," said David. "If I'd been caught, I don't know what he might have done. Luckily he was in too much of a hurry to notice."

"Obviously, or you would not be here to tell the tale," said Darcy.

David's eyes widened. "You didn't tell me the cove's *dangerous*, gov'ner, or I would've charged you more."

"I think you already have as good a bargain as you were likely to get," said Darcy. "Now, are you going to tell me where he went?"

"He said he was going to the West India Docks," said David. "Do you think he's planning to leave England?"

"Very likely," said Darcy.

"I done good, didn't I, Mr. Darcy?"

Darcy could not help smiling at the impish eagerness on the young lad's face.

"You've done well, young McKee."

"So, are you going to give me that job you promised? On account of me wanting to save some money to open a gambling hell."

"You're not going to do any such thing," said Darcy, "not if you wish me to employ you."

"But, sir, you *promised*."

"And I will deliver on my promise to employ you, as long as *you* promise me not to open a gambling hell in the future."

Young McKee grinned mischievously. "Well, I could always promise, couldn't I?"

"You, my lad, are truly incorrigible," said Darcy, smiling.

"Whatever you say, gov'ner. So, when do I start?"

Back at the Darcy townhouse, Darcy put down his quill for the third time that morning. He had several different business matters to settle, but since Bingley had left for Netherfield, Darcy had been unable to concentrate on anything else. How could he have any peace of mind when he kept imagining that at this particular instant in time, Bingley was very likely talking and laughing with the Bennets? He wished so desperately to be there with him. Unlike Darcy, Bingley was certain of his reception. It had been that way from the beginning. Darcy had started badly and his situation with Elizabeth had gone from bad to worse at every juncture. Bingley, on the other hand, had always been a favorite. It was Darcy's bad advice that had hindered his friend's relationship with Miss Jane Bennet.

The clatter of hooves stopping outside the townhouse drew him to the window. He had been listening for them, hoping for an express from Bingley. He was not disappointed. A lone horseman had arrived and was handing over a letter.

Darcy sat back at his desk, drumming his fingers against the mahogany surface, waiting impatiently for Franklin to bring him the letter.

"An express for you, Mr. Darcy," said the butler, balancing the salver carefully on the tips of his gloved hands. No doubt he thought he was being very dignified, but Darcy had no patience for such things just now. He had given Franklin a severe talking-to for withholding information about David's visit. Franklin's version of sulking was to walk so slowly across the room that Darcy had to fight the urge to run up to him and snatch the letter from him.

Then he had to wait for Franklin to slowly make his way out of the room before slipping the letter knife under the seal and opening up the sheet of paper. Bingley had not written much, as usual. He rarely filled up both sides of the missive. He did not have the patience to write letters and today was no exception.

Dear Darcy

The deed is done. I have seen Miss Bennet and I have asked for her hand in marriage. She has accepted me, so congratulations are in order. As I write these words, I can scarcely believe it. I am the happiest man alive! It transpires that she has suffered as much as I from our separation. Who would have thought it? If only I had known! I was such a fool to stay away! Had I but returned to Netherfield sooner I must have spared us both a great deal of torment. Miss Bennet has the sweetest temperament possible. She has entirely forgiven me my neglect and has not uttered the smallest reproach for abandoning her so suddenly. I wish she would, as I am quite consumed by guilt.

Mrs. Bennet is insisting that we obtain a special license and I believe I shall. I do not do it to oblige Mrs. Bennet, of course, but to indulge myself. I cannot possibly wait until the reading of the bans. We have already wasted so many months of happiness; I will not postpone it a moment longer. You know how impatient my temperament is. Whatever I do is done in a hurry. I wish to set the date as soon as possible. I intend to hold the service at Netherfield, and have already consulted with the parish clergyman.

I will be travelling to Town in the next two days to purchase a special license, in order to set a date and make preparations. I hope it will not take the archbishop's office too long to issue it. I have heard it may sometimes take as long as a week. A week is an eternity!

I hope you and Georgiana will ride back with me to Netherfield. I would love to have your sister meet dear Jane before the wedding.

Ever yours,

C Bingley

Darcy dropped the letter onto the table before him. He should have been happy for his friend, but instead, a strong sense of oppression settled over him. He was honest enough with himself to recognize the sensation as envy. Bingley's happiness only served to emphasize his own lack of it. Bingley talked of his suffering but it was all over now for him, whilst for Darcy there was no end of it in sight.

He would help Bingley obtain his special license, of course, but it was out of the question for Darcy to go to Netherfield or any place where there was a possibility of meeting Elizabeth. He would not even go to Pemberley for fear of finding her at his doorstep. It had happened once, it could happen again. At this moment in time, he longed to go somewhere no one had ever heard of him, to remain incognito until he had overcome the aching in his heart and learned to live his life normally again.

Perhaps that was what he ought to do. He had hired a Bow Street Runner to discover where Wickham and Mr. Drabble had gone. Perhaps, with the excuse of finding them and bringing them to justice, he could leave England until his heart had had a chance to mend.

Meanwhile, there was no chance at all of him either riding back to Netherfield with Bingley or of attending the wedding. They could do well enough without him.

~~x~~

When Bingley arrived the next day, he was bounding with joy. There was a special glow on his face that Darcy had never seen before. Darcy tried in vain to overcome the bleak feeling he felt at his friend's success in love. He loathed himself for feeling jealous, but he could not help it. Knowing he *ought* to rejoice made no difference at all; he could not force himself to pretend a benevolence he did not feel.

Even worse, telling Bingley that he would not attend the wedding proved to be ridiculously difficult since his long term friend would not accept no for an answer. He tried to soften the blow at first by refusing to accompany Bingley to Netherfield.

"Darcy – I will not have you sitting about and moping. Come with me to Netherfield. You need not see Miss Elizabeth. We will fish and ride – anything is better than London at this time of the year."

"You know very well that we will not be doing anything of the sort – that you will spend your time with the Bennets, and leave me to mope at Netherfield alone. I would far rather mope in my own house, thank you, and I will have Georgiana to keep me company."

"Georgiana can keep you company in Netherfield," said Bingley. "I would not dream of excluding her from the invitation. It makes no sense not to come in any case. You will have to encounter Lizzy – Miss Elizabeth – at the wedding. You may as well do so earlier."

Lizzy. To think that Bingley was entitled to call her by that name, while he could not! It was a bitter pill to swallow, and it strengthened his determination to stay away completely.

"I am sorry, old friend," he said. "But I will not be attending the wedding either."

Bingley stared at him in horror.

"Surely you do not mean that," he said. "You are joking."

"I assure you," said Darcy. "This is no joking matter. I have never been so earnest in my life."

Bingley took up a glass paperweight from Darcy's desk and began to toss it from hand to hand in agitation. Darcy watched the paperweight closely, wincing at the idea that it might slip out of Bingley's grip and come crashing down on the floor, or worse, come flying at Darcy's head.

"I know you have your reason to stay away," said Bingley, "but this is taking it too far."

"You do not know how sorry I am. Under any other circumstances, I would like nothing better." said Darcy. "However, I stand by my decision."

Bingley put down the paper weight and came to sit at the corner of Darcy's desk.

"Come, Darcy, you cannot possibly mean such a ghastly thing. You cannot be absent on my wedding. I *depend* on you. You are as close as a brother to me, and brothers always attend their brothers' weddings."

Bingley's appeal only served to make matters worse. It made Darcy feel morbidly sorry for himself because he felt the loss keenly. Not only was he depriving himself of seeing Elizabeth Bennet, he was also hindering himself from celebrating the happiness of his closest friend.

Knowing that Bingley would not let off until Darcy had given in, he tried to distract his friend with a different approach. He had learned long ago that distraction was the best way to avoid an unpleasant subject in Bingley's case.

"You will be much better off without my presence," he pointed out. "As you know, I am the object of unfavorable gossip in Meryton. People there think me arrogant and proud and the moment I appear on the scene;

all eyes will be on me. I will only draw attention away from the happy couple and cast a pall upon the proceedings."

"As to that," said Bingley, laughing, "it will be a small ceremony with only family members attending. You need not concern yourself with the rest of Meryton; only us. I know what you are doing, Darcy, since you always do it. You are trying to distract me."

Darcy gave a twisted grin. Bingley was often more perceptive than he appeared to be. Any merriment quickly dissipated, however. He realized that nothing but the truth would stop Bingley from insisting.

"Look here, Bingley," he said, feeling awkward at having to bare his emotions, "this is no reflection on my affection for you. I, too, see you as the brother I never had. Our friendship means a great deal to me. You and your sisters have become like a second family to me. You have supported me through thick and thin."

As he pronounced the words, he understood how true they were. His connection with Bingley had drawn him out of his loneliness and given him a sense of confidence. It was quite the opposite of his connection with Wickham, which had always been a source of conflict. Bingley, with his easy-going ways, had accepted Darcy for who he was when they were at school together. Later, Bingley had helped him shoulder his responsibilities after his father had died by making light of everything. He had always managed to coax him out of an ill humor; Bingley could make him unbend like no one else.

There were limits to everything, however, and this situation was one of them.

"I do not choose to absent myself from you in your moment of happiness. However, much as I would like to attend, you know very well I cannot, and you know the reason. I am trying to recover from my lamentable obsession with a certain lady, and I am much like an opium addict. I can only recover by avoiding the source of the obsession. You of all people should understand how that feels. You have experienced the uncertainty of love. If you are truly my friend you will not insist."

Bingley examined him gravely for a few moments, in which Darcy felt like an insect under a microscope.

"Very well," said Bingley. "I will not pressure you any further. You must wish me felicity, in that case."

Darcy rose to his feet, relieved, and shook his hand's friend warmly.

"I wish you all the happiness in the world. I am confident you will do very well together. Now go, take your special license, and be happy."

After Bingley left, Darcy sank into dejection. Part of him hoped that Bingley would return and talk him into going, while the other half was fiercely opposed to the possibility. However, when Georgiana tried to reason with him, he knew there was no chance at all that he would change his mind.

"I have no objection to you going, Georgiana. In fact, I quite insist upon it. Young Ebenezer will take you there. You need not fear going among strangers. You know almost everybody."

"I will not go without you, brother," said Georgiana.

"Then I am afraid you will not be going at all," he said, and that was the end of it.

Chapter Twenty Two

Bingley made no further effort to convince him to come to the wedding, beyond a brief letter telling him the date of the wedding and saying that he would be sorely missed. Bingley was happy, Darcy supposed, and did not wish to have his happiness ruined by Darcy's lack of it.

The day of the wedding came and went. Nothing earth shattering occurred. Darcy felt irrationally vexed that Bingley could marry without him, but he supposed now he owed more loyalty to his wife than to his friend. Darcy felt as if he had been consigned to oblivion, as though he was no longer needed. He had always thought that, just because Bingley had depended on him in their schooldays to protect him from the bullies, Bingley had always needed him. Now he suddenly acknowledged that he, too, had needed Bingley all these years. His friend could always be relied upon to buoy him up whenever he felt discouraged. Bingley had never left him in the lurch. That is, he had never done so until now.

Nobody needed him any longer, not even Georgiana, who had managed to connect with some old school friends in town and, although she had not yet started her Season, she was slowly developing an independent circle of acquaintances.

Thus it was that Darcy was sitting in the library one afternoon, morosely pouring over accounts and wishing himself somewhere else completely, when Georgiana came in.

"I have been invited to a Venetian breakfast," she said, "and I would really like to go, but I do not wish to go alone."

"I am not fond of Venetian breakfasts," said Darcy. He turned back to his accounts.

"You know, brother," said Georgiana, "you are becoming a regular curmudgeon. You are far too young to turn into a recluse, and you still have not resolved the issue of my coming out Season. Surely, you do not wish to deprive me of a chance to marry well. It is your duty to ensure it, you know. You may have been unhappy in love, as I was, at one point, but surely, I am not to be punished for it. Once I am married, you may retire and sulk all you wish, but you cannot do so quite yet."

Darcy heard her through a haze. Most of what she was saying bypassed him, but the word duty rose up and wagged its finger at him.

He roused himself out of the gloom with a tremendous effort.

"A Venetian breakfast, you say?" said Darcy. He considered the possibility. It was a bore, of course, and he was in no mood for socializing, but he had to admit, a breakfast was infinitely better than a ball. At least he would not have to dodge the matrons thrusting their unmarried daughters at him and expecting him to dance and make merry.

"Oh, do say yes, brother!" said Georgiana, sensing capitulation on his part.

Darcy looked at his sister's eager face. He had scarcely noticed her the last few days. She seemed to be creeping about in the shadows. As long as Mrs. Annesley was keeping an eye on her, he had been content to have her do as she wished. She was right, however. He was not being fair. She had her whole life in front of her, yet she was being forced to tiptoe around him as if he was some invalid elderly uncle. What kind of a person was he turning into?

"I *have* been a bit of a bear, have I not?" he acknowledged. "I am sorry, little sister. You are right. I cannot hide away forever. I do mean to remedy the situation and you shall have your wish. I will escort you to the Venetian breakfast."

Georgiana clapped her hands. "Huzzah! I am so glad to hear it. It is on Friday morning."

He was glad he had made her happy at least. It would be an insipid affair, no doubt, given by one of the debutante's families as an opportunity for her to practice her social skills. He would excuse himself and leave early. He was quite certain Georgiana would not even notice.

~~x~~

On Friday morning, Georgiana came down the stairs dressed in a lovely white mull dress with delicate silver embroidery and a silver sash. She was in remarkably good spirits. The sparkling look on her face made him feel guilty for not taking the time to escort her elsewhere. He had been neglecting her and it really was not fair to be left so much to her own devices.

"You look very pretty, Georgiana. That is a very fine dress you are wearing – perhaps a little grand for early in the day, but perfectly charming. Is it new?"

"Yes, Mrs. Annesley and I have been shopping. I have acquired several new items since we it looks like we will be staying in Town for a while, and I am going out more often. I hope you approve?"

"Of course. You must look your best. You will be the Nonpareil of the Season, I promise you."

Georgiana giggled. "I do not believe I will ever be that, since I am far too plain, but I thank you for wishing it, brother."

Darcy looked surprised. Was she really not aware how pretty she was? "Your modesty does you credit, Georgiana, but you cannot truly believe that. I am no judge of the current fashion in beauty, but you are exceedingly handsome."

"You are very kind, brother, but I know I am too tall, and too slender to be truly considered a beauty," she said, "and my mouth is too wide, and my eyes too close-set—"

"Enough!" said Darcy. "If you continue this way you will soon have me convinced that you are a veritable ogre! Come now. I will not have my little sister disparage herself. You must take my word for it that you are exceedingly pretty and that I will be obliged to spend the whole Season fending off your suitors."

Georgiana giggled. "If you say so, brother."

He offered her his elbow. She hooked her arm around it and they walked down to the waiting carriage together, with Mrs. Annesley following behind.

"Where is this Venetian breakfast we are attending?" said Darcy, realizing that he did not know the name of their host.

"It is in Berkeley Square," said Georgiana, "Oh, look. Did you see that strange dog that is trying to cross the road? What an odd creature!"

Darcy strained his neck but saw nothing.

"Look, over there. Oh, it has disappeared now."

"It was almost as strange as Ursus was," said Mrs. Annesley.

Darcy looked at her, surprised. Mrs. Annesley hardly ever talked about her past.

"Ursus? The Bear?" said Darcy.

"Indeed. When I was first married, we used to have a strange-looking dog that resembled a bear," she explained. "He had a black tongue. My husband was captain of a clipper and he brought him back from China. He was a type of exotic dog called a Chow Chow. I used to carry him everywhere with me and when he died I was cast down for months."

In view of this unexpected personal revelation, Darcy felt obliged to question her about the dog and its unusual features, and so the time passed until they found themselves in Berkeley Square.

There were not many invitees, it appeared, hardly what one would call a crush. However, there *was* a line of carriages, and as they waited their turn in the queue to draw up to their destination, Darcy deliberately did not allow his gaze to wander over to the Bingley townhouse. He could not help wondering, however, if the Bingleys had returned from their honeymoon, and if a certain young lady was visiting her sister Jane in Town. It did not bear thinking of, and rather than sink into the dismals again he threw himself whole-heartedly into the ladies' observations of the occupants of other carriages.

Finally, their carriage crawled forward and a pair of footmen let down the stairs to descend. Darcy helped Georgiana and Mrs. Annesley out then stepped out himself.

"What is this?" he exclaimed, staring at the familiar building before him. The door was wide open and everyone, it appeared, was walking in that direction.

There was no time at all to react, for at that moment Bingley came bounding out towards him.

"Darcy! Do stop standing about so stupidly and come on in. You are already late."

Only now did he realize that he had been tricked. There was no sign of either Georgiana or Mrs. Annesley, who must have hurried in to avoid being questioned.

Darcy hesitated.

"I cannot stand out here all day on my wedding day, Darcy."

"Wedding day? But I thought you were already married. I thought you were to marry from Netherfield."

"Do not be absurd, my dear friend. You know I would never marry unless you were present. We have been waiting for you. The vicar has been growing impatient."

The words brought a lump to Darcy's throat. He had been feeling sorry for himself, thinking that no one cared for his presence, when all the wedding plans had been altered to accommodate him. He was so touched that for a moment he could not utter a sound.

There was no going back now. The carriage that had brought them had already moved on and besides, now that Bingley had gone to all this trouble to accommodate him, he could hardly refuse to enter.

"Are you coming in?" said Bingley.

Darcy swallowed hard and smiled. "I would not miss it for the whole world."

~~X~~

The Bingley townhouse was full of well-wishers, family members and children. Georgiana, shy because she knew no one, tried to find Miss Bingley in the chaos but Mrs. Gardiner spotted her first and approached her almost as soon as she arrived.

"My dear Miss Darcy. I am delighted to see you. I hope you have good news for us. Is he here?" she said, looking over Georgiana's shoulder towards the doorway.

"He is," said Georgiana, "though I *will* admit I was terrified he would notice where we were any minute. I have to give credit to Mrs. Annesley for managing to keep him distracted."

"And a great deal of nonsense I had to speak," said Mrs. Annesley, nervously. "I still do not feel happy about the deception, but if you say it is for a good cause…"

"It is for a good cause indeed," said Mrs. Gardiner. "It is now up to Mr. Bingley to see to it that Mr. Darcy is brought to his senses."

"I still do not approve of deceiving my master," sniffed Mrs. Annesley as Mrs. Gardiner led her away.

At that moment, Elizabeth Bennet came down the stairs, followed by her sister Lydia.

"I do not care that you have a stain on your gloves, you are not to borrow mine, Lizzy. My dear Denny bought them for me, and I would rather not lend them to anyone. It is quite your fault that you do not have a husband to buy you clothes. If you had but listened to Mama and married Mr. Collins, you would have had as many gloves as you could have cared for."

"I hope Mr. Denny is more sensible than to buy you more than two or three pairs, Lydia."

"And what if he did? You must not begrudge me my clothes, you know. I do believe you are jealous."

Elizabeth was looking as vexed as could be when she caught Georgiana's eye.

"Oh, Miss Darcy, how do you do?" As Lydia began to turn away, Elizabeth caught her by the sleeve to remind her to be polite. "I do not know if you remember my sister Lydia."

Lydia curtseyed briefly. "You were at my uncle and aunt's house when I returned with my husband, were you not? I was too busy at the time to take much notice of anyone, but I suppose you must be Mr.

Darcy's sister. Very pleased to meet you, I am sure. I hope you will excuse me. I must go and find my dear Denny."

Elizabeth frowned at Lydia's back. "I feel I must apologize for my sister's rudeness, Miss Darcy," she said, ruefully. Her gaze, however, quickly shifted as she began to look around the room.

Georgiana hid a satisfied smile. It was as she had hoped; Miss Elizabeth was searching for her brother. She knew the exact moment Miss Elizabeth saw him. There was no mistaking the tension in her body, the sharp intake of her breath or the intense expression in her eyes. She put up her hand as if to wave at him then let it sink when William did not notice her.

Then someone announced that everyone was to assemble in the hall, which had been set up for the wedding and the moment was gone.

The wedding ceremony was all one could have hoped for. Jane Bennet looked as if she would never stop smiling, and Bingley could not take his eyes off her. Mrs. Bennet sniffed a great deal into her lace-edged kerchief, and Mr. Bennet comforted her every now and then by reminding her that she still had three unmarried daughters at her disposal.

Miss Elizabeth Bennet sat very upright throughout the ceremony on the left side of the room, looking neither to the right nor to the left, while Darcy sat equally upright and unmoving next to Georgiana at the right side of the room.

Just as the vicar pronounced the couple husband and wife, the sun emerged from behind a cloud and a sunbeam slanted across the room from the window and settled on the newly-weds, surrounding them with a halo of bright light.

Everyone rose to their feet and a buzz of excitement replaced the silence of the church service as the wedding breakfast was announced.

Bingley planted a gentle kiss on his wife's lips then came over to Darcy.

"Darcy, I will arrange for you to have a private moment with Lizzy in the library. This is your moment. Remember the speech that you practiced at Pemberley, and please, for everyone's sake, get it right this time."

Darcy looked from Bingley to Georgiana. She smiled at him encouragingly.

"I have faith in you, brother," she said. "I cannot wait to hear the good news."

A wild look came into Darcy's eyes and Georgiana's heart sank as she realized he was not going to do it.

"No," said Darcy. "I cannot. Not now. Not this way."

He ran out of the door. Georgiana exchanged glances with Bingley and shook her head.

"I tried my best," she said, unhappily. "I can do nothing more."

Bingley looked despondent. He gave a brief nod. "Well, I suppose I must get on with it," he said. "I have my own bride to think of, and she is waiting for me."

Then Jane walked through the doorway and he gave her his full attention, the radiant smile on his face proclaiming his love.

Georgiana swallowed hard as tears welled up in her eyes. She wanted this so much for her brother. They had been so close to making it happen.

Then the bride and groom walked past her and she remembered the grains of rice in her hand. She tossed the white grains over their heads and they fluttered down like tiny bits of paper, settling on the married couple's hair and clothing. The front door opened and they stepped into the sunlight.

Georgiana watched them go sadly. It was time for her to leave. She had to go back to the Darcy townhouse to help William pick up the pieces.

~~X~~

239

Darcy clutched the flowers to himself. They were not his first choice by far, but in his headlong dash he had gone in the wrong direction and these sprigs of lavender were the only flowers he had been able to buy. He did not want to delay further. He was deathly afraid that Elizabeth would leave and then where would that leave him?

He ran back to Berkeley Square. There was a lone carriage waiting outside the Bingley townhouse, the line they had encountered earlier had dissipated.

Please let Elizabeth still be there. Please let her not be gone. The little prayer thudded through his mind in time with the rhythm of his feet hitting the ground. He picked up speed. The scene of lavender intensified as he crushed the flowers in his urgency. He ran up the steps and ran through the open door – straight into Elizabeth and Mrs. Gardiner.

"Elizabeth – Miss Bennet – thank heavens! I had thought you were gone."

"Lizzy stayed behind to gather up Jane's things," said Mrs. Gardiner.

Elizabeth looked wide-eyed and quite out of breath. He supposed he had knocked the breath out of her – something else he needed to apologize for. Her gaze went down to the lavender in his arms.

He handed the bundle to her and she took it, not looking at him, only at the flowers.

"That is a very large bunch of lavender you have there, Mr. Darcy," said Mrs. Gardiner, her eyes twinkling. "Perhaps you would like to find a place for it somewhere, Lizzy – in the library, perhaps? Mr. Darcy will no doubt know where the library is."

Elizabeth nodded. Darcy was grateful that he was being given time to catch his breath. He did not quite understand why Elizabeth was taking his flowers to the library, of all places, particularly since this was Bingley's house, but he was not about to question the opportunity handed to him on a silver platter. He would be able to speak privately to her.

He bowed and led the way forward towards the library. Once inside, he closed the door and leaned against it.

Elizabeth stood there, clutching the flowers to her as if for dear life. Would she welcome what he had to say?

240

Before he had a chance to say anything, she began to speak.

"Thank heavens," she said. "I have been hoping to talk to you for a long time now, Mr. Darcy. I know it is quite indelicate of me to bring it up, but I must. It has been haunting me and I cannot rest until I address it. I have spent many a sleepless night tossing and turning and I cannot keep it inside me any longer."

She was looking down at her hands, avoiding his glance. Her cheeks were flushed with embarrassment. He probed her face, trying to guess what she meant to say. Could it be that she loved him? His hopes soared. They rose up with a joy so fierce it burned him up. He did not know if he had the patience to hear what she was saying. In two strides, he could have her where she belonged, his arms wrapped around her, kissing her until she did not have a breath in her body.

Fortunately, the fear of bungling again held him back. He knew this time he must not be ruled by impulse. Patience was needed, patience and saying the right thing. However much he wanted to hold her, he had to get it right. But he was dying for her to speak. He could not bear the distance between them. He had to cross it or he would go mad.

He schooled himself to stand still and wait.

"I need to know what I can do about the jewels," she said, in a voice so faint he could hardly hear it. "That is—Georgiana led me to believe. Oh – it is no use – I am mortified to think that my stupidity – my bullheaded obstinacy – led to the loss of her family heirlooms. I do not know how I can make up for it – I am so indebted to you and to her." She raised her eyes to his. Their dark depths were full of torment and confusion and distress.

He plummeted. From the high reaches of the sky, he was tossed down with no way to protect himself. It was like being thrown in the river with weights dragging him down. As in a nightmare, all his joy turned to anguish and he thrashed about, struggling to resurface.

"I care nothing about heirlooms," cried Darcy. "I would give them away, again and again, if it meant saving you from the clutches of men like Mr. Drabble. What value could they have to me if I kept them and lost you?"

241

She did not understand him. She would never understand him. He had tried to tell her how much he loved her in so many ways, but she was blind to it all. What use was it to bare his soul when she felt nothing of what he was feeling? It was a lost cause. It *had* been a lost cause all along. He had come to the abyss and there was nowhere further to go.

It was time to leave.

He cast a last glance at her. Her eyes were fixed on him and there was something in their depths that kept him rooted in place.

Hope resurfaced – again. He had to give it one last try.

He swallowed convulsively. Somewhere, from the back of his mind, he dredged up the speech he had never thought he would use.

"Miss Bennet," he said. "I know I have been a fool. I know I have behaved badly and I do not blame you if you cannot bring yourself to forgive me for the terrible things I said."

She began to laugh.

His stomach clenched. No, it could not be. Was she mocking him?

Still, he was determined. He would not let her laughter stand in his way.

"I am aware that I am a figure of fun – from the first day we met, I have made mistake after mistake—"

"I am sorry, Mr. Darcy! I did not mean to laugh. I have an unfortunate tendency to laugh at the ridiculous."

"You think me ridiculous for asking again, no doubt—"

"No! It is not that at all," cried Elizabeth. "I am not laughing at *you*. I am laughing at myself. It is *I* who am ridiculous, Mr. Darcy. It is *I* who has been a fool."

She was looking at him in a strange way. There was something in her gaze that he had never seen before, a kind of wonder and something else. If he were not terrified of having his hopes dashed again, he might even have thought it was love.

"Miss Bennet," he said, in a voice that trembled, not daring to hope. "You are too generous to trifle with me. If your feelings are still what they were that day at Longbourn, tell me so at once. One word from you will silence me on this subject forever."

"They are not," said Elizabeth. "They have changed so much I scarcely recognize myself. I have been a fool, Mr. Darcy and because of that, I almost lost you. You need not attach any blame to your words at Longbourn. What did you say of me that I did not deserve? Your reproof, so well applied, I shall never forget. False pride has dogged my steps all the way."

Darcy wanted to stop the torrent of words. How could she say such things when it was obvious that he had treated her so abominably?

"No, Mr. Darcy, do not stop me. You must hear me through. I must tell you all because it is the least you deserve from me. You cannot imagine the torment caused by your words to me on that last day at my uncle's house when you said you would not be going to Netherfield. I had resolved to talk to you then, but there was finality about your manner that prevented me. I felt as if the door had been slammed in my face."

He listened in amazement to her words.

"I thought then that it was too late, that I had lost you forever. Then when my sister Jane told me you would not be coming to the wedding, I knew I would never see you again. It was then that I knew the meaning of despair. When we were in Brighton, I became accustomed to your presence. I began to discover that there was more to you than I had imagined. Your dedication to finding my sister despite my rejection at first roused my guilt, then my gratitude. Nor will I ever forget your heroic effort to rescue me. You thought nothing of the danger you exposed yourself to by going to such an isolated area. I was terrified when you did not return. I felt humbled by your persistence, by your concern for my parents – even though I knew your opinion of them – by your solicitude at every turn. I came to know the person you truly were, a person whose kindness and generosity were no longer hidden from me. A person I have come to love."

The last sentence was said in a kind of a whisper, and Darcy was not quite certain he had heard it correctly.

"Could you repeat what you said, Miss Bennet? I am not quite certain—."

She smiled widely. "Indeed I can, Mr. Darcy. I said I have come to love you, with all my heart."

He stood there, dumbfounded, hardly daring to breathe. How could it be possible? Was he dreaming? Was he deceiving himself because it was something he wanted so very desperately? His heart was ready to burst and he could not endure it if he was disappointed this time. It would shatter him to pieces.

But there she was standing in front of him, looking as real as could be, her eyes glistening suspiciously. Tears? Could she be shedding tears? In all the time he had known her, he had never seen her cry.

"You are crying," he whispered.

"I only cry when I am happy," she said.

In two strides he was standing before her. For a moment he hesitated, still uncertain. Then as he gazed deep into her eyes he saw his own feelings reflected there. He saw the raw emotion and the desire, the flame that was burning deep inside them both.

He crushed her to him, his lips seeking hers in blind instinct. He drank from her frantically, his thirst for her so deep he could never quench it. His fingers dug through her hair, drawing her to him until every part of their bodies touched. She gave a tiny mewl then her lips opened up to him and he gave a hoarse growl, wanting to taste more of her, to reach for her with every fiber of his being. He pressed his body against hers and his hands slid down to her shoulders, exploring her soft skin through his fingers, dizzy with the joy of touching her.

Later, he did not know how much later, there was a knocking at the door. He had the feeling it had been going on quite some time. He came to himself as abruptly as if someone had flung cold water at him. What was he doing, seducing a young lady in someone else's house under the very eyes of her aunt?

He stepped back shakily and saw with enormous satisfaction that Elizabeth was just as shaky and dazed as he was.

The crushed lavender fell to the floor between them.

He looked at it and began to laugh.

"I hope you liked the lavender flowers I brought you," he said, whooping with laugher, unable to stop himself. He was feeling so elated, so happy, so full of rapture he was afraid his heart could not contain it and he would die of happiness. Elizabeth – dearest, sweetest Elizabeth -- began to laugh, too. A chorus of laughter rose up between them, filling the air along with the intoxicating aroma of crushed lavender.

The door opened and Mrs. Gardiner appeared in the doorway, beaming.

"I brought you a vase for the lavender," she said. "I could not find one sooner as the house is so full of flowers and all of the vases are in use. Also, it is not my home, so my knowledge is limited. One of the servants kindly brought this down for me from the attic."

"Thank you, aunt," said Elizabeth. "We have been talking about how best to arrange them."

"You seemed to have taken an interesting approach, considering that they are lying on the floor."

Darcy realized now that in the heat of the moment he had not proposed to Elizabeth. He wondered if he could ask Mrs. Gardiner to leave so he could give her the speech he had prepared. He wanted to do it just right. When he glanced at them, however, he could see Mrs. Gardiner was waiting expectantly for an announcement.

The devil take it! Never mind about the speech he had prepared. He had never had any success proposing in any case. The fewer words he used, the better. There were other ways of persuading Elizabeth of the power of his love for her.

He strode over to where the flowers lay on the ground, picked them up and went back to Elizabeth. Going down on one knee, he knelt in front of her and held out the lavender.

"Miss Bennet. I hope you will accept this humble token of my affection for you. I may not be able to express it in words, but I know I will love and cherish you for the rest of my life. I only ask that you will give me the opportunity to prove it." He paused, suddenly nervous. "I offer you my hand in marriage, Miss Bennet. Will you consent to take it?"

The heated look in her eyes left no doubt about her answer. His pulse surged as she leaned over and took the flowers from him, her hands sliding against his, provoking an intense surge of heat through his veins.

"Yes, Mr. Darcy. I will."

Then he could bear it no longer. He rose to his feet and took her into his arms. A whoop rose up from Mrs. Gardiner.

"Allow me to be the first to congratulate you," said Mrs. Gardiner. "It has been a long time coming, but I am glad it has finally happened."

Darcy smiled wryly. If only he had enlisted Mrs. Gardiner's help in Pemberley, instead of trying to conceal his affection!

"Do not say anything yet, aunt. Mr. Darcy still needs to speak to my father," said Elizabeth.

"I will leave you alone for another few minutes to talk about your plans, but then I am afraid I will have to steal Elizabeth away from you for a while."

"Thank you," said Darcy, amused at Mrs. Gardiner's blatant attempt to play chaperon.

The moment the door closed, Darcy slid his arm around Elizabeth's waist and kissed her gently, over and over, glorying in the feel of her against him.

"You cannot imagine how happy you have made me, my dearest Elizabeth," he breathed, as he planted a row of kisses down the side of her neck.

"I *can* imagine it," said Lizzy, "because I feel the same. I never thought I could be so blessed. I do believe you have enchanted me, Mr. Darcy."

He drew her to him tenderly and put her head against his shoulder, feeling her heartbeat mingle with his, a soft, steady throb that filled him with blissful peace. He thought about his dream of returning to Longbourn as a knight in armor and receiving her kiss as a trophy.

He tossed the dream away, without regret. The reality of Elizabeth in his arms was far better than any dream could ever be.

THE END

About The Author

Monica can be described as a gypsy-wanderer, opening her eyes to life in London and travelling ever since. She spent many years in the USA before coming back full circle to London, thus proving that the world is undeniably round.

Monica's first novel was *An Improper Suitor*, a humorous Regency. Since then, she has written two traditional Jane Austen sequels: *The Other Mr. Darcy* and *The Darcy Cousins* (both published by Sourcebooks) and contributed a sequel to *Emma* in Laurel Ann Nattress's anthology *Jane Austen Made Me Do It* (Ballantine). She has also published a futuristic *Pride and Prejudice* spoof, *Steampunk Darcy*.

Mr. Darcy's Challenge is the second volume of her series, *The Darcy Novels*, which are traditional *Pride and Prejudice* 'what-if' variations focusing on Darcy's transformation through his love for Elizabeth. It can be read independently, but might be more scrumptious when read after *Mr. Darcy's Pledge*.

Monica Fairview is an ex-professor who enjoys all historical periods starting with the Regency. She discovered that the Victorian period can be jolly good fun if seen with retro-vision and rose-colored goggles, and also loves the Edwardian period as exemplified by Downton Abbey. She adores Jane Austen, Steampunk, cats, her husband and her impossible child.

If you'd like to find out more about Monica, you can find her at
Web page: www.monicafairview.com
Blog: http://austenvariations.com www.monicafairview.blogspot.co.uk
http://www.facebook.com/monica.fairview Twitter @Monica_Fairview